SAVE THE CITY

SAVE THE HUMANS | BOOK 1

AVERY BLAKE
JOHNNY B. TRUANT

Copyright © 2019 by Sterling & Stone

All rights reserved.

No part of this book may be reproduced in any form or by any electronic or mechanical means, including information storage and retrieval systems, without written permission from the author, except for the use of brief quotations in a book review.

The authors greatly appreciate you taking the time to read our work. Please consider leaving a review wherever you bought the book, or telling your friends about it, to help us spread the word.

Thank you for supporting our work.

SAVE THE CITY

1

"First thing we're gonna do," the boss told the thief, "is we're gonna break your kneecaps. Lotta people think that's old-fashioned, but I got an affection for it. Fingers and knees — both classics, and harder than you'd think. The goal is to get the joints moving backward. If you can bend a leg the wrong way, you're really doin' the Lord's work. Know what I mean?"

Hollis, two chairs from the boss and three from the thief, with Mia Davies practically in his lap, hand casually across his junk, watched the thief swallow without a word. The thief's name was Jayson — not that it mattered. He wore a too-tight short-sleeved collared shirt made of some eco-friendly fabric with penguins on it and had a mustache that Hollis, whose mind tended toward sophisticated things, thought of as a pussy tickler. There was no beard or stubble, just that little mustache. Waxed at the ends. Hollis wondered if, when Jayson's head was buried in the boss's garden, his wax would be bad for the plants.

"Thomas," Jayson said, "I *swear* I wasn't planning to steal the—"

The boss didn't seem bothered by the thief's protest, but he did hold up a polite hand to stop him. Thomas Davies wasn't a fan of bullshit. "Please. Let's not make this worse."

The room murmured. There were twelve people at the round table, and to Hollis it looked like they were about to start a very important meeting. The mysterious attaché case — the subject of Dead Jayson's lust and affection — was on the polished wood, nearly at the center, closest to the boss's big fat hands, on display like Exhibit A. The room was dim, and the chandelier overhead put the silver case in a spotlight. Hollis, who'd never seen or heard of this very important case, had no idea how to react and so instead simply tried to fit in.

The boss's phone buzzed. Again. Lots of people wanting to contact him this morning, and at the worst possible time. He tapped the screen to silence it, then put his hand on the case, flat like a tired spider, gaudy rings winking at the ceiling.

Mia's hand was elsewhere. She was in a red dress that looked sprayed on, calf-length, so tight she must have taken lessons to walk in it. The boss's wife played with everyone, like candy with boobs, but no one was supposed to play back. Nobody told Hollis when he started working at the big house in the hills. It was the kind of thing a man just knew, like how sticking his fist into a wood chipper was an awful idea.

"Do you actually know what's in here," Davies asked of the case, "or were you just thinking it looked pretty?"

Jayson swallowed again. Hollis, like all the others, was only at the table for spectacle. But he knew a leading question when he heard one and willed the mustached fool not to answer.

The phone buzzed again. Hollis reached for his pocket

out of habit, but of course it wasn't his device. Only the boss was allowed to have a phone inside the house for security reasons. Except Mia. Not that she could fit one into her skin-tight ensemble.

Thomas silenced the phone. "You hearing me? What gave you the idea to take it?"

Don't answer.

But the dumbshit did.

"I ... I'm sorry, okay?" Jayson's words came out like hot melting panic. "This guy I know, he—"

"*Sorry.* Everyone's *sorry* in this fucking town. You can't turn around without invading someone's safe space. The girls at Austin Java have armpit hair. You're a bad guy if you don't tip at Amy's just because they throw your ice cream in the air. You know how many petitions to save this or fucking that I've been asked to sign? Why do you think there's a fence around this place? Why do you think I've got the dogs? It's not just my enemies. It's to keep the fucking hipsters away."

"Thomas, I—"

"But I can handle the hipsters," Thomas went on. "Just like I can handle my enemies. Just like I can handle the fucking armpit hair. You know why? Because if you're not a flexible person these days, you're never able to change with the times. So I say, bring on the weirdoes. I've got guns, all of 'em legal and registered. I've got guys, and someone hot who likes to fuck."

Hollis flinched, dislodging Mia's hand.

"It gives me peace, you know, to live here in my own house, behind my fence, with all I need. My own 'safe space,' you might say. And that's why, when I find a cancer *inside* my little bubble, it really sets me off."

Thomas hadn't raised his voice. He sounded eminently

reasonable. Yet Hollis felt cold — and looking at the others ringing the dimly lit table, he knew they felt the same.

"Just tell me who sent you."

"Nobody sent me."

Thomas shrugged. His facial expression looked like a tube of pastry dough in the act of self-sculpting.

"Come on. I can break your knees the wrong way to get it out of you, or you can just tell me. Deny it again and I'll just get more annoyed. Bad things will happen then. When—"

The phone buzzed again. This time Thomas snatched it from the table and threw it against the marble section of the wall, shattering it. He was composed within milliseconds, hands demurely laid one over the other on the tabletop. But the temperature had dropped another hundred degrees, and now even Mia's usual Dragon Lady act was paused, her back straight, porcelain features wary like a feline. Yet another sign that she wasn't the brainless sex toy Thomas made her out to be — and far more fiery than the boss had ever seen.

"I get impatient, and break things I shouldn't."

Now Jayson looked like a fish. All mouth and eyes. His lips worked as if searching for air.

Then, he finally broke.

"Okay! Okay! I'm telling the truth. Nobody sent me! I just wanted a nice little nest egg to ..."

Thomas raised his eyebrows. "Sixty million dollars, for a nest egg."

"I made a mistake," Jayson blubbered. His eyes were watering.

"Yes. You did."

The tough guys around the table mumbled and nodded. Hollis, a second late, did the same. He was one of them, wasn't he? Just more free-thinking, and a little more intelligent. He had plans of his own and was looking for a nest egg himself. A small place on the ocean, a picket fence, maybe a grandma down the road to sell him pies. Hollis was a simple man, with desires to match. Someday, he'd settle down, repay all his debts, and either make nice with his casual enemies or get the hell off their radar.

Only Brendan was angry enough to kill him. The rest were petty grievances — half over a woman. The goal was always to get away from both. Work for Thomas until he earned enough to pay Brendan back, then settle somewhere off the radar.

"I'm sorry."

"Again with the sorry."

"I'm sorry, Thomas! I fucked up. I *know* I fucked up! You've been good to me! I was just weak! Nobody told me to do it. I just thought ..."

He stopped, seemingly unsure *what* he thought. Which, Hollis reflected, couldn't have been much. There were always a few wiseguys in the house, armed to the teeth. The security system was always on, and in the event of a breach, it called out to a private security firm that, rumor said, didn't always follow the law.

Thomas sighed. To the man next to him, he said, "Benny, give me your knife."

Jayson started shouting. The men to either side grabbed him and held him fast.

"I'm sorry! I'm sorry! I don't know what else I can say! I would never have gotten to the front door with that case, Thomas. You gotta believe me!"

Thomas turned the knife to inspect its blade. "Damn right, you wouldn'ta."

"I mean, I would have dropped it! I would never have

gone through with it! I love you, man! Team Davies! One hundred percent, shit!" Then incomprehensible sounds that were a form of begging.

Hollis's stomach turned, but he stayed where he was. The boss had set this spectacle on purpose. Round table, dark room, attaché case on display. A dozen seats — eleven witnesses versus the accused.

Mia leaned toward him, in full sight of everyone, and purred, "Watch this, Hollis. Someday, he'll do the same thing to you."

She gripped his crotch. Hollis scooted back, drawing stares. Beyond the door, one of Thomas's house guards ran past, yelling for another. Trouble elsewhere in Dodge, Hollis supposed.

The boss, who'd caught Hollis's eye, returned his attention to the thief. Hollis, because he didn't want to look at Mia or watch a knifing, put *his* attention on the attaché case.

Sixty million dollars?

It'd have to be negotiable bonds. That much cash would never fit in so small a space.

No wonder the hipster had been tempted.

Mia's slim, soft hand slithered beneath his chin like a serpent. She pressed her palm flat on his cheek, and on it, Hollis could smell her expensive lotion — lilacs and intercourse.

She turned his head toward the thief, almost directly across from the boss. She lowered red-painted lips to his ear and, hot air on his skin, whispered, "Watch."

"I'm sorry," Jayson blubbered. "I'm so sorry. Please, don't hurt me."

Another two men rushed by the entrance. Hollis thought he could hear something outside, like muted shouts.

Finally, Thomas sighed. Instead of extending the knife, he offered a hand.

"Look me in the eye, shake my hand, and tell me you're acting alone, and I'll believe you."

Jayson, a relieved expression claiming his features, slowly extended his hand.

Thomas took it, slammed it palm-down on the table, and used the big knife in his other hand to pin it to the wood.

Chairs scooted. Hollis stood and Mia, standing as well, stagger-stepped away, managing to keep balance in her too-tall heels. Someone shrieked like a woman, but Mia was the only gal in the room. A big man with two gold-hoop earrings was in the corner, gagging.

Better not puke, Hollis thought at the man, *or you'll be next.*

"Cut him up," Thomas told the men between him and the thief.

But as Jayson screamed in pain and bled all over the lacquered oak, and as bad guys shifted to comply, an alarm started to scream. Those Hollis had seen rushing by poured into the room. They gaped at Jayson, stared at the two men moving to take him away and obey the boss's last order, then turned to the boss and stood at semi-attention.

"What the fuck," Thomas said.

"I'm sorry, sir," said the first of the men, swallowing before he continued. "The perimeter communication line is failing. The house is unprotected, and we can't close it down."

"The system uses cellular," Thomas told them.

"Yes, sir," said the other. "But all the cell networks are down, as well."

2

SHOUTING. About the gates, about the alarm, about the cellular networks and the security system's fault without cell service in place. Hands patted pockets, everyone forgetting they'd surrendered their phones at the gate.

How could *all* the networks be down? The guards said they were overloaded, with every line occupied.

But how could that be?

Had everyone in the world suddenly decided to call their mother?

Hollis was looking at the attaché case. Alone in the middle of the table, now that all the chairs were abandoned.

He looked up. Mia was watching him. More importantly, she'd been eyeing the case a second before.

Both of them froze.

Between them, a foot from the case, Jayson's hand had paled, playing Pat-a-Cake in a spreading pool of blood with that giant knife enforcing the rules.

Hollis stared at Mia.

Mia stared at Hollis.

Her hand twitched. So did his.

His leg twitched. So did hers.

Finally Jayson, seeing them both, lunged for the handle. How he planned to get away with half his blood draining from an in-progress pithing, Hollis had no idea. That's why he pivoted and, without thinking, punched Jayson hard enough to throw his weight backward and elongate the wound in his hand.

The case scooted away, toward the table's edge. Mia dove for it, failing to summit an intervening chair, and managed only to graze its far edge. Hollis tried to recover it, but the case had ideas of its own. It canted upright like the Titanic going under, sliding between wheeled chair and table to strike the floor.

The boss turned. Followed by the guards.

Hollis hit the floor, hands scrambling for the sixty-million-dollar prize. Mia was already under, gripping the thing with both hands. Hollis got an edge and pulled, but Mia had a double grip to his single.

She yanked and freed it, then her face lit with a partial-second victory before momentum threw the thing's edge into her jaw, opening a tiny gash.

"What the fuck?" someone above the table shouted.

Hands raked chairs away from the table, throwing light below. But at the same time the alarm changed pitch, growing both louder and more shrill.

Thomas bellowed, "SOMEONE SHUT THAT FUCKING THING OFF BEFORE I START SLITTING THROATS!"

Feet moved in the other direction, dragging chairs, banging a cross-member across Hollis's face. Hands gripped his feet, tried to drag him out by his trademark alligator boots.

Hollis, knowing he was already in for a penny and therefore might as well go for the pound, stomped backward hard and crushed his assailant's balls. The man wheeled backward. Hollis grabbed the case.

Mia, turned halfway around, put a foot against the case and shoved. It slid across the polished floor, striking a tacky plaster pillar with a bust on its top.

Open floor. Too much chaos, and only seconds had passed. Half the people in the room hadn't grasped what was happening over the protesting alarm techs, shouting guards, and threats from the boss.

Hollis rose and dove, sliding like a kid down a waxed hallway in stocking feet. Unfortunately, Mia did the same and they found themselves holding the case together, two hands each, flat and humping the floor, Mia's dress slit torn upward in the tussle to reveal her upper thigh.

"Let go!" Mia hissed.

"Tell you what, I'll make you a deal. If—"

She punched Hollis in the face, drawing blood.

Then she was up, case held against her chest like a swaddled baby. She dodged one way and then the other around the table.

She's not protecting it. That bitch is taking it for herself.

Over his dead body.

Hollis, losing options as men circled from left and right unholstering their guns, took the only logical shortcut. He dove across the big table, barely avoiding Jayson's hand but not the blood puddle. The table ended too soon, and he struck the ground face-first on the opposite side.

Hollis was up in a half-second, barely avoiding a grab, crashing through Thomas Davies in pursuit of Mia in a way unlikely to earn him further employment at the house.

He leaped and took her in a flying tackle. They both

struck the ground, Hollis atop Mia, front to back. Both held the case, wrestling for possession.

His dick made a discovery.

That's interesting.

With the cavalry coming, Hollis raked up Mia's dress, elongating the rip, and slipped out the hard metal thing that had given him a close encounter — a tiny pearl-handled pistol, almost adorable, but deadly enough for this particular dance.

He pointed with one hand, using the other to hold her flat. For the time being, she was too preoccupied with indignity to run. That would change, but for now Mia was shouting that he'd ruined her dress while trying to cover her underwear. Oh, well — served her right, keeping a get-out-of-jail-free card so close to her hoo-ha.

Thomas raised his hands when he saw the tiny muzzle, but he laughed, too. "Please ..."

Now that Hollis was mostly into the hallway, he could see the security guys were the tip of an iceberg. There was something seriously fucking wrong going on, and it didn't seem confined to the house. From here, Hollis could see the windows and the rest of Hill Country spread out below. Whatever incident caused the cell networks to overload had also caused a hell of an accident on 2244 headed toward 360. Smoke plumed in a dozen places, and Hollis could hear sirens even from up here.

"Look," he said, swinging the gun back and forth in a game of firearm whack-a-mole, forever aiming at whoever seemed most likely to draw. "Something tells me everyone's got their hands full around here. I'll just get out of your hair."

A personal bodyguard named Morton chose this moment to casually step between Hollis and the boss. He slowly drew his gun from a shoulder holster and, despite Hollis's protests that he'd shoot if provoked, flicked the safety off and pointed his weapon at his forehead.

So Hollis rolled, putting Mia between Morton and himself. He stood, pointing the little gun at the side of her head.

Mia began swearing loudly. She slapped at him everywhere using every appendage. Holding on wasn't easy. He still had the sixty-million-dollar attaché case in his other hand, and that arm was doing double duty trying to hold her still. Mia seemed unaware that he had a pistol against her skull.

"Come on, Hollis," said Thomas. "This isn't you."

"Well, then who's it holding your gal?"

"You turn on me, you lose your protection. Brendan Banks isn't as reasonable as I am." Thomas looked at the case in his hand. "And believe me, you really don't want to owe us both."

Morton pushed closer, trying to get a shot at Hollis around Mia's head. Thank God for the study doorway and the bottleneck it offered. Without it, the rest of the room's goons would have surrounded him in a crescent.

Hollis pushed the muzzle against Mia's head, mussing her brown hair. He jerked his head at the window, where something large had just exploded.

"Tell you what. You stay here and fret on Brendan, and the Missus and me'll head out into whatever-the-fuck and take our chances." He moved back, aware of the hallway. If security guys came now, Mia's angle wouldn't protect him. "Tell 'em to open the gate."

Thomas shook his head. "You won't hurt her."

"Says you. This was my favorite shirt."

"Where are you going to go?"

"Don't you listen? Shopping."

The men pressed forward. Hollis, delighted to see that the little gun had an exposed hammer, cocked it for drama.

A uniformed guard appeared at the hallway's end, saw the Mexican standoff, and froze.

"Hey, Chappy!" Hollis shouted. "How 'bout you do us a favor and open the outer gate?"

The guard looked at Thomas, who gave a reluctant nod.

"You really sure you want to do this?"

"Sure, I do. My fortune teller says I lived too long already."

He backed out, sure he'd be pinned at any moment. The house had to be full of security, and he couldn't face Mia toward all of them. But the ruckus beyond the gate claimed an unfair share of attention — something Hollis saw as he dragged Mia kicking and screaming and biting and swearing past the big windows. The staff seemed to be mostly out on the lawn, looking toward the sky.

"Let me go!" Mia screeched, raking her nails across the exposed skin of his wrist.

She bit him. He slammed her into the wall.

Out onto the rear patio. Through the open, which felt incredibly exposed but turned out to be entirely safe. The clot of goons came as far as the door, then spilled out slowly like spreading ooze. Hollis managed to keep them all at bay by throwing the little gun here and there, training it mostly on Mia's brain.

Fortunately, the wireless dongle was resting in the console of a Testarossa sitting unoccupied in the long driveway. Hollis knew there was a fob in the maid's minivan because he'd taken it on an errand earlier, and it had auto drive, but fuck a dramatic escape in a *minivan*.

Hollis threw Mia into the passenger seat, and of course

she'd locked him out by the time he got to the driver's door. Good thing he'd grabbed the dongle. He used the gun to drive her back, then pulled the seat belt out to the stop, used the Leatherman knife in his pocket to cut one end, and the now-extra-long strap to tie her arms to her sides then her body to the seat. A sloppy job, but if she squirmed he could shoot her, or threaten it.

"You got the car! You don't need me!"

"Well, lady, I hate singing alone on road trips."

Gunfire invaded the garage. They weren't even inside; they seemed content to fire blind. A slug pocked the vehicle's side. Shooting something so beautiful should be illegal.

Reverse.

Floored it.

With guns blazing beyond the window, Hollis swung the car around and managed to get into first without dying. He revved the engine to a ridiculous speed before remembering he'd need to shift, then hit second by the time the gate came into sight. Closed, of course.

Mia, now paralyzed by his driving, was ramrod straight and white as a sheet.

Hollis was wrenching the wheel. Gates in Texas were usually designed for privacy. The Davies gate was no exception, so he aimed the Ferrari's pretty red hood at the shrubbiest part between two hedges and floored it. There was a bang and a jostle, but the car emerged with nearly undiminished speed on the other side, now raising gravel on the driveway.

He hit the wipers to clear the window of leaves and twigs, then turned to Mia with his winning smile.

"Well, lookie there! Ain't nothin' gonna stop us now, baby."

She thrashed, her eyes furious. But the belt held, and so

Hollis put the pistol in his lap, anticipating the need for both hands as they approached the first of several accidents looming ahead.

Occupants were outside of their smoking cars, duking it out. Hollis spied an impossible amount of bottled water, sleeping bags, and what looked like a camping lantern in the backseat of one. The other's trunk was popped from the fender-bender, and Hollis saw three big green military gas cans, along with a lot more water.

Hollis pulled around them on Thomas's fancy-pants street, then made a slalom toward Bee Cave, slowing only to glance at the quarreling motorists — in whose eyes he saw absolute, abject terror.

He thought of what the guards had said, about the cellular networks being overloaded. About the fires and sirens. If he had his phone, Hollis could play cell tower lottery, reloading pages until he got a signal. But of course his phone — along with Mia's, judging by her skin-tight outfit and lack of a purse — was back at the house under lock and key.

"What the hell do you think is going on?" Hollis asked.

Mia, only now seeing the furor around them, didn't respond.

3

THE RADIO WAS FILLED with assholes.

As the car turned hard right, blowing burned rubber into the atmosphere, Hollis managed to punch the thing on and fill the cabin with the last-played station. He wanted news, but got music instead — a 70s station playing "Little Willy" by Sweet.

"Do we really have to listen to this?"

"I'm just trying to find news, sweetheart."

"Well, good job."

Hollis grunted. But truth was, he agreed. Sweet was not exactly thrumming getaway music. Next, they'd probably play some Bee Gees. This maybe being the end of the world and everything.

"I think I'm getting brain cancer," Mia said.

Hollis had played fast and loose on Marley but wasn't about to take chances on Bee Cave. The road was a swerving roller coaster through the hills when clear and had become a thrill ride of obstacles and dumb people in SUVs, most of whom were honking at folks they could just go around.

Hollis saw a pair of black pickups in his rearview.

Nobody owned pickups souped up for power and speed, let alone a pair of them. Except maybe Thomas Davies, who probably wanted his wife back.

Oh, who was Hollis kidding? Thomas wanted his case back.

The song ended as he executed a quick left-right-left, nearly painting the Ferrari's windshield with a trio of oblivious runners on the berm.

News, finally.

Except it was old news, from yesterday.

He could see people on their porches and on the roadsides, looking at their phones and then at the sky.

Hollis strained low to glance upward. Not a good idea. He clipped the car next to him as his foot nudged the Ferrari past 90 MPH. All of these rubberneckers were staring at nothing.

The news ended its story about the newest acts booked for Austin City Limits then went on to recap the latest speech from Governor Jefferson Garrett, who was always talking about guns, freedom, and secession. "A Texas for Texans." To Hollis, he always sounded like Yosemite Sam.

There was a slam, and the entire car shook. Out of pure instinct, Hollis managed to keep the wheel straight. He goosed the accelerator to give some distance, then glanced back. The big black pickups were right up their butt. Up close, they looked big enough to drive right over top of the little red speedster.

"Just pull over," Mia said. "Let me out, and he'll let you go."

Hollis begged to differ. Mia didn't just peck at Hollis and her husband's other guests, she also told him how to run his business. Guys like Thomas didn't like fielding the opinions of others, and there was a fair chance he was cool with her abduction. Either way, Hollis was dead if he stopped. Unless she wanted to jump out at high speed, Mia was with him for a while.

"Look out!"

Hollis had jockeyed onto the berm to dodge the trucks, wheels flirting with roadside gravel. Bikes loomed ahead. He made a split-second decision, opting for a strong nudge into the car on his left. The bikers, hearing the Ferrari's hungry engine, got the message and pulled to the far right.

It wasn't enough.

Just before Hollis's bumper hit their back wheels, both corrected too hard and rolled into the gravel and grass as Hollis screamed by.

Once clear, he floored the accelerator. The car leaped, widening the distance between them and their pursuers.

These damn hills and curvy roads. If Hollis could get onto a clear straightaway, he'd leave his pursuers in the dust. But he wasn't used to driving stick, and taking those corners without at least easing the pedal made him want to crap his pants. Hollis was probably supposed to drop a gear and slam it hard after a slowdown, but without that finesse he kept the shifter where it was, and the trucks held their pace.

Cars ahead. Normal traffic. Might as well be folks out for their usual errands, going to the grocery store and whatnot. The light turned green, and oncoming cars were starting to move. Folks were freaking out, but still obeying the rules of the road. At least for now.

"You got your seat belt on?"

Mia, still bound tightly in the modified belt, gave Hollis a look of intense loathing.

He took a breath.

"Guess I lived long enough," he said.

Dropped the shifter. Finessed the clutch, in and out.

Slammed the gas.

Hollis whipped the wheel to one side and then the other, carving a tight C-shape around the traffic ahead, into opposing traffic, then barely threading the needle to squeak back to the right. Miraculously, he hit nobody, but everyone behind started honking and swerving in delayed reaction.

Which caused just enough chaos — and closed the gaps just enough — that when the first of the black pickups tried to follow, it hit the vehicles on both sides. Hollis watched the rearview, seeing the pickup flicking the front ends of two vehicles apart like flippers in a pinball machine.

There was a long line of people emerging from a subdivision, all pointing up, by the side of the road. The gathering was peaceful — a stark contrast to the aggression they'd witnessed elsewhere.

Whatever was happening, it was brand new.

Hollis pointed the Ferrari straight ahead, checked the rear, and mapped enough of the road ahead in his mind to divert his eyes for a second.

"LOOK OUT!" Mia shouted.

Hollis was just looking up when glass and metal slammed off to their side. A car in the right lane not fifty feet ahead, T-boned by a vehicle speeding out from a side street, and ignoring the stop sign.

"Jesus Christ. Jesus Christ." Either Mia had seen something in the accident that Hollis hadn't or delayed reaction was only now hitting her. Her chest was rising and falling too fast, nearly hyperventilating.

He returned his attention to the radio. The tight suspension obeyed his every movement.

The car swerved, and Mia screamed.

"Settle down, will ya?"

"Watch the road!"

"I need to figure out what's going on." He tapped the radio. A touchscreen — state of the art, and totally non-intuitive. What happened to knobs and dials? "You hear anything before we split?"

"I was too busy being dragged out by my throat."

More to himself than Mia, Hollis muttered, "This city, man. The lake's up, right? Maybe that Stevie Ray Vaughn statue got his tootsies wet."

He found a news report just as Mia shouted for his attention.

He looked up, swerved to barely avoid a couch — a fucking *couch* — that some dumbass had lost on the road. A big engine revved from one side, near the back quarter panels, and Hollis saw that they had company again.

He slammed the gas, watching the remaining pickup vanish behind.

Ahead, where Bee Cave ran into 71, a line of cars had grown. His brain was trying to square it with the news report, but was only paying a tenth of his attention. The rest was focused on getting away, staying alive.

Cars. Clogged in both directions. A massive jam ahead had clotted the large intersection.

And the pickup was closing.

Hollis looked left. Just before the intersection, a slightly smaller big old mess. An opening. And they were approaching too fast.

Mia saw his glances, the gridlock ahead, and the black truck full of armed men behind. She must have guessed that he was about to do something idiotic. Her face changed.

"Wait," she said.

But then Hollis yanked the wheel hard left and Mia struck the passenger-side door, his shoulder almost touching her headrest.

Into a parking lot, over a speedbump, rattling the undercarriage. The truck behind them tried to copy the maneuver, failed, and struck the rear of a stopped Tesla before jockeying the wheel and turning to follow.

Blitzing between rows of a grocery store parking lot at better than sixty, Mia gripped the seat beneath her. "WHAT THE HELL DO YOU THINK YOU'RE DOING?"

"Gotta stop at HEB for some cereal."

A woman pushed a cart into the aisle in front of them, saw the Ferrari too late, and dove out of the way. They smashed into the cart, sending groceries hither and yon. A box of Cinnamon Toast Crunch landed on the windshield as the bashed cart spun away.

A grin broke across Hollis's face. He pointed at it and half laughed, half spoke. "H-hey! Lookie that!"

"HOLLIS!"

Which was supposed to be a warning about the family ahead, who he managed to avoid killing with a hard right, not quite managing the full turn. Hollis raked a line of red paint across the rear of several cars a lot less impressive than his ride as they slowed to fifty then bolted down the aisle in the wrong direction.

The truck, far less agile, cut the distance by taking an angle.

"You know what? Fuck HEB. I ain't that poor. There's a Whole Foods on the other side of the street."

And a second later he was out the plaza's front, hard right onto 71, a sloppy angle, reaching all the way out into the turn lane before correcting. On the corner was a little dry cleaner with multiple signs stating that drivers shouldn't cut the corner through their lot, but Hollis was feeling creative and disobedient and cut it anyway, hitting another speed bump, roaring around the massive logjam and heading in the exact opposite direction as before, the grocery plaza now on the right.

Somehow, Mia had gotten her hands free, but both were on the dashboard, elbows locked.

Adrenaline surged. The chase had gone from blood-chilling to fucking awesome. Now feeling the Ferrarri's tight handling, Hollis looped around the jam, onto the berm and then the grass, meaning to get back onto 71 in the same direction he'd just left before the jammed intersection had stopped him. But douchebags had blocked the turn lanes and there was a curb ahead the low vehicle couldn't handle, so he turned into the opposite plaza, past a liquor store and a sporting goods store, past the Whole Foods he'd joked about a minute ago.

Then he hooked a thumb over his shoulder, pointing at a barbecue joint near the entrance, and said, "You and Thomas ever go there? Good brisket. *Aaaalmost* as good as Smitty's."

"What?"

Hollis looked over his shoulder, seeing how far back the truck was now, and considered looping back to taunt it. Then he remembered dying and decided otherwise.

"This car's got her some pick-up. Watch this."

"I don't want to watch any—!"

Accelerator to the floor. A Barnes & Noble blurred by on the right, then Hollis circuited a traffic circle inside of two seconds flat. There weren't many cars at this exit, so he pushed around one, the Ferrari's passage shoving it tighter to its neighbor.

Hollis felt the door crumple and watched the glass crack and prepare to fail. The sporty ones weren't really made for pushing others around. But it held, and the car tipped but kept its feet, and then with a cacophonous bump they were back on 71 heading northwest, away from the city.

Their pursuers might be back there somewhere, but the little red jet was in its sweet spot now, mostly straight roads, able to top out and turn itself into a blur.

Only once the rearview was clear could Hollis hear the radio. Finally able to focus on what he was hearing — what, he supposed, his deeper mind had gathered from the start but was only now willing to believe.

"Pull over," Mia said.

Hollis's mouth was open.

The voice on the radio repeated: "... an armada of what appear to be alien ships approaching from Jupiter's orbit, with the popular Astral app predicting an arrival within the next six days ..."

"Pull over!"

"Fuck you, 'pull over'! ET's on his way, and my ass doesn't plan to be around to see him—"

Mia reached over like lightning and ripped the wheel toward her while stepping over the console and stabbing her unshod foot hard on top of his, finding the brake only after smashing Hollis's toes.

The Ferrari skidded to a stop beside some kind of ranch fence — halfway the hell out of Dodge already.

He stared murder at Mia. Then, he looked at the door.

"Fine! You wanna go free, get the fuck outta my car!"

But Mia didn't move. Her head slowly shook. "No. We have to go back."

4

MIA SAT IN HER SEAT, hands finally free, using that freedom to defiantly cross her arms. She'd had just about enough of Hollis Palmer's bullshit. He was handsome and knew it, and like a lot of good looking guys who'd always had things easy, he was obnoxiously cocky.

But unlike Hollis, who'd acted on impulse, Mia had plans before today had gone so totally wrong. Hollis and this absurd alien panic had thrown a wrench in those plans, but that didn't mean she was ready to surrender. Not after all the time, money, and effort she'd spent to line up the dominoes.

Governor Garrett, now blaring through the radio, said, "We are *Texans!* If spacemen are really on their way to our planet, I say we raise our militia and tell them, 'COME AND TAKE IT!'"

"You hear me?" Again, Hollis gestured at her door. "You wanna leave? Then go on, git!"

"This is my car more than yours. It's going where *I* say it's going."

"Are you forgetting the part where I stole it? I'm not exactly interested in chain-of-title, missy!"

"Don't call *me* 'missy'!"

"Okay, *sir*."

Mia crossed her arms harder.

"Pout all you want. I like my kneecaps intact."

Mia rolled her eyes. "I don't want to go back to the *house*. I meant, we can't leave the city yet."

"Why the hell not?"

She was thinking fast, trying to adapt on the fly. Mia knew what she needed, but not quite how to get it.

"The attaché case," she said.

"What about it?"

"Open it."

"Why?"

"Just do it. What, do you think little old me is going to take it away from you?"

Hollis shrugged, reached into the back seat, and brought the silver case forward. The locks wouldn't open, of course. The case remained stubbornly closed.

"Wonderful." Hollis said. "What's the code?"

"I don't know. And you can't open it without one."

"Sure, I can. There's a Lowe's back there. I'm sure I can find a crowbar, or some other code inside."

Mia shook her head. "That's a Dvinsk impenetrable attaché. Thomas has three of them. They cost fifty grand each, and one of the three he uses as a party game. He likes to bet guys they can't get out whatever he puts inside, and he's never lost. I've seen that case beaten with rocks, pried with crowbars, shot ... even blown up once, at a quarry outside of town. Oh, and at the quarry? They tried a jackhammer, running it over with one of those twenty-foot-tall rock-movers, anything you can imagine. And even if you *could* force the lock or break it open, a mechanism inside destroys the contents. So, yeah. If you have the code, you've got sixty million dollars. If you don't, enjoy your brick."

Hollis monkeyed with the thing for a while, eyed the direction of the Lowe's because why not, then tossed the case back with disgust. "Fabulous."

Mia turned in her seat. "But Thomas has a safe deposit box at the big Chase downtown on 6th. He keeps all sorts of important information in it. Like the code to that case."

"He keeps the key to his briefcase ... at the *bank.*"

Mia acted frustrated with his slowness. "Yes! It's not the kind of box you access with a key. It's the kind of box you access by *being Thomas Davies*. You know how paranoid he is! That box is the most secure place he can put anything. The thing is harder to get into than a bank vault. Nobody can invade his home and find that stuff — and safe deposit boxes, filled with paper, can't be hacked like a computer. The only way to get what's in there is to go through all sorts of legal hoops after he's dead — at which point, he won't care if his cases get opened."

"Still not seeing how this helps me, seeing as neither of us are Thomas Davies."

"You think he doesn't have a second signer? What happens if he's detained and needs someone to get inside?" Mia put a hand on her chest.

Hollis laughed. "I'm supposed to believe he trusts *you?*"

Mia gave a coquettish chuckle. "Oh. You poor *men*. None of you know how easy it is to control you. All I need, for Thomas to give me anything, is for him to be straight."

"Yeah. Right."

Oh, this next part was going to be fun. Mia put a soft hand on his cheek and purred, "Is it really so hard to believe? I got a guy with everything to lose to fuck the boss's wife."

"You wanted that," Hollis muttered.

Mia moved the hand to his leg, high up. Hollis swatted it away, but hilariously, a bulge had already grown beneath his jeans. She laughed.

A car roared by at well over a hundred miles per hour, its roof stocked with camping supplies and bottled water. They watched it round a slow bend, their argument suspended. The Texas governor prattled on, decrying America's lackluster response to this coming alien menace and pointing out how Texans could clearly do better.

"You believe this shit?" Hollis asked, still uncomfortable.

"I don't know. Get me Internet and we'll see."

"I meant, do you believe how hard all these folks are freaking out?"

"People freak," Mia said. "We're not a terribly hearty species."

The governor promised swift action. If the US government wouldn't act, drastic measures would be taken.

Hollis switched the station. "That asshole is going to cause a panic."

"Look around. There's *already* a panic."

"This state, man. Little blue Austin surrounded by a sea of red. Garrett must be happy, having one more reason to turn everyone against each other." Hollis pointed at the radio. "*This* is why we've gotta get out of here. Can't be too long before he does something stupid."

"What, you think we're going to secede from the nation?"

"I know a guy who's tight with him. He's got a fucking arsenal in his yard. And three tigers, by the way. People like *that* are prepared for Texas to go it alone. You heard the governor. He might not have mass support, but he's got enough to cause some problems."

Actually, Mia hadn't heard much of the governor's ranting. For one, she had no appetite for politics or taste for bullshit. But mostly, she'd been occupied by sparring with Hollis.

"Look. I don't like you."

"Thanks," Hollis said.

"You're a self-centered, arrogant, sarcastic asshole with no sense and tunnel vision."

"See, now I think you're just trying to get my pants off."

"But no matter *what's* going on, I don't want to end up alone while roving gangs form."

"Certainly not in *that* dress."

"You've got a case that's worthless without the code ..."

"Maybe I should be happy to get away with my life, rather than doing something stupid like heading downtown?"

"... but it's not just paperwork Thomas has in the vault. Guys like my husband, they don't get safe deposit boxes so much as safe deposit *rooms*. He has guns, Hollis. Passports and cash. Phone numbers for guys who can doctor them with whoever's photo we'd want."

"Which would be great, if we were able to call anyone." As he spoke, he watched the road.

The radio station was all news, the reporter going on and on about alien ships and all sorts of other things a sane world should never see. The Astral app was mentioned a few times — and that, Mia of course knew. She, like the rest of the civilized world, had used it to watch Antares go supernova right on her little screen. If the app had seen ships coming, that would explain the mass freak-out. Forget NASA cover-ups. The people would have been alerted at the same time as the government.

"Even if something's really coming, the radio says we've got six days before it arrives. I'm only asking for an hour or two. Look." Mia pointed at 71, at the southbound lanes. "Nobody's going into the city. Everyone's coming *out*. The news must've just broken. That's why the cell networks overloaded and set off the security alarm at the house. Bankers aren't reactionary. They'll at least finish the day. But we need to go now."

"What if you're wrong?"

"Then we'll be no worse off than we are right now. What's the risk?"

"Getting jammed into some kind of clusterfuck and not being able to get out."

"If you're so worried, we can park away and take scooters." This was getting annoying. Mia didn't like asking for permission. "Come on, Hollis! Be a man!"

"Being a man don't mean being stupid."

Mia wasn't so sure of that.

"Try to think practically for a second, will you? We've got no supplies, no weapons, no phones, no way to buy anything unless you want to risk being tracked with a credit card. And a case we can't open."

"So now it's *our* case." Hollis eyed her, probably wondering for the first time whether she'd tussled with him over the case to protect it for her husband ... or because she'd wanted the thing for herself.

"If we go to the bank, we'll at least have options. And *then*, once we're not running helpless, we can head off to Dripping Springs or wherever you want."

"Oklahoma."

"Louisiana is closer if you just want to leave the state."

"Fine. Louisiana."

"And you weren't taking us in the direction of Oklahoma *or* Louisiana."

"I was going to double back."

"Where?"

"Shit, *you* wanna drive?"

Yes, she did. But now that Mia had the beginnings of agreement from Hollis, she didn't want to push it.

His head turned, now looking toward 71. Which would take them to 290. Which would take them to Mopac, then all the way downtown.

"If it looks bad, we can always turn around."

Hollis stared straight ahead. Then, with a self-loathing shake of his head, he mashed the clutch and shifted the Ferrari into first, waiting for an opening to make a U-turn.

"Fine," he said, mashing his alligator-booted foot down on the gas.

5

THE TRICK WAS GOING to be getting away from Hollis, then to the W Hotel three blocks from their supposed destination. But for that, Mia already had plans.

In the meantime, she'd settle for keeping him calm and on-task. *Of course* heading into downtown was risky. Mia was a rational person and resisted the idea of an alien invasion with every sensible fiber of her being. But it didn't matter if the aliens were real, if the Astral app and the scientists and the congresspeople on the news were right in their assertion that an armada would reach the planet inside of a week.

The *panic* was real, and right now that was the bigger obstacle. Downtown was probably a mistake under any circumstances, but she had few options. Mia had made her contingency arrangements at the W, not knowing she'd be battling mass hysteria to claim them.

"This is stupid," Hollis said.

And sure, it was. But Mia kept reassuring him, focusing on the money and the guns. Men understood that. With money, you could buy your way past anything. If that failed, you could blast your way through with bullets. Nuance was lost beyond that.

Right now, we have nothing. How will we get by as the world goes further to shit without anything to our names?

And Hollis would say, hearing Governor Garrett's proclamations between alien updates, *We should be heading away, not into the chaos.*

We'll run as far as you want, she'd say, *once we have money and guns.*

It was almost insulting. Hollis should have caught on, down to the way Mia kept touching him, talking to him like a baby. But his hands stayed white on the wheel, his jaw clenched.

Mopac north at 290 was closed due to something on fire, and the area was swarming with people out of their cars, lapping businesses and a baseball diamond for no apparent reason. A preacher on a literal box sermonizing to an impromptu congregation not far off, only he was wearing a Pink Floyd shirt, had hair down to his ass, and was swaying on roller skates.

With incomprehensible muttering, Hollis steered around.

"Lamar," Mia said, pointing south.

"Barton Springs," Hollis countered.

So he nudged through and along the access road that ran aside Mopac, honking his way through crowds on foot, and after twenty minutes of mostly civil traffic, they made it to the Barton Springs turnoff. Surprisingly, traffic lightened up as they passed Zilker Park. There were a ton of people wandering the grass, but cars were mostly going the other way.

Hollis pulled in.

"What, you want to go swimming? Play some Frisbee golf?"

He didn't return her playful tone. "This shit in Thomas's locker. Is any of it in backpacks? Bags you can throw over your shoulder?"

"Yes. All of it." Mia had no idea. She wasn't even sure Thomas had a box. If he did, his trophy wife sure as hell wouldn't have access.

"If there's guns, I assume there's ammo? In boxes?"

"Tons."

Hollis drove the Ferrari into the park, down a few switches and turns, then buried it on an obscure side road. Apparently this was to make sure nobody spotted and swiped their ride, so Mia pretended he'd chosen an excellent spot. She didn't care, and wasn't planning on seeing the Ferrari again.

They walked for a few minutes to a parking lot by the Barton Springs pool. Nobody was interested in swimming with aliens on the way, so the lot was nearly empty. A few scooters were lined up along the walkway.

"You know you need an app to start those things," Mia said.

"Already thought of that."

Hollis waited, then headed toward a family marching across the lawn. The father raised his hands as if he thought Hollis planned to rob him, but instead Hollis had what looked like a civil discussion, and the man — but not the wife or children — came back with him.

"Hi," Mia said.

"Hi," the man replied, not looking up.

A quick shuffle, then the man was gone. Hollis was taking one of the scooters, nodding Mia toward another.

"They're unlocked?"

"I traded the guy a hundred dollar bill I found in the console of your hubby's car for two scooter rentals."

Mia looked. The man was returning to his family, who seemed relieved that he hadn't been murdered.

"Why didn't you just take his phone?"

Hollis gave her a surprisingly wounded look, so very unlike the schemer who'd worked with Thomas for the past few months. "Shit, Mia. He's got kids."

He mounted his ride and moved off. Mia had never used one of the scooters, but found it easy enough to ride once she removed her Manolo Blahniks.

Downtown — or at least the approach to it, along Barton, was less of a frenzy than Mia imagined.

"You've gotta be kidding me," Hollis said as they passed.

They saw Torchy Banner in the park — a street preacher one hell of a lot more interesting and storied than the Pink Floyd fan from earlier. And also, a lot more fun. Whereas Floyd's soapbox sermon looked dire, Torchy's was more like a hippie rave. Everyone was blowing bubbles, laughing, and dancing. Torchy himself was visible among them, sporting low-profile sunglasses to accent his black rockstar hair. He appeared to be wearing a half-dozen belts.

"I heard that guy owns Torchy's Tacos," Hollis said.

"I heard he's crazy," Mia countered, yelling to be heard.

"So, it's possible?"

As they moved out of sight, Torchy addressed the congregation, his accent thick. "You are stupid! Aliens will not land if you are stupid!"

Then more cheering and bubbles.

Farther on, they passed a row of street vendors who Mia was pretty sure didn't normally set up where they had.

They'd smelled a special event and moved to capitalize. Vendors were dressed as if this were any other day, smiling as they passed. One was selling beard conditioner. Another had wooden toys that looked antique but were clearly new. A woman with a buzz cut had sculptures made of recycled doll parts. There were also two taco trucks, a brisket smoker, and the Gordough's Donuts trailer, which they'd dragged down from its usual location on South 1st. The people here weren't running so much as milling and taking in the sights.

"They must not know," Mia said when they stopped at an intersection.

"They know," Hollis replied.

Downtown proper, once they left the green area, was less weird, and a little more normal-world. Here they found more folks fleeing as expected, plus long lines of stopped traffic that made Hollis brag with artificial humility that he'd made a smart choice by leaving the car behind. Assuming they kept their scooters close and unlocked, they'd be able to get in, take whatever was supposedly in the vault, and get back.

They made it all the way to 6th without incident, taking the Lamar bridge. The beautiful day was overshadowed only by the obvious threat hanging over everything and everyone. Fear bubbled around them like dry ice in water, everyone moving but unsure of what to do — other than *get out*, like Hollis had wanted.

On their way up to 6th, they passed the W on 3rd. Mia looked at it longingly, the mood of all the people around them finally puncturing her stoic shell. And she realized, against what her logic kept trying to tell her, that she was afraid.

Aliens coming? I don't believe it.

Am I a bigger fool if I worry, or if I insist I'm the only one who knows the truth?

Mia needed to see. Talk to someone who knew — find a source of information better than the paranoid rants of their divisive governor — and set this uncertainty to rest.

But first, she had a rube to lose.

6

Hollis glanced at Mia. Nerves had clearly begun to take hold in her.

If he weren't so occupied trying not to freak out himself, he might have felt bad for her. Might even have tried to comfort her. Not that it'd do any good. Mia Davies was cuddly like a sea urchin.

"You okay, Pixie?"

"Let's not nickname each other," she said.

"Okay, be like that. But you can't stop me. Pixie."

Mia made a sound that was thoroughly disgusted, thoroughly over him and his attempts to be cute. They were lucky she was right and the bank was still open.

"Everyone's looking at us."

"It's 'cause of the scooters." Hollis was holding two things, and they'd have to shoot him to take either away — the attaché case in his right hand and the scooter, by the handlebar, in his left.

Hollis met her gaze and his intuition prickled. Yes, she was nervous. But it wasn't just the panic around them, nor the adrenaline of fleeing from Thomas. Something was bugging her, and it had ramped up when they entered the bank.

"'Scuse me," Hollis said to a well-dressed older woman moving purposefully from one end of the lobby to the other. "You work here?"

"Yes, yes," the woman said. "I'm sorry for your wait. Many of our younger employees have decided to leave early, to be with their families."

The implication was that everyone still in the building either had no family or cared more about the bank than anyone waiting at home. It was sad, so Hollis dodged the comment.

"Can you help us? The lady here needs to get into her safe deposit box. Ain't that right, honey?" Hollis took her arm as if they were a couple, using his case hand. Their scooters clanged together.

But Mia was distracted, and it took her a long second to reply. Her smile took too long, and looked forced once it was showing. He'd interrupted her in thought and felt unsettled by the idea in a way he couldn't quite articulate.

"You sure you're okay?" he whispered to Mia.

"Fine, fine." She brushed his hand away from hers.

"This way, please," the woman said.

They crossed the lobby, heels clacking on tile and echoing off the marble — or fake marble, or whatever the stuff on the walls was.

The woman led. They followed. Hollis felt a wash of surreality. Were they really about to enter a bank cubicle to do business as usual? *Really?*

The woman sat behind a desk. No family photos, just three of a dog — all fluff, like brown cotton candy.

"I wondered if y'all'd be open," Hollis told the woman, mostly to soothe her nerves.

"Yes, yes. Well. We need at least some stability, am I right? What with all the news."

Mia perked up at that. "What have you heard?"

"Same as everyone. Something near Jupiter. Like big silver balls."

"Wait. You can *see* them?"

"Sure. Do you have the Astral app?"

"We lost our phones," Hollis said.

The woman was clicking around on her computer. At least she had a connection. Either a dedicated bank line, or the congestion had eased up.

She took a phone from her jacket pocket and slid it across the desk. "Take a look. Service is in and out, but it saves the pictures every time it hooks up, I guess, so you can see them any time."

Fascinated, Hollis took the phone. He opened the Astral app with Mia huddled beside him. Both gasped.

Silver balls in the void of space, with Jupiter's red-eyed mass small in the background. Hollis studied the spheres. More than he could count.

The woman took the phone back and returned it to her pocket. The computer seemed to be where she needed it, so now she crossed her hands and prepared for business.

But Mia wasn't quite ready. "Are they really saying those things will reach Earth in six days?"

"I think so, yes." Her voice matched the troubled look on her face.

"And *then?*"

"I've been listening to the news whenever I can. Nobody seems to know. Nobody can even *guess*. But the problem is, we're not even a little prepared. We could be, but we're not."

"What do you mean, 'we could be'?"

"The president says they aren't even *considering* a first strike."

"That seems sensible, don't it? Why strike if they might be friendly?" Hollis's mind went back to the Keep-Austin-Weirdoes along Barton Springs Road and inside Zilker Park. *They* sure seemed to think the arrival was cause for celebration rather than worry.

"Well, he's not even *considering* it." The woman's tone seemed to scold Hollis for his naiveté, disappointed that he was as soft on violence as the president and congress. "They're not securing our borders or gathering militias to help the police and National Guard ... we're just sitting here with our pants down! And the Texas legislature is as bound as the rest of them!"

Ah. So that's it.

The woman must have been listening to Lonestar One News, famous for its allegiance to the governor. Unlike this woman, Hollis wasn't a fan of "cutting the tethers to give us the freedom to act without federal interference." If he opened his mouth, they'd argue. And then probably not leave with what they wanted.

Hollis and Mia looked down at their hands, saying nothing, while the woman clicked around her screen.

Then she sighed and forced a customer-service smile. "No use worrying, I suppose. Can I have your key for the safe deposit box, please?"

Hollis looked at Mia, then said, "We don't have the key."

"Well ... you've got to have the key to unlock your box."

"It's not the kind of box that needs a key. See, this here is ..." Hollis looked at Mia for positive identification, but his voice trailed off when she passed a note across the desk. The banker's eyes went wide as she read it, then they darted around the room, searching for someone. Probably guards.

Fuck. He really should have seen this coming.

Mia saw the recognition in his eyes. She snatched the attaché case and, when Hollis tried to take it back, swung it around and hit him. The corner struck his jaw, slamming his teeth together, bringing blood. He reached for her again, but the banker was already waving for guards, and the lobby was full enough that Hollis wasn't going to get out unhanded — not with a scooter in tow or the attaché case Mia was now backing out of the cubicle holding.

Hollis touched his chin, looked for the advancing aggressors, and reached for Mia.

"Now wait just a goddamn—"

"RAAAAPE! THIS MAN IS TRYING TO KIDNAP AND RAPE ME!"

That broke what was left of the guards' paralysis.

They rushed forward as Mia skated backward, out of the closing circle. She dropped her scooter but clutched the case tighter and hauled ass for the front door, running with purpose, knowing where she was going.

There probably was no safe deposit box. She'd needed a public spot and a police presence. *Bitch*.

The guards closed, hands on their weapons. None had drawn. They shouldn't, given that Hollis was one unarmed man. But they seemed happy to have a focus for their agitation — versus the distant and vague threats approaching from above — and might do anything if provoked.

Hollis held out an arm, his palm facing them. "Now hang on just a second."

"Sir? Kneel on the ground for me, please."

"I ain't hurtin' nobody."

"Sir? On the ground!"

Mia. Out the door. Gone, and getting away.

"All right, all right ... just let me ..."

Hollis pretended to set the scooter aside, but instead threw his weight in one direction and swung it the opposite way. The thing made a big, clumsy arc, hitting one of the guards and rebounding into a second. There was a third, plus a bunch of slack-jawed bystanders, but it was better to take his chances at getting jumped or shot than to end up in jail during the apocalypse.

So he bolted. Right at the third guard, who tried to unholster his weapon but got an elbow in the face first.

A half-second later, his alligator boots were pounding the sidewalk.

And lucky him — Mia was in sight, hauling ass south, a half-block ahead.

7

Hollis burst through the bank doors behind her. Damn this straight shot. She should've gone the long way around, cutting down one block then back, to kill his line of sight.

Her feet pounded the pavement, any pain she'd normally feel nullified by the fog of pursuit. She'd hiked her dress so her legs could run free. The air was brisk, and it felt like she was running a thousand miles an hour.

But Hollis was faster. He wasn't carrying a big, stupid case. His legs weren't taking a beating with every running step.

Mia reached the corner at third, jogged to one side, and finally spied the W's entrance, out of his view.

She looked back and wondered if she could get inside before Hollis closed enough of the distance to see her, then realized she didn't have a choice. Hollis was longer-legged and faster — and that was without her holding the sixty-million-dollar case.

Mia hauled ass for the lobby doors. She almost collided with a man in a fedora — a proper gentleman checking out after his stay, apparently indifferent to the armada on its way.

The lobby, unlike the bank's, was deserted. The lights were off.

It gave Mia the chills, as if she'd run to someplace forsaken.

Another glance at the glass front. She didn't see Hollis. Maybe she'd gotten away.

No time to think. Mia shot into the elevator, which worked fine — the lights were out, not the power.

Her room was on the ninth floor. Paid for by the month from a solo account she'd set up two years ago. She'd had the place for two months and had visited once. Too bad *this* would be the second and final time — it was a nice room and she'd planned to spend at least one night. That wouldn't happen now, not with Hollis coming and aliens on the way.

The world would splinter over the next several days, and Mia didn't want to spend those days in a city. Like Hollis, she didn't particularly want to spend it in Texas. Too many guns and folks who'd rather handle the invasion in their own way.

The elevator doors slid open with a *ding* on the ninth floor. Mia trotted down to 909, fished the room key from her tiny garter wallet, then opened the door. She pulled her go bag from the closet, unzipped it, then opened the safe to retrieve the items she hadn't wanted to leave around for the maids to explore. Once she had it all together, Mia dug through the contents like a dog, making the fastest possible inventory.

But it was only mental masturbation. A delay tactic invited by fear. She didn't need to assess the bag's completeness — she'd done that when she'd packed and brought it here. The point was to split on a moment's notice with no additional preparation. As long as she had the room key and could reach the hotel, she'd be able to get the hell out, away from Thomas, and disappear forever.

Fucking Hollis ruined everything. He had to choose *today* for his chaos?

Her gaze found the attaché case.

Fortunately, she'd stumbled across the right thing to steal as Mia made her final getaway. Sixty million was better than she'd hoped. Decent alimony for two years married to a killer.

The bag had her money, secret credit cards linked to a hidden account, fake IDs, and of course a much bigger pistol. She didn't like the thing but knew how to shoot it just fine.

Mia zipped the bag and threw it over her shoulder, then had a moment of panic and dropped it back on the bed. She hadn't seen the transponder for the Tesla Prime in the W's parking garage. She'd emptied the safe bag, but that little dongle wasn't in there. How could she get away if ...

It was on the floor. She'd dropped it, was all.

Mia went to pocket the thing. But of course, the tight red dress had no pockets.

She checked the screen on her burner, noting the time, heart in her throat.

Calm down. You're fine.

Reaching back with effort, Mia unzipped her dress then slithered out of the fabric like a snake shedding skin. Next she opened the bag and, after rifling through the contents, pulled out a utilitarian bra, slim jeans, and a tee. *Then* she pocketed the Tesla dongle, along with the room key.

She was straightening her shirt when there was a knock on the door.

"Housekeeping."

Mia ignored the voice. She searched the floor, the closet, the bed. Satisfied she'd left nothing behind, she shouldered the bag and grabbed the case in her right hand.

Another knock. "Housekeeping."

"No thanks!"

But housekeeping was insistent. The door cracked, hard, and then flew inward, splintered around the lock, smashed by a large sphere of ornamental marble Mia noticed when getting off of the elevator.

Hollis.

She tried to shrug off the bag, meaning to dig out the gun, but he crossed the room first, tackling Mia, throwing her to the bed.

"Get off me!"

"What? You gonna call security again?"

Mia raised her knee very hard and very fast into Hollis's groin.

He rolled off and hit the floor.

She sprung up and dashed.

Hollis took her around the waist before she could reach the doorway, and together they rolled halfway into the hall. The carpet was soft, but she hit it hard. Her vision blurred then cleared. She saw sconces and tasteful decor. Her own bloody footprints leading to her room's door — apparently what had given her location away.

"Now don't go rushing off. I was just getting to like you!"

Mia didn't need a fancy battle routine. Or mind repeating the same winning move over and over. So this time, when she found her advantage, she drove her fist into his balls.

"Bitch!"

But her feet were tangled, he managed to grab her calf and reel her back down.

Hollis stood, wincing, and then had her by the ankles, dragging her back into the room. If her fingernails could just scratch grooves in the floor, it'd be a scene from a cartoon.

He grabbed her, then threw her onto the bed. Without missing a beat, she hit him in the gut. But Hollis seemed to have steeled himself in advance. He held her fast, groin turned enough to the side to deflect future blows.

"Got yourself a little nest here?" Hollis's hair hung in his face. His patience was gone. "I *know* you didn't rent this room just now. I know 'cause I stopped by the concierge to find a really nice five-star steak place and nobody'd seen a crazy chick who—?"

She went to rake her fingernails across his cheek, but Hollis pulled back just enough for a playful scratch. Then he pinned her hands by the wrists.

"This where you wanted to come all along? Ain't no business in the bank, huh? Just wanted to bust me. Shake me loose, then steal my shit and run off." He looked over her neatly prepared stash. "I guess there's a car?"

"Use your own car."

"The Ferrari ain't exactly inconspicuous. Plus, it'll be shit for off-roading."

His hands went to her hips. She flinched as he fished in her pocket, emerging with the dongle for her Tesla.

He stood and looked around the room, now seeing it fully for what it was. Married women didn't keep rooms in the city — especially ones hosting packed bags, guns, money, and an extra ride — if they were on the up and up.

"Birds of a feather, huh? Guess you're just as big of a thieving piece of shit as me. Difference is, I'm honest about what a piece of shit *I* am. What were you going to do, fuck your due out of Thomas, then fly the coop?"

Mia was still on her back, gaze on the ceiling, silent.

With a huff, Hollis grabbed her bag and the attaché. Then he turned to go.

"You're leaving?"

"Honey, you wanted to be free. So, go on. Spread your wings. Frankly, I don't need the hassle."

"Hollis?"

"What?"

"Don't you want to know what's in the case?"

Hollis stopped.

"It's not cash, you know," Mia went on. "Sixty million won't come close to fitting into a space that small."

"Maybe it's a check." Then he moved toward the door again.

"Too bad you came when you did. I was about to find out."

"Using the combination in the bank vault?"

She laughed. "Thomas isn't exactly an intellectual. He uses the same three passwords over and over. Only one sequence of numbers ... say, for a case."

"Oh, and he told you?"

Mia sat up. A smile had formed on her lips.

"You're lying," Hollis said.

"Fine. I'm lying. *That's* why I went out of my way to take it at the bank, then haul it all the way back here, banging it into my legs and slowing me down. Because I *don't* know how to get what's inside." She laid back again, ignoring his eye. "Have fun trying to open it. Forcing the lock will destroy the contents."

He returned to the bed and set the case on the comforter. "All right. You got the code? Prove it."

Mia shook her head. "So that you can take my husband's

property, plus my bag and car, and leave me with nothing? No, I think not."

"I'll give you ten percent of whatever's inside."

"Not a great deal, considering you can't get any of it without me."

"I'll leave the bag, too. And the car. I can swap mine out later."

Mia was staring at him, not giving him the satisfaction of shaking her head.

"Fine," Hollis said. "Fifty-fifty."

Mia nodded. She stood and pulled on shoes. Sneakers, this time. "Deal."

"What you think you're doing?"

"Putting shoes on, stupid."

"You're not coming with. You say you can open this case? Good deal. Open it now."

"No way, cowboy. I open it now, you'll take what's in there and run."

"Well, what good's coming with me?"

"Oh, come on. Smart guy like you? You'll know someone who can turn whatever's there into cash, even if he'll only pay fifty cents on the dollar. Get us in front of that person, and *then* I'll open the case and walk away. Until then, we're a team."

Something blew up outside. Glass rattled in the window frame.

"And maybe we should hurry," Mia said. "Something tells me money and guns are about to be the best assets in town."

Hollis watched her closely, his folksy humor gone. He was cute and sly and cocky, and that one time they'd been together, there'd been heat for sure. But she'd never liked the man, and the feeling was mutual. Right now, the only consolation for teaming up with Hollis was that she'd hate it the same as he did.

He was scoping her in a way he hadn't ever before. For the first time, he was seeing Mia for who she really was — who she'd been before Thomas, and who she was when her husband wasn't looking. Ironically, they were more alike than different. Hollis only thought about himself. And Mia, when her masks were all off, really only thought of Mia.

As she squeezed past Hollis and into the hallway, Mia took her go bag from him. The transponder had been in the same hand, and it hit the carpet. She snatched it before he could. If Mia was done with the damsel-in-distress act, then for goddamn sure nobody was driving her car. Especially not Hollis Fucking Palmer.

"You know what they say about compromise," he finally said. "It's what you call it when two people make a deal that neither likes, where nobody is happy."

There was a scream from the street. A kind of rebel yell — something you'd expect to hear from a good ol' cowboy leading a charge.

"Sounds about right," Mia agreed.

8

"Ardmore?"

Hollis put his finger on Mia's map. She'd looted it from the little stationery store in the lobby. Who knew that people still sold paper maps? Good thing, he supposed. Right now, the app on Mia's burner worked most of the time, but that might change. When the alien armada was first spotted, the cell networks jammed — the disconnect that triggered Thomas's gate alarm and started this freak show. Six hours later, you could make a call or surf the net just fine if you wanted. People lost their minds but got distracted that fast.

Paper maps. Along with the shit Hollis planned to stop by a Walmart to buy or steal. It was best to diversify, get away from a reliance on digital.

Hollis looked at the little cluster of lines representing Ardmore, Oklahoma. He eyeballed the distance from Austin, then moved his finger in a clockwise ark and tapped another cluster.

"What about Texarkana?"

"It's farther. Same for Shreveport." Mia's finger moved now. "Maybe Beaumont."

"Beaumont is still in Texas."

"Orange, then."

"Also in Texas."

Mia seemed annoyed. They both felt the ticking clock, and every second spent on reconnaissance was one more chance they might end up on the wrong side of a war hammer. Picking a destination and route before driving was necessary, but at least they could do it quickly, and with a minimum of wiseass.

"You get my point, Hollis. *This direction.*"

"I want to go north. Arkansas or Oklahoma. Louisiana is Texas's buddy. Give 'em time, and they'll decide the federal government isn't working for them, either."

"Maybe that's not a bad thing," Mia said.

"So you're a secessionist now?"

"I'm just saying, where's the National Guard?" Mia looked out the window. "I think we're on our own."

Hollis wadded up the map and shoved it into an outside pocket on her bag. He stood with decision. "Fine. Tell you what. You stay here and hang with the citizen's army when they start coming in from the outskirts with their guns blazing. But maybe put your slutty dress back on first. And be prepared to hear how you got a purty mouth. Buy yourself some protection."

"Oh, I see. I have nothing to offer an organized group just because I have a vagina."

"Actually, I think I just said the exact opposite."

Mia glared. Enough that Hollis thought she might be changing her mind about going — might stick around the W after all and let him do his thing on his own.

Wishful thinking. She stood and glared lasers into his eyes.

Hollis shrugged. "Ardmore, Oklahoma, it is."

They took the stairs. She'd been dumb to use the elevator the first time. The city was already a mess, and Hollis could see the post-apocalyptic writing on the wall. Not only had watching the lobby display told Hollis which floor she'd gone to, it also might have died with her inside. Stairs never did that.

"Where's your ride?" Hollis asked once they were underground.

"I don't know. I parked it here two months ago. I'll click the dongle."

Hollis considered making one of several sex jokes at the mention of "dongle." Instead, he waited as she clicked it and a horn honked across the garage space.

A black Tesla Prime. Fine car, and not nearly as conspicuous as the Testarossa.

Mia shoved Hollis out of the way when they reached the vehicle, planting herself in the driver's seat.

"I'm driving," Hollis announced.

Mia looked up at him, bowed lips and green eyes feigning confusion. "Weird. Doesn't look that way to me." She reached down, shutting off autodrive and putting the car into manual, to deepen the sting.

Rather than fight, he said, "Pop the trunk."

Hollis rooted through the bag and plucked out the money, the pistol, the phone, and the map. After stowing the bag and case, he got in the passenger side. Then he looked through the stack of cash. Buried in it were several fake IDs, all with Mia's photo. He turned toward her. "Ramona Cruz?"

Mia started the engine.

"You don't look like a Ramona. And you definitely don't look like a Cruz."

She steered the car to the exit. Sun pierced the windshield, dazzling after the garage's dark.

"Maybe I *married* a Cruz."

"I hope it worked out better than your marriage to Davies," he said, flipping through IDs and credit cards. She'd done an excellent job preparing her bag. Only a professional con like Hollis could do better. "You got quite the collection. Separate bank accounts. New identities, probably with their own credit histories. How long you been planning to rip him off and run away?"

"None of your business."

"Are you fucking someone else on the side? Got an accomplice to help you, once you cut and run?"

"Why would I need an accomplice, Hollis?"

"What if you need someone to hold your makeup mirror while you drive?"

Mia shook her head, clearly considering a comment about him being a misogynist pig. He knew the look. And got it often.

"Just tell me where to go."

"Ardmore."

"Right or left?"

"Right."

"You didn't even look at the map."

"Maybe you didn't hear. Men don't ask for directions. Ain't that right?"

"Jesus. You're such an asshole."

He leaned forward, pointing. "Right. That's west. I'm not completely useless, believe it or not."

"35 is on the east side of town."

"Yes, and 35's *never* clear, not even at 3:00 a.m. on Sunday. You want Mopac."

"We just came from Mopac."

"Get on at 5th, ahead of that last pileup. Shit, Pixie. How long you lived in this town?"

"35 is faster."

"35 is suicide."

Mia shook her head. "We should be taking country roads."

"Sure. Once we're out of the city. Ain't no country roads down here. But I'd take Lamar over 35. In fact, let's. I'm hungry."

She must have known he was being sarcastic and didn't reply, but she did turn right, which was an excellent call.

Traffic stopped, and Mia reached for the phone. She mapped a route to Ardmore, then touched to navigate.

Looking at the route, he said, "This takes us right through Dallas."

"So?"

"So, you don't think Dallas will be a problem?" He laughed in condescension.

Mia's mouth firmed. She seemed close to hitting him again.

"I know a better way. We'll get off onto smaller roads once we're north of downtown. We can go by this guy I know's place. He's got tigers."

Mia didn't reply.

"Honest, no-shit. Tigers."

"I heard you the first time."

But now that she was annoyed, this was fun. "And big guns."

No response from Mia.

"Name's Brendan. He even—"

But that was a slip. Mia jumped on him in a second.

"Isn't that the guy Thomas said you were hiding from?"

Dammit. "No."

She glanced over, then broke into a smile that would have been pretty if it wasn't at his expense. "Yes, it is. I'm good with names. Brendan ... *Banks?*"

Now Hollis was the mute one.

"Maybe we *should* stop by. I want to see the tigers. And you? You could relive old times. Is that why you took Thomas's case? To pay back Mr. Banks?"

Yes. Sort of. But then aliens came and all bets were off. Hollis said, "Turn here."

She let it go, but a ghost of that smile was still on her lips.

"How 'bout some tunes?" Hollis said thirty seconds later, tapping the radio on.

A drawling, upscale hillbilly voice filled the cabin, talking about the aliens and the governor. Hollis recognized it immediately.

"*This* asshole?"

"Who?" Apparently Mia didn't know the voice.

"Forest McCafferty."

She wasn't getting it, probably because the context was wrong. So he prompted her. "The actor?"

"Why's *he* on the radio?"

"He lives here. You've never heard him mouthing off about the state of Austin?"

"No."

"Every big issue. Every election. Every time someone doesn't recycle. McCafferty is there with his cape on."

"I've never heard any of that."

Hollis shrugged. "Well, you're probably in Thomas's lap when it happens, bobbing for dollars."

There was nothing in the street ahead. Mia swerved around a corner, whipping Hollis sideways and slamming his head into the car door.

On the radio, McCafferty was complaining about the governor. "The last thing this city needs right now," he said in a voice that always sounded like he had a reed between his teeth, "is a bully."

Another voice — the station interviewer, probably — said, "A bully?"

"That's what Garrett is — a bully. Nothin' more than a hardass with a small dick who—"

"Now, hang on just a second."

"I'm sorry. It's a family show." Pause. "But you know that thing is tiny."

"Mr. McCafferty, we should—"

"Secession," McCafferty said. "Now what kind of stupid talk is that? I don't know if you're seeing the same Austin as I am, Chuck, but this city in particular isn't looking to go it alone, or with 'the great Republic of Texas.' We don't have a militia. We've got a million folks with itchy trigger fingers. That's not organization. That's no reason to snub the federal government, whose help we might need when our out-of-town visitors show up in six days. But okay, let's say we *do* have a problem with the way the president has handled this alien thing so far. What, we're going to do better?"

"Jefferson Garrett says he has a plan, using the Texas State Guard."

"Sure. *He says.* But Garrett doesn't speak for Austin. If Texas wants to secede from the US, maybe Austin should secede from Texas."

"You're not seriously—"

"Of course I'm not. Austin being on its own is as dumb as

Texas being on its own. But let's just for a second look at what's underlying all of it. It's bigotry."

"Bigotry?"

"Sure," McCafferty said. "Rejecting those who are different from us."

"Well ... it is *thousands* of alien ships. It's natural to be worried that their intentions are—"

"Because we just assume they're like us? Hell, Chuck, human society was founded on the backs of others. You know what I'd do, if I was in charge? I'd sit back in a lawn chair with my hands behind my head, grab a cold beer, and watch the ships come."

"Without fear? Doesn't that strike you as a little naive?"

Mia stabbed a finger to change the station. "Yes," she answered in McCafferty's place.

9

ACCORDING TO THE MAPS APP, when it was working, I-35 had turned into a parking lot. Just for fun, Hollis entered start and destination spots on the app that were a half mile away from each other, just to see what it would say. It predicted the trip would take thirty hours.

Mopac was almost as bad. The autodrive kept wanting to turn on, and take them onto the expressway. Mia kept them to the access roads whenever she could. But they were shitty, too.

She slammed her hand on the dashboard, above the speedometer, which read *0 MPH*.

"What?" Hollis asked.

"*What?* Look around you, idiot."

"Green grass. Blue skies. It's a lovely motherfuckin' day." He'd even rolled down his window. There'd been a pack of joints in the glove compartment — *Mia's*, mind you — and lit one up. She wasn't even getting a contact high with the window open, and her blood pressure felt through the roof. She wanted to take her foot off the gas just so she could kick it through Hollis's face.

"Where were you going to go?" Mia asked, just to keep her mouth busy.

"You mean before you told me to drive us right into the center of the city? Into all these people and all this traffic? Is that what you're referring to?" He puffed, held, and waited for her to respond, but of course she didn't. "Dripping Springs."

"Why?"

"Dunno. I had people out there a while ago, before it got big. I know a few places. If you stay out of downtown, it's still pretty quaint and there's not too much traffic."

"I thought you wanted to get out of Texas."

Puff. "Yeah, well, one thing at a time."

Hollis turned to her, saw what must have been visible fury, and did something strange. Held the joint toward her, pinched between his thumb and index finger. "You want a hit?"

"No."

"Don't tell me you don't smoke. Last I looked, this was your car."

"No, thanks."

"So, you *like* the tight-ass vibe, huh? Cool."

Traffic opened. Mia dodged around a few cars on the berm and managed to get back into line without getting honked at, run into, or shot.

Hollis held the joint between his lips, then used both hands to operate the phone. Mia saw him flip to the Astral app, scrolling past the pictures and stats they'd already checked a hundred times. The alien spheres were still too far off for the moon telescopes to see as more than big silver marbles, but the contact time kept constantly updated. It was labeled ARRIVAL and read 5d:2h:15m. Adjustments came in fifteen-minute increments. It was admirable that whoever was in charge felt confident being so specific.

A chill ran down her spine.

Speaking from his mouth's corner, Hollis said, "So. You don't dig McCafferty's take on the aliens. Too woke for you, huh? Do you dig the governor's?"

"Not since he threatened to close the borders in front of the Senate."

"We'll be okay. The legislature doesn't reconvene until 9:00 a.m. By then we'll be partying with the Sooners."

Mia looked at the line of traffic. "If we ever get out of here."

"Maps says it's okay once we get past Cedar Creek. This is just maximum rush hour." He looked at his watch. "We got all night to get through it."

Mia said nothing. She wasn't so sure "all night" would be enough time. Not if the newspeople kept hinting at doom and the people panicked and the likes of Jefferson Garrett and Forest McCafferty were there to fan the flames. That last bit was what bothered Mia the most. She was scared, and the fights and confrontations they kept hearing about on the radio made her angry. People should be banding together, not breaking apart.

But even beyond that, she hated all the grandstanding. It didn't seem like Garrett, McCafferty, or any of the others were really trying to do any good for anyone. From where Mia was sitting, it looked like they were jockeying for political positions. One got attention by riling up the right-wingers and the other was baiting all the lefties. Bad juju for the little blue island in the big red ocean, and one more reason Mia didn't particularly want to be around when the two sides decided to enforce their anti-alien plan as the *only* one there was.

"Fine," Mia said, finally giving in and clicking on the autodrive. She flexed her finger at Hollis's hand. "Pass that over."

10

WITH NOTHING ELSE TO DO, Mia got very high. It seemed sensible. If she stayed sober, she'd have to face a whole lot of things she didn't want to. That her old life was over. That ,by now, Thomas had probably snooped enough in pursuit of Hollis to have uncovered Mia's plotting, as well. That in just over five days, alien ships would arrive with unknown might and mysterious intent. And that the only person on the planet she had to count on during these uncertain times was Hollis Fucking Palmer.

That wasn't how her relationship with the guy was supposed to go. She was supposed to play with him like a cat with its prey. Until it came time to end his misery.

But with the autodrive on and only joints to occupy her mind and hands, Mia puffed and then some. She didn't realize how high she was until going to shift her position on the seat and found her seconds slipping by in fits and starts.

"Right?" Hollis said.

Mia had no idea what he was referring to, so she nodded along. Everything was really interesting. She was also pretty sure the last half hour had taken sixteen years, but she wasn't bored. The conversation had been fascinating. Or so she assumed.

A gap opened ahead of them. The car did the opposite of moving up to close it.

"Mia," Hollis said.

"I'm not driving. It's the autodrive."

"Well, do the thing."

Mia tried to do several things, but the car didn't respond. It felt floppy, like a big metal fish.

The vehicle behind them let out a braying honk.

"That guy doesn't like you," Hollis said.

Mia pressed the starter. Nothing.

"The car's dead."

"Why?"

"I don't know. It's dead!"

"But ... why?" Then he looked out the window.

"Hollis!"

"What?"

"I think it's the battery."

The car behind them honked again. So did several others.

"Is there some sort of emergency charger?" Mia asked.

"That'd be a good idea."

"But is there?"

"Everything is *somewhere*."

Fucker. He was higher than her.

She forgot what the big, pressing problem was. While grasping for recall, the car behind them honked again then gunned its engine, sped forward three inches, and hit the brakes behind their bumper hard enough to jump on the shocks and squeal the tires.

Oh, right. The battery. The car's battery was dead. And that was a problem because ...

The guy behind them rammed their bumper, shaking the cab.

"Hey!" Hollis shouted.

He was getting out of his car, coming toward theirs.

Oh, right. It wasn't a car *with* a battery. It was a *fully electric car*. They'd noted the low battery warning what felt like hours ago, but traffic had been moving so slowly that they hadn't seen a single recharge station.

That meant they had to ...

"Hollis."

"Yeah?"

"I'm really fucking high right now."

The man rapped on Mia's window. She looked up and saw fury. She couldn't quite remember why he was angry, just that he had good reason. They were probably lucky he hadn't come to the window with a gun. Hollis had one on the floor in front of him, after all.

Mia tried to roll down the window. But the car had no power.

The man did not see the rational explanation. He got more pissed, and slammed the window with his fist.

"Hang on, hang on!"

Mia opened the door. The sky had gone dark. But there were a few streetlights along the expressway, and in that glow Mia saw the weed cloud blow away like Cheech and Chong at a traffic stop.

"You see that gap ahead of you?" the man demanded.

Mia looked. It had gotten wide enough that cars from the other lane were gobbling up the opening, taking all their spots. That couldn't be making the folks behind her any happier.

"Our car is dead."

"Then get it off the road!"

"But we can't even get gas. We'll be stranded here."

The man sniffed the air. He looked at Mia with disdain. Here he was, trying to fend for his family, and some idiot pothead thought it was time to party right in his way.

"Well it's not like you're not going anywhere staying the fuck in front of me!"

Hollis got out. Thankfully, he left the gun inside. But others behind them must have anticipated a fight after all the yelling, because several men and a few women were getting out of their vehicles and coming forward. One woman held a tire iron.

"Can you give us a ride to a station?" Hollis asked.

Mia wanted to laugh at him. You couldn't take fuel to an electric car like you could to a gas guzzler. Damn her, choosing the Tesla. There were still plenty of dinosaurs and hybrids on the roads, and all would be better than the brick their ride had become.

The man didn't answer. He pushed Mia out of the way, then ducked inside the car to slip it into neutral. With a series of gestures, the group mind got its many bodies behind the Tesla and pushed until the vehicle was fully on the grass in front of a shitty steak restaurant Mia had visited once.

Then, honking at the other-lane cars who tried to eke in and fill the space Mia and Hollis had occupied, the people returned to their cars and resumed moving.

"What time is it?" Hollis asked.

Mia wasn't sure. She may have slept.

But she was wearing a watch — the little silver one Thomas had gotten for her, ornamentation left over from her earlier formalwear.

"Four."

"*Exactly* four?"

"It's ..."

"I'm betting it's slightly *after* four AM," Hollis said with a grin.

"Why does that matter?"

"Sliiiightly," Hollis repeated.

He laughed, but Mia already felt more sober. Probably her will, dominating that fake sense of well-being.

She grabbed the gun and slipped it into her belt, safety on, shirt draped over the top. Phone in her pocket and ... what the hell, she took her sunglasses from the visor. Next, the attaché case from their trunk.

Time kept slipping. The world wasn't static. It might have been the weed, or maybe that everything had changed forever.

"Get the bag," she told Hollis.

"Where are we going?"

Mia answered in the only way she could.

"Somewhere else."

11

HOLLIS HAD SLEPT a little before the car died, or maybe he'd passed out. But he'd been walking for two hours with a loaded duffel over his shoulder ever since. He kept asking Mia to switch, to trade him for the attaché case if only for a while, but she refused.

He didn't like it — her with the case, its combination, and the gun. So he stayed close, within physical distance should she try to draw, but by now it didn't feel like a real possibility. Two were stronger than one, and with the roads as they were, Mia had nowhere to go. She'd wait to try and ditch him, if she was smart.

Still, when they paused at just after 6:00 a.m. to rest, he casually pulled the gun from her belt.

"Give me that," she said.

"Nah," Hollis told her.

The gun went into the back of his pants instead. Mia kept trying to pull the same trick, falling back so she could grab him from behind. But Hollis kept her to the side or in front, and when she finally complained aloud, he told her she could have the case or the gun, but not both. She chose the case.

Two hours of walking took them a disappointingly small distance. Insult turned to injury when, around 4:30, some logjam in the traffic broke and the cars beside them began to move at almost normal speeds. Mopac was still slower than usual, but quickly reached forty miles per hour, maybe more. If Mia had chosen a gas vehicle — or fully charged the Tesla instead of assuming and finding it half-empty — they'd be out of the city by now, well on their way to the border. Hollis knew that was an accident, but in the moment, with the clock incessantly ticking, it was hard not to be angry.

Around the same time, they'd heard what sounded like shooting not far off. A handful of miles at most. There'd even been one big bang. Some sort of explosion.

Now it was six o'clock. The first hints of daylight were kissing the sky.

"You never told me where you were going to go," Mia said.

"That's right. I didn't."

They walked in silence. Gravel crunched underfoot. Cars with better-prepared drivers rushed by.

"Lots of people coming into the city."

Hollis looked. "Yeah. So?"

"Wouldn't people want to get out, not in?"

"Why? Here, there ... what difference will it make when the aliens come?"

"I don't know. I just assumed cities would be a problem."

Hollis looked back, toward downtown. "Yeah. Because of *people*. You get too many in a small space, and differences really start getting apparent."

"You sound like Forest McCafferty."

"McCafferty's a tool. But he's right about the problems that come with fear. We don't know there's a problem with these aliens, but people are fucking each other up as they make their way here, just the same."

He didn't need to explain that. Mia had heard the breaking news reports and read them on the news sites, same as him. Austin's transgressions (setting aside the crazy governor and his surprisingly large group of followers) were minor compared to some of the things that'd been reported elsewhere in the last twenty-four hours. Looting, riots, spontaneous violence — humanity had never felt more like a civil rind around a rotting center.

There was a roar from the expressway. In the growing light, the vehicle making the noise wasn't hard to see.

"What the shit," Hollis said. It wasn't a question.

"That was military."

"Yeah. But so are those."

He pointed. The rightmost lanes coming into Austin were a never-ending line of green trucks. Some were canvas-topped carriers with troops inside, but others were vehicles that Hollis could only guess at. They looked like big weapons. Armored Jeeps with guns on top. Even — if his eyes weren't deceiving him — a few tanks in the distance.

"The stencil on the side says 'Texas State Guard.'" Mia looked at Hollis. "What's the Texas State Guard?"

"They said something about that on the radio. Hang on."

Hollis took Mia's phone. The signal had been in and out, but right now it was in. He typed 'texas state guard' and waited.

Wikipedia gave him the basics — a largely symbolic Texas defense force under sole command of the governor, established in 1941 at 23,000 strong to "protect public utilities, transportation arteries, and war plants; to maintain law and order; to suppress subversive activities; and to repel invasion if necessary." In the early part of the century, it'd dwindled to around 2,000 people with no official armament and no power.

But the KXAN website gave Hollis its more recent history. Through the previous governor's tenure (and especially since Jefferson Garrett's election on his secession platform), the Guard experienced hockey-stick growth, ballooning to well over 30,000 "ultrapatriot" members before getting re-armed by a quiet initiative in the Texas legislature that Washington, reportedly, didn't like at all.

The most recent news hit for the organization, just a few hours old, reported a clash between the Texas State Guard and the US-official Texas Army National Guard. Tensions flared and sure, a few folks had been shot. But it'd all worked out, and the good Army Guard women and men at Camp Mabry had since either joined the Texas Guard or been dismissed to flee the alien invasion. There was only one imperative in town now, and apparently it'd seemed silly to spend any more time than necessary fighting fellow Texans when there was a much bigger threat just five days away.

"Jesus," Hollis said. "That must have been the shooting we heard. Mabry's not far from here at all."

The line of green traffic continued to march. The tanks were closer, but slower. Seeing them cross lanes of traffic was surreal. Whatever the Texas State Guard's armament had been before, it was recently upgraded. Hollis found himself thinking of that scene from Die Hard... *Now I have a machine gun. Ho, ho, ho.*

"What's it mean?" Mia asked.

"That our lack of mobility is no longer acceptable. Come

on." He shuffled in a half-run, curving toward a neighborhood surrounding an upcoming exit.

"Hollis!"

She had the case he'd nearly given his life to get, and still he was leaving her in the dust in his rush to get away. That, more than anything, finally shook his veneer, and Hollis found himself truly, nakedly terrified.

"Hollis!"

He stopped and forced himself to wait for Mia. The case was slowing her down more than the duffel was impeding him. Everything was moving too slow.

Breath huffing, Mia came alongside him. "What the hell? Where are you going?"

"We need a ride."

"Why all of a sudden?"

He pointed back toward Mopac, no longer visible. "Tell me that didn't look like a coup to you."

"So?"

"So, I don't think anyone's waiting for a legal okay to do whatever Garrett wants. From the news, looks like his crazies have gotten a lot of support overnight. Wasn't hard to take Mabry at all — some because a lot of regular civvies joined the Texas Guard on its way in, some because the Army National Guard was all ready to throw up its hands and hop on the state cause before they even showed up."

"No way. The secessionists are fringe. Everyday people wouldn't—"

"They wouldn't, huh?" Hollis handed Mia the phone with the news site still up, a handful of damning reports on the homepage. "Austin is the seat of government. If Texas the state becomes the Republic of Texas, I guess people figure this'll be where the action is. *That's* why we've seen so many people coming into town. Austin's not just for hipsters anymore. Everyone's coming down from all four corners to help keep it weird."

Mia scanned the screen, but she was a smart girl. She already understood even if her higher mind didn't want to. They couldn't see the caravan coming into Austin anymore, but they could hear it. Plus, now that they listened, there were helicopters, too.

Hollis was shameless. Looting rules applied. He picked up a brick and began smashing the windows of houses with the lights all out, usually with skid marks in the driveway and often with garage doors still open. Even without a clear and obvious reason to do so, a third of the neighborhood seemed already to have cut and run. It was only a matter of time before he found ...

"Got one!" Hollis leapt back through the window, holding a set of old-fashioned metal car keys. Mia was crossing the lawn, holding the case, obediently nearby. She seemed to have given up running. Right now, it was all hands on deck.

Mia's head swiveled as she looked toward the curb for the car that went with the keys. She moved toward one, but Hollis said, "Nope, garage."

Hard to find all-metal keys these days, unless you were driving vintage.

Inside the detached garage was a vehicle covered with an off-white sheet. Hollis peeled the cover back and found himself facing a beautiful robin's-egg-blue Dodge Charger, circa 1978.

"At least we're hauling ass in style," Hollis said.

They threw the bags in the rear. Before sitting, Hollis took the pistol from his belt and set it in the center console. He didn't think. That's just where it seemed to go. And Mia didn't touch it. She knew where her bread was buttered, and right now both wanted it melting in Oklahoma.

"Time," Hollis said as he cranked the engine. The Charger came alive with the sound of roaring lions.

Mia looked at her watch. *6:08.*

"Buckle up."

He had to dodge and drive on a few lawns, but leaving the neighborhood was easy. Same for reaching the access road and getting onto Mopac. They rolled without incident for nearly twenty clear minutes, at decent highway speeds. All the way to just shy of Cedar Park. Hope blossomed alongside the miles.

But Hollis's thoughts were darker.

Five hours. Even in ideal conditions, another state is still five hours away.

Governor Garrett was moving fast, putting his chocolate in the US Military's peanut butter. The secession rhetoric that seemed so ridiculous and radical just a day ago was now almost mandatory. If Garrett *didn't* get the Texas legislature to secede, everyone who supported him would face charges of treason.

Mia seemed to be thinking the same thing, making the same calculations.

"They'll puff their chests for a while. They're all insecure men with something to prove, so they'll all wag their dicks for a day before anyone has the guts to declare ..."

She stopped talking when the sea of taillights glowed a deeper red ahead of them. Traffic slowing, preparing to stop.

Hollis looked up. Ahead, a southbound tank crossed the median and rolled to block the berm of northbound Mopac. A few Jeeps were already in place, and they'd laid out a line of enormous Czech hedgehogs that looked to Hollis like a pile of jacks dropped by a giant.

Hollis — and the rest of the northbound traffic — pulled to a stop.

"Shit," he said.

The borders — not just of Texas, but of its capital as well — were already closed.

12

THE PHONE DIED by 8:00 a.m. It would have lasted longer, but Hollis kept checking it, obsessing over a trio of checkpoints — the Astral app, which occasionally showed new photos but mostly boasted only a countdown, local news sites, and his email for some reason.

He wasn't getting messages. *Nobody* got email when alien ships were on their way. It was a tic to keep him busy. She kept glimpsing over to see Hollis deleting automated spam, trying to unsubscribe, mumbling through the first time, after he'd worked to recover his password. Once, she'd seen him checking LiveLyfe. That almost made her want to take the gun and use it.

And now the phone was a brick. The car didn't have a charger. Mia had packed one for a wall outlet, but they'd yet to find anywhere they wanted to stay long enough to juice it up. Public spaces were dangerous. Even beyond the soldiers, there were clearly a lot of new folks around. And they were *not* interested in keeping Austin weird. They wanted the city sober and focused.

Malls, stores, arenas, restaurants, schools, and all the

other public buildings had become impromptu gathering spots — and, it seemed to Mia, turf worth controlling for any of several competing parties. More than once they'd driven by and seen two distinct camps eyeing the same spot, each distant enough to claim they were only in the neighborhood.

In the parking lot of a restaurant called Jack Allen's Kitchen on route 360, they saw those two parties advancing toward each other like Jets and Sharks, getting ready to rumble. They hadn't stuck around to see what happened, but as they went south, a line of military and police vehicles rushed north. the Texas State Guard with all their big guns, ready to intervene when the locals and out-of-town visitors began drawing smaller ones.

"Where are we going?" Hollis asked.

"I don't know."

"Then maybe you should stop driving."

"Maybe I want to go back to Thomas's house. Turn your ass in. Beg for his protection." It was an idle threat. Thomas wasn't sentimental, and Mia was sure that begging or not, he'd chop her into small pieces and stick her in the garage freezer.

Hollis dragged her out as a hostage. But it wouldn't be hard to find something that would make Mia look less like a doting wife and more like a thief in the making.

Two more weeks, she'd been telling herself. That was the longest she had been willing to keep letting it go on. She'd reserved her room at the W. She'd packed her bag. She'd had her car. All she'd needed was the score, and she'd have slipped away forever. If Hollis Palmer hadn't ruined it.

"You're full of shit," Hollis said.

Oh, hell no. He did not *just challenge me.*

It made Mia want to take the Bee Cave exit for real. She'd die, sure. But in good company.

Mia stepped on the gas. The Charger was built for speed and slammed them back into their seats.

"Hey!" Hollis blurted.

Traffic had thinned. Word got around that the city exits were blocked. Without jobs to do or places to go, the citizenry seemed to be staying put. Mia swung the Charger around a minivan, driving on the shoulder and rattling the rumble strip, then back onto the road.

"Seriously, what the fuck are you doing?"

"I told you what I'm doing."

They passed a church on a hill. The road, between cleaved walls of striated rock, dove down and then up.

"Mia!"

"Tell you what, Hollis. I'm happy to go somewhere else. Why don't you look on the phone, find us a nice hotel. Five stars, please."

Hollis looked at the dead phone, resting in the console.

"Or maybe check your LiveLyfe." Mia turned her head, eyes fully off the winding road. "Maybe take a selfie and make a post. You'll need a caption. How about, *Trapped with crazy bitch. About to die.*"

"This is about the phone?"

"It's about you. You and your stupid fucking—"

"Hey, I wasn't the one who dragged us back downtown. Way I remember it, I was the one who wanted to—"

"—head off without money, credit cards, a gun, or a phone?"

"I had ideas. I would have gotten us all that stuff."

"When? How?" Mia barked laughter, shaking her head. "You're such an asshole, Hollis."

"Is that why you let me fuck you in your husband's bed?"

"*Let* you!" She laughed again. "I got mine, shithead!"

"Okay. Enough's enough. Pull over."

The Bee Cave exit was ahead. They were fifteen minutes from Thomas's house, tops. Mia floored it. The car leapt again, aimed for the exit.

"I said pull over."

"That's just what I'm doing."

"Not at the exit!"

"Why? Worried I can talk my way out of this but you can't?"

He reached for the wheel. The car swerved. Mia's arm went up to deflect, but she accidentally landed a perfect elbow to Hollis's mouth. He reached up, wiping blood from his gums. The car swerved back, both of them racking the doors.

"Are you crazy?"

"All women are crazy. Handsome stud like you — don't you know that?"

He reached for the wheel again. This time, after deflecting, she glared right into his eyes, the Charger's wheels rattling loose stone on the berm.

"Touch the wheel again, and I swear to God I'll drive us into oncoming traffic. Think I care? I've lost my life, got barricaded in my city under martial law, and have *you* for a companion. Don't test me. I very much don't want to be here."

The bluff made Hollis back off. There was a difference between knowing what buttons to push and understanding a person's core. She'd pushed his charm to an extreme, gone so wild that he didn't know how to cope. It was like a dog chasing cars, then finally catching one. Where was all his macho bullshit now?

The car went faster and faster — far too fast for the exit

ramp ahead.

"Okay," he said, raising his hands in pacification. "Mia? Okay. I'm with you. We can go wherever you want. The gas stations all still seem to be open. We can gas up and drive the roads all week. But don't go back to Thomas's." He swallowed. "I can't let you take me back there."

Mia felt herself sliding into a fugue. The past few hours had gone both slow and fast. She'd been inside her head, driving in circles without paying attention. Where *were* they going? The facts were the facts, and only now did Mia see that she'd kept them all at arm's length. But sooner or later, unless she truly planned to crash or return to Thomas, she'd have to face those facts.

As mad and confused and scared as she was, Mia eventually had to stop circling and start doing.

They could no longer leave the city. And in less than five days, an alien armada would reach Earth ... and do God knew what.

Her foot was still on the gas. Her hands still on the wheel, knuckles white, steering toward the exit.

If she went back to Thomas, he'd probably kill her ... but at least that would show Hollis — and this whole stupid military-invaded, alien-infested, panicking new world they'd entered yesterday — who was boss.

"Mia?"

She gave a primal scream, wrenching the wheel hard left. Instead of roaring down the exit ramp at lethal speeds, they raked across a triangle of grass and back onto 360's southbound lanes, still at lethal speeds.

Mia screamed again, and again, and again. Because fuck this world. Fuck her bad luck. Fuck Hollis and fuck Governor Garrett and fuck stupid Forest McCafferty. But most of all, fuck the visitors in the sky. Nobody knew what they wanted or what they'd do when they arrived, but Mia wished they'd hurry up so she could rip those ships to pieces for what they'd done to all she once had.

Mia slammed the brake, hard. Hollis managed to catch himself with his hands, avoiding a concussion.

But neither of them could avoid whiplash as the Charger stopped halfway into the roadside grass, where the bluebonnets bloomed in spring and families pulled over to snap ridiculous portraits.

What about next spring? Will there be anyone left to stand in the bluebonnets?

She gripped the wheel, feeling dizzy. Feeling it all.

Then all the tension left her at once, deflating her taut body and mind like a withered balloon. Everything she'd been holding back crashed like a wave, and Mia fell forward over the wheel, sobbing uncontrollably.

Now he'll run. Now he'll open the door, grab the case, the gun, the phone, and the money, and he'll get the fuck away from this out-of-control broad.

But the door didn't open.

Hollis sat in his seat, waiting for it to pass.

13

MIA KEPT WAITING for the smartass remarks. But they never came. She waited for Hollis to treat her like fragile glass, but he didn't do that, either. He had the wheel now, and she had the gun in her lap. No particular reason. It just felt better that way.

They'd been driving silently for a while.

Finally, he said, "Let's open the case."

She looked back. The attaché was innocent, just as impervious under alien threat as it had been before. Seeing it made her think of the man who'd tried to steal it, before she and Hollis had done their hot-potato act on the way out the door. What had happened to that guy? Had Thomas still felt as vengeful, with the case in new thieving hands and a fresh threat on the way?

"When it's time."

"It's time now." Hollis paused, flicked his gaze toward her, then went on in his calmest, most reasonable, least cocky voice. "Look. I keep rolling it over and over in my mind. We ain't goin' on a road trip no more. We're stuck here. And that means its value is available to a much more limited audience. Shit *will* get real when the ships arrive, and I was hoping to be far-gone from all these people when that happened."

He was being careful with his tone, adding a look of *not-that-I-blame-you* before continuing.

"I know a guy who lives on an island off the coast of Georgia, and he's kinda built himself a fortress. I owe him money and might have screwed his sister, but that's true of half the folks I know. I coulda charmed him, and man, that woulda made for a great little hiding spot. But now?" He looked at the passing road, slowly shaking his head. "Well, we're gonna need a way to grease some palms if we want safe harbor in the middle of a fuckin' metropolis."

"So ... the case. Do you know anyone in town who'd buy it off of us?"

He hesitated. It was only a second, but Mia knew the pause for what it was. A resounding *yes*, with one obvious candidate who for reasons unknown, Hollis didn't want to mention.

"Maybe. But that depends what's inside. If it's bonds, no problem. Ain't hard to find someone who'll pay cash for discounted legal tender, even when there's aliens on the way. If it's something else ... well, the field narrows. So why don't you help us out, seeing as we're apparently in this together. Pop the top, and let's see what we got to trade."

Mia felt a flash of nerves. "That wasn't the deal."

"Fuck the deal. The game changed. First you wanted the case, then I dragged you away and took it myself, before you tried to bolt with it. I guess now we're stuck with each other until something better comes up. We sealed that old deal before the borders closed. It's a new world now."

Mia avoided Hollis's eyes. "No."

"*No?*"

"You heard me."

"W ... *why?*" His irritation back, full speed ahead.

"Because what matters hasn't changed. Once the case is open, you'll ditch me and take what's in it for yourself."

"That's horseshit." He picked up the pistol and handed it to Mia butt-first. "Here. You take the gun. I get grabby, you have my permission to shoot me."

"It's not that simple. Even you knowing what's inside tips the balance of power."

"Not if I can't get the damn case open again! I'm not askin' you to just pop it and *leave* it. Open the thing, then close it again. I don't care."

Mia shook her head. This turn of events was tricky, and she hated every second.

Hollis huffed. "All right, fine. You open it and peek. I won't look. You don't even have to tell me what's in there. Just tell me what *class* of stuff we're dealing with. Is it cash-equivalent, or something only a certain person would want?"

"I don't trust you, Hollis."

He swerved to the shoulder, then put the car in park and killed the engine. He glanced at the case, then at Mia.

"Well, then I guess I'll have to trust you." He nodded at the passenger-side door. "Go on. Take the case. Go as far away as you feel you gotta, and I'll stay here. Open it, close it, then come back. I don't need to see with my own eyes."

"Aren't you afraid I'll run?"

"Not so much. But if you wanna try, I suppose I can't stop you." Hollis leaned past her and opened the door, pushing it wide. "Go on. That sixty-million-buck case ain't worth shit if we don't know what's inside. I'm willing to take the risk."

She thought. "Give me the gun."

Hollis shook his head. "That's a bridge too far. You take

the case, I keep everything else. I think there's no reason for you to run, and if you're smart, you'll agree. I know people who can help us both, and you know damn well I'm smart on my feet. But like I said, if you want to try this on your own? Well. That's a chance I'm willing to take."

She looked at the open car door.

"Oh, come on. You want me to turn my back?"

She searched to articulate her answer. "You'll be able to read it on me."

"I'll be able to tell what's in the case," he said in his best *I-just-want-to-make-sure-I'm-understanding-this-bullshit* voice, "just by *looking* at you."

"You're a con man!" she said, as if that explained everything.

"Yeah, and so are you. Keep your poker face." He looked at the grassy hill beyond. "Seriously, Mia! You wanna die with an ace still in the hole? Right now, we're fucked. But right *there*" — he stabbed a finger at the case — "are sixty million ways we could get *out* of being fucked!"

Mia closed the door without exiting the car. There was a moment of silence, in which Mia looked resolutely forward and Hollis stared in disbelief.

"Find us someone who'll make a bargain, and *then* I'll open it."

"Jesus, woman. Use your brain. I can't figure out who to sell it to if I don't know what's inside."

Mia shrugged. "Then you'll just have to guess."

Hollis's mouth hung open, thinking his ears must be lying.

Then he depressed the clutch, moved the car into first, and got them back onto the road.

"We need somewhere to stay. And something to eat."

"Straight ahead," Mia told him.

14

Walmart, it turned out, engendered no employee loyalty. Without the for-sure promise of a payday at the end of the world, nobody who worked there came in, though looters had shown up in droves.

"Look at this place. It's disgusting," Hollis said as they crunched through spilled merchandise, one eye on the other looters and one hand on the gun, just in case someone got feisty.

"Walmart?" Mia asked.

"Society. We're a quarter-inch from being savages, and it's getting worse. Used to be, it took a famine to turn civilization wild. Nowadays, cities lose their shit if the Internet goes off for a day or two." He looked at the ceiling, as if he could see the sky. "And to think, some folks thought a threat from outside would unify us."

"How do you know it won't?"

Hollis picked up a broken knickknack of some sort. Like a Hummel figurine, only mass-made and much crappier.

"You kidding? Look around. Everyone's out for themselves." He kicked the other half of the figurine, sending it across the wide aisle. "Smash, grab, run."

"Like you, stealing from Thomas."

"That's different."

"How?"

"I decided to pinch that case *before* I knew the world was ending." He gave her a rare sincere smile. "Just like you did, with your little hotel hideout. We're a higher class of criminal."

"And yet, here we are, looting Walmart."

"Hey. We didn't break the seal, but we'd be dumb to just walk away once it's broken, don'tcha think? Where else are we gonna get" — he picked up another broken figurine — "a little statue of a chubby kid with his dick out?"

Mia inspected the figure. "I think that's a hose. I think he's watering flowers."

"Yeah. With his dick." Hollis tossed the thing away.

They went back for a shopping cart each, then loaded up on food first. Shockingly — as far as looted stores went — there was plenty left. Hollis wondered if that should give him hope for humanity. It'd only been a day, but the stores hadn't been emptied. For now, there was still sustenance for the low-grade lawbreaker.

They took water, some fruit, dry goods, and a bunch of cans. Hollis wanted meat, but when Mia figured out he assumed she'd cook it for him, he nearly got another elbow in the eye. They settled on tuna. Hollis also got cocktail wieners, because he found them hilarious.

"Hang on," Mia said. She was headed for the kitchen goods.

"What, you wanna bake a cake?"

Something metal flew at him. He caught the can opener. Dammit, he'd have forgotten. Ditto paper plates and plastic silverware. A man could make do with his fingers, but why should he have to?

They took their loot to the car. Hollis considered staying to guard what they'd gotten so far while Mia went back in, but then he decided against it. For one, neither was comfortable leaving the other alone with the case. But for another, there was still plenty left in the store and people, accordingly, were being more or less respectful. Why steal from them when there was still enough in Aisle Six?

The Charger, being from the seventies, had a massive back seat and trunk. Even after moderate theft, they would have plenty of room.

"You know what we never do anymore? Take romantic weekends away."

"What are you—?"

But Mia stopped asking when Hollis threw a compressed thermal sleeping bag at her face. She caught it just in time to field another.

Then a tent.

Next a cook stove.

"You know we can't leave Austin, right?"

"Actually," Hollis said, moving to the electronics section a few aisles down, "I don't know that at all. They set up roadblocks, okay. But how hard would it be to leave off-road? You know they're not watching every inch of the border."

"With the car?"

"Well, we'd probably have to leave the car," Hollis admitted.

"So we *can't* leave."

"You have a very narrow view of things." Hollis gave her a frame, perfect for strapping backpacks to, filling with food and clothing. "Besides. This is a hippie city. We could camp a hundred feet off the expressway. Or in the green belt."

"I forgot about the green belt."

"In fact, maybe we should head to REI so I can go climbing."

Mia had stopped paying attention. She was moving toward the clothing department.

"What you lookin' for?"

"Clothes."

"I figured that much out."

"There's only a few changes in my bag, and you've got nothing. No offense, but I don't really want to smell you if I can't help it"

"Guess I need soap and deodorant."

"Already on my list." Mia tapped her head. She was looking through racks. "Only problem is, there's no clothes here."

"What do you call all of this?" Pointing at the entire department.

"Costumes, if you want to look like part of a welfare line. We should hit the mall. Hell, even a Kohl's would be better."

"Listen. I'm not really that interested in—"

"Non-negotiable," Mia said, cutting him off. "You need me around because I can open that case for you, and if I'm going to be around, *believe me*, you don't want me in elderly activewear. I'm allergic to polyester."

"So maybe you just look at the labels," Hollis said, taking a shirt and peering at the tag.

"Allergic," Mia repeated, walking away, "to polyester."

Hollis expected any shopping trip to be life-and-death, but the city turned out to be strangely hit and miss. Some stores, like Walmart, had been abandoned then ravaged. Others were as functional and staffed as the bank. They even drove by a gym with windows for walls, and through those windows they saw dozens of people exercising. Treadmills, barbells, the works.

"Is there any chance," Hollis wondered aloud, "that these folks just don't know ET is on his way?"

Mia shrugged. She, like Hollis, seemed to doubt it. "I guess people just do what's comfortable and normal when they don't feel like they can count on anything else."

Hollis wasn't having the mall. But they did run across an outside plaza stuffed with shops, and it struck them both as open enough to chance. Hollis found a miscellany store — like a Target, but smaller and locally-owned — then emerged with a handful of external cell phone batteries, plus a car charger. Mia waited outside.

"He was up and running," Hollis said of the store behind him. "Probably the owner. But nobody's gonna take credit cards. I don't think it's preference, though I sure wouldn't want credit right now if I owned a store. I think the network is down. You still got cash?"

Mia flashed a wad. There'd been five grand when they'd gone to the W, and very little had been spent.

"Good. Gimme the thingy." He extended a hand, flexing his fingers. Mia, becoming fluent in Hollis, gave him the phone. He cabled it to a battery, powered it up, then checked his rounds. The Astral app now put the arrival at four and a half days. They looked over the newest photos in chilled silence.

Then, the news sites.

"Great," Hollis muttered.

Mia looked over his shoulder and read the article.

"Great," she repeated.

"Let's finish our shopping, 'fore the redneck cavalry arrives."

While Mia picked clothing for them both at a string of

unnecessary boutiques, Hollis sat on a bench outside and thumbed through more articles, catching both the inside-Texas perspective and the larger American outlook, painting Texas in a far less flattering light.

The news wasn't good. Not only had the Texas State Guard sealed off all major arteries into and out of Texas and done the same with all roads in and out of Austin, they'd been fortified by what was being termed "concerned local citizens."

To Hollis, the concerned citizens who'd joined the Guard in safeguarding Texas independence looked like a lot of guys with beards and shotguns. The show-offs had more advanced weaponry, like machine guns.

USA Today featured an article headed with a photo of Governor Garrett surrounded by soldiers holding a rebel flag. The motley crew of men all trying to raise it at once made the photo look like the Iwo Jima memorial. The headline on the article ready simply, *Yaa-Hoo!*

Mia emerged holding two big bags in each hand.

"I ain't had a wardrobe that big no matter what's invaded in the past," Hollis said.

"They were practically giving things away. Not much call for pricey clothes right now, and I think the owner figures she'd better get what she can before people start stealing or start burning."

Hollis held up the phone, showing the *Yaa-Hoo!* photo. "If we have to stay here, I'm not dyin' to do it out in the open. Seems like right now, everyone's rememberin' the Alamo."

"The woman in the store said that Forest McCafferty is rallying some sort of 'city defense force.' There are fliers and everything." Mia held up a piece of paper, but Hollis wasn't interested.

"Thought that's what the militia was doing."

"That's Texas. This is for Austin."

"I'm not seeing the difference."

"You know Austin. The hipsters aren't going to let Garrett and his radicals off so easily."

"The Guard and militia people have guns out the ass. How are McCafferty's people going to push back? Harsh language?"

"Probably mustache wax," Mia said.

"Pork pie hats."

"Irony."

They looked at one another, moods lightened by the joke. But after a few seconds, reality returned.

Hollis stood. "Point is, folks'r about to stop being friendly. It'll get worse. Sounds like we got an oppressed population, only they're being oppressed by a group that just got done feelin' oppressed themselves. My money's on the group with the guns, but getting there ain't gonna be pretty no matter what. And seein' as I don't really want to choose a side ..."

"Me, either," Mia said. They were an army of two — or two armies of one, once they finally found a buyer for the case and split the spoils.

"Then we should go. Shopping's over." He looked up. "I know we got all that nice gear, but personally, I don't feel like camping. Too many opportunities for butt sex."

"Or, less graphically, being robbed and killed."

"You say po-tay-to, I say po-tah-to."

"There's a Holiday Inn not far away," Mia said.

"All that fancy-pants stuff you just got, and you want to stay at a Holiday Inn Express?"

"There are better hotels down—"

Hollis held up a hand. "I was kidding. I don't want to stay in a hotel. *Any* hotel. It's too contained, not enough ways out. And like you said, anything that's not a total fleabag is gonna be in a crowded area, and I'd rather not do crowds."

"All right," Mia said. "So what are we going to do?"

Hollis nodded slowly, rubbing his chin.

"I got an idea, and if we play things right, it might be two birds and one stone."

15

There must have been an intercom in the door — concealed so that Hollis took it for a person speaking just on the other side of the wood. But the person who said, "Who is it?" when Hollis rang the bell emerged from behind a hidden portal to his right, pressing the rough muzzle of a shotgun against his cheek.

"That's not Hollis Palmer," said the man with the gun, sawed off enough to make it an oversized handgun. If Hollis hadn't been about to piss his pants, he'd have thought it looked like a 1700s dueling pistol.

"Brendan, hey."

"Brendan?"

"Stay back, sweetheart," Brendan said, eyeing Mia as he stepped forward, as the shotgun pressed harder into Hollis's face. His home's entryway was a tip of the hat to paranoia. His front door appeared to be a decoy. The real entrance was the one he'd come out of — perfect for catching unwanted visitors unaware, as they waited for the fake door to open. He was holding something like a CB microphone with the cord cut — the other half of the intercom, probably. He was also in an open bathrobe, with striped, baggy boxers and a stained white T-shirt. A raggedy, brown cowboy hat perched atop his head, several sizes too small.

"Brendan," Mia repeated, meeting Hollis's eyes. "As in, the guy you were running from when you were working for Thomas. *This* was your great idea."

"*Thomas?*" Brendan asked.

"My husband," Mia said.

"And who the fuck are you?"

"Thomas's wife."

"I can explain," Hollis said.

"Oh, I'm sure you can." Brendan used his free hand to cock both hammers.

"Let's all just settle down," Mia said, raising her hands.

"You stay out of this, Thomas's Wife."

"Brendan? Brendan, listen. I've got a deal for you."

"What makes you think I'm interested in any deal you got? Last 'deal' you brought me got five Russians up my ass and cost me my boat. You know how much I *loooved* that boat, Palmer."

"Hell, Hollis. This really was a great idea."

Brendan tossed his head toward Mia, then spoke to Hollis. "Who *is* this bitch?"

"*Excuse* me?" Mia said.

"Go see if Thomas wants dinner, bitch."

"So, it's nothing but misogynists from here on out, then?"

Brendan, whose property they'd entered through two gates and past four *No Trespassing Or You Will Be Shot* signs, surprised nobody by pulling a second weapon from his waistband and pointing it at Mia. This one looked like a Beretta, but it was hard for Hollis to inspect it without getting his teeth blown out.

"Funny thing is, I could kill both your asses right now and nobody'd care. Not with aliens on the way and an army in town."

"We're not alone," Mia said. "Do you really think we'd come to see *you* alone?"

Hollis heard what she was trying to do, but she was entirely transparent. She'd emphasized *you* as if she meant Brendan specifically, yet she'd already said that she hadn't known who Hollis was taking them to see.

"What's that supposed to mean?"

"It means we've got friends. Three of them, in the woods, watching us right now."

"Thomas's Wife is funny, Hollis. I can see why you're banging her."

"He's not banging me."

"That's right. You're banging Thomas. What kind of pretentious assbag goes by Thomas instead of Tom? Guys whose wives got shot after making up some bullshit about friends in the woods, I guess." Something seemed to be bothering him — a loose end in need of taming. "Thomas who?"

"Thomas Davies," Mia said.

The gun lowered. But the one against Hollis's cheek pressed harder. Brendan's teeth gritted.

"Oh. You made a *big* mistake, Hoss."

"Brendan? Brendan, that's not what this is." He began to talk faster, words spilling like liquid from a broken cup. "I *was* with Thomas. *Was*. But only until I could make my move. I was there, at his house, when—"

"Sounds like what you did to *me*."

"I came to make it right!" Hands up, wanting to back away but now with a wall to his back, Brendan in his face.

"Do you even *know* how much money you owe me?"

"It's gotta be at least half a million, and—"

"Plus a boat."

"Plus a boat! And compensation for the Russians!"

"That's right. For the inconvenience.'"

"I came to pay it all back!"

"Just like that? World's ending, and you decided to square with me? Tell the truth, Hollis."

There was silence. Mia had backed out of striking distance. Their gun was still in the Charger. Hollis said it'd be a bad idea to go in packing. The guy who lived here was easily spooked.

"We need protection," Hollis finally said.

"I see. Well. Good thing I like you and owe you so many favors."

"I brought something to sell!"

"What? *What*'d you bring me, shitstick?"

"Something of Thomas's!"

Brendan's eyes flicked between them. "What about her? Why's she here? You playing both sides?"

"No!"

"I'm here because I want to be here," Mia said.

"That's cute," Brendan replied. "But *you're* not the one who just got a visit from some dicktip with a rep for double-crossing. I guess you made some kind of deal with him, right? He helps you fence something from Davies, and the two of you ride off into the sunset? He's lying. Hollis always lies. Only person he looks out for is himself."

"Listen. Brendan. We didn't plan this. We were at Thomas's compound when the first news of the aliens hit, then decided we'd rather not stick around. We got a case. It's—"

Now the shotgun was pressing Hollis between it and the wall. *"I don't want trouble with Davies!"* he barked. "I got all I need! I don't need his shit, I don't need his people up my ass like some fuckin' Russians, and I don't need you on my property! All I'm trying to decide right now is whether to shoot a hole in you right here and ruin my brickwork, or shoo you toward the dooryard and leave a mess for the morning!"

A shuffling noise came from behind them, from the still-open doorway to the house. A quiet voice said, "Brendan?"

"Hang on," Brendan said to the unseen speaker.

"Brendan, are you out there?"

"Yeah, Ma. I'll be right in."

Hollis and Mia traded a glance. They looked away just before Brendan caught their curious expressions.

"Brendan, listen," Hollis said. "I'm not going to trick you. Ain't no reason to. We coulda gone anywhere. I *chose* to come here. Out of all the places we could go, even knowing how bad I fucked you up, even owing you all that money. You're the most prepared guy in the state."

"That's right. I thought ahead. So why should you benefit?"

There was movement from the doorway. An old woman walked unsteadily into the evening air, wearing a long and well-worn nightgown.

"Go back inside, Ma," Brendan said.

The woman seemed to notice neither the shotgun nor the tension. She smiled at the visitors. "Oh, hello."

"Hi," Mia said.

Brendan glared.

"Ma, please. Watch your show. I'll be right in, I promise."

She seemed indecisive. "Well, all right. But come right back. I miss you, Sweetie."

It was hard to laugh with a shotgun pressed against his face. Otherwise, Hollis might have, and died. He'd known

Brendan's mother was still around, but last he'd heard she was living on her own a few miles away. When they'd worked together, Brendan kept scheduling their capers around errands, like running groceries over to her place. Apparently, her senility had dropped a notch too far and she'd moved in.

She disappeared, leaving the three of them alone.

Brendan pulled the shotgun away. Hollis could feel twin zeroes still pressed into his flesh.

"Just go," Brendan said. "But if you come back, I'll cut you in half."

"Let me repay you," Hollis said.

"Bitch, I figure you owe me at least a million dollars."

Hollis pointed at the Charger. "What I have in there, is worth *sixty*."

Brendan's eyes went to the car. His body language softened.

"Give us a place to stay the night, and I'll sell it to you for whatever you think is fair."

It was a delicate play, but after the appearance of Ma, Hollis thought it was worth the risk. Brendan was a criminal and a killer and easily the most insane person he knew, or had ever met, but even his paranoia and armament stemmed from a sense of fairness.

He'd turned his property into an arsenal because he thought it unfair that the government told him he couldn't own whatever deadly things he wanted. He waved guns because he found it unfair that he should own property and not be allowed to defend it. He'd supported Jefferson Garrett when he'd run for governor because he felt the USA treated Texas unfairly, taking its stated independence as a joke. And, if the news sites were correct, he'd started actually working with Garrett to build a citizen's army because compared to the US military, the newly liberated Republic of Texas was unfairly outmatched.

Unlike Hollis, Brendan Banks wasn't in the business of ripping people off. He fought and he plotted, but never did anything that struck his odd sensibilities as unjust.

Ironically, offering the attaché case for whatever Brendan felt it was worth would net them the best — and possibly only — deal they were going to get.

"Fine," Brendan said, "but you're sleeping with Tigger."

16

"Tigger" turned out to be a 450-pound Bengal tiger. He spent most of his time prowling Brendan's extensive grounds — seven acres near the western edge of the Guard blockade, purchased by his parents before Austin really started to grow — but preferred to bed down inside for the night. He scratched at the back door with his massive claws to be let in ... a door Mia noticed was barely still intact.

Tigger had a miniature harem — two females named Hobbes and Tony. Apparently, Brendan decided on the names before learning the reality of tigers. Too many males led to aggression, sexual power displays, and fighting. Just like with humans.

The tigers had their own room. It smelled like fur and meat. It was also the location of his only guest beds — two bunks which, thankfully, were high off the ground.

Brendan showed them the space, pointed to the bathroom, and told them he didn't want to hear about their bullshit tonight. They'd arrived in the dark, and by Mia's watch it was nearly nine. It was early to retire by pre-alien standards, but the day had been impossibly long. Even among tigers, Mia felt ready to sleep.

"Don't do anything stupid," Brendan warned. He indicated the tigers, all of whom had stretched out, their girth yawning across a floor full of dirty pillows. "These three like me a lot. Decide you want to fuck with me, and they'll tear you apart. Not much you can do to stop it."

"Unless we shoot them," Mia said.

Hollis flinched. He was still walking on eggshells, but in Mia's opinion, fuck that.

"Yeah," Brendan said. "You try that."

He ambled off. His robe was still hanging open, the ratty little cowboy hat still perched on his head. They heard one door slam then another, and the house went quiet.

"So," Hollis said when they were alone. "You wanna play Tiger Tag?"

"How's it played?"

"Get me a sharp stick and a bleeding steak and I'll show you."

"No thanks."

He nodded. "You need the bathroom?"

Mia rubbed her neck. "I really need a shower."

"Really? Here?"

"Well, I had a really nice suite downtown at the W. But someone didn't want to go back there."

"You wanna? Be my guest."

She shrugged. "Nah. The case is here. And I'm sticking with the case."

"Plus, the news says the Citizen's Army is massing on 6th Street."

"Right."

"And McCafferty's holding his City Defense Force rally tomorrow on Caesar Chavez."

"Yeah, that."

"So I did okay, bringing us here."

Mia laughed. Was he seriously fishing for an atta-boy while they were calf-deep in tigers, in the home of a man with antiaircraft guns on his lawn?

"No," she said. "You did not."

"You'll say different when the fighting breaks out and we're safe in here with millions of dollars."

"Yeah, I'm sure I'll come around."

Hollis's grin, as she took her toiletry bag and turned toward the hallway, was almost pleasant. Almost cute.

She closed the bathroom door. Felt the quiet slip another notch deeper. A small window in the room was hung with ratty red curtains, and a cool bite from behind told her the sill was open.

She slid the curtains aside to close it, then paused to look at the moon. It was visible, nearly full, between the dark fingers of nighttime trees.

Never before had the moon struck Mia so clearly as nothing more than a rock floating through space. As was Earth. A big boulder orbiting a ball of burning gas in the cosmic void. Terra firma had always felt so ... well ... *firm*.

The world was supposed to be solid, unshakable, eternal. The foundation of all that was, even if science said it was only an illusion. But now, she saw right through the farce. On the far side of the rock she saw in the sky was a telescope that had spied Earth's first known visitors. As to the rock she'd lived and would die upon? It was one in trillions — nothing special to those coming to judge it.

Suddenly cold, Mia closed the window and curtains. She undressed, then stepped into the shower. As ramshackle as Brendan's house was, the water pressure and temperature were downright luxurious. The past day had been hard, as had the one before it. Two days of Hell, endured without a shower. Hot water was a slice of normal. One comfort she felt comfortable holding onto.

She dried off, wrapped herself in a towel, then took her time applying more hygiene and beautification than was strictly necessary. More normality-seeking. Even flossing felt good. Brushing her hair, even in preparation for mussing by a pillow, was the height of pleasure.

"Shit," she told the empty room.

Because she hadn't brought a change of clothes.

She left the bathroom light on and entered the hallway. But the light didn't wrap around the corners, and in the tiger room she found herself tiptoeing blindly around warm forms, hoping Brendan's promise that *they won't bite, unless you really piss them off* was true. Hollis must have been asleep. All was still.

She could do this by feel.

A light clicked on. Hollis, sitting on a chair by the room's desk, had snapped on the lamp. He'd been looking at the phone. He was shirtless, wearing only sleep shorts.

Mia's hand went to her chest. Her heart was already slowing, but he'd given it a start.

"Need the light?"

"I'm okay. I just wanted to ..." She held up her fist full of clothes, but of course her panties flapped most obviously. Not pretty ones. White cotton, utilitarian, fraying at the waistband.

She was suddenly hideously aware of being naked. Cool air played beneath the towel, which barely came to the top of her calves. She hadn't taken enough time to make sure the tuck knot was secure. She'd planned to get in, out, then back to the bathroom, expecting to see nobody and for the lights to stay off.

Instead of commenting on her state — which would have been perfectly in character for Hollis — he picked up something from the desk. A silver chain, with a tiny locket on the end.

"This yours?"

Mia came forward. Her hand moved from her chest to the hollow of her throat. She no longer noticed the locket. It was simply always there. The idea that it had fallen off was deeply troubling. Even as Hollis held it up — safe, not lost — Mia felt the nerves of a near miss. She could have dropped it anytime, anywhere. It was dumb luck that she'd lost it here, and that Hollis had found it.

"Oh, my God. Yes. Thank you."

Her hand was out, but he didn't offer it. He stood.

"Is it a locket?"

"Yes. It was my mother's."

"What's inside?"

Mia's instincts told her to snatch the thing. That's what she would have done in the daytime, instead of playing his games.

Into the quiet, she said, "Open it."

Hollis did. He looked inside. "This you?"

"Fourth grade."

"You were cute." His eyes ticked to the other side. "Who's this?"

"My brother."

"I didn't know you had a brother."

"He died three years ago."

Mia thought he might say *sorry*. Ask more questions, pry more out of her. She hated her vulnerability, standing here, nearly nude in both body and soul.

Why *would* Hollis know she'd had a brother? He was nothing to her.

But instead of saying anything, Hollis closed the locket. He stepped forward, holding opposite ends of the chain in each hand.

"Turn around."

And she did.

His arms wrapped her, laying the locket against her chest. Then his fingers whispered against her bare skin as he fastened the clasp. "There."

His breath tickled the back of her neck. She closed her eyes and murmured, "Thanks."

Then she turned. They stood face to face. The room was perfectly silent. Shadows played across his features. Funny, in this light, he didn't look like a son of a bitch.

From down the long hallway, someone coughed.

Mia blinked. Hollis looked away.

"I'll ... I need to change."

"Of course," he said.

"Thank you for finding my locket."

He nodded. "Ain't no thang."

Mia tiptoed back to the bathroom and closed the door. Before removing her towel, she planted her hands on the porcelain sink and hung her head, looking deep into the drain's bore. Dark hair circled her field of vision. She ran the tap, splashing cold water on her face. Then she dressed, vaguely uncomfortable, every movement strange.

When she finally tiptoed back to her bunk, the lights were off and all four bodies in the room were breathing deeply, soundly asleep.

Mia lay on her back, looking up at the shadowed ceiling.

Her hand went to her neck, fingers resting on the locket.

Five minutes later, Mia was as asleep as the animals.

17

Hollis awoke to the sound of popping grease and the scent of frying bacon.

His eyes stayed open for a while before he thought to move. He just stared at the ceiling, taking it all in. Today would be important. And tricky. Managing a sleepover at Brendan's was a victory. It meant he was at least intrigued by their offer and willing to forgive for a big enough buyout.

The rest, hopefully, would handle itself.

Four days left.

He heard Mia rising, rummaging below. She'd be sorting her stuff, getting ready for the day without tripping over the man-eaters who were already outside. From the corner of his eye, Hollis saw the tigers prowl past the window.

He rubbed his jaw, feeling the past two days of abuse finally catching up. He'd been hit a lot in his life. Often by women. But before Mia, not with such unending consistency.

He rolled, moving his feet to the high bunk's edge. "Mornin', sunshine."

"Morning," said the other person in the room. But it wasn't Mia.

"Mrs. Banks," Hollis said, now fumbling. He had an absurd desire to pull on clothes.

Brendan's mother was a southern woman from a generation back, so it seemed like she might prefer strange men in her home to be dressed. Possibly in white suits and bowties, with shallow, flat-topped hats. While sipping grasshoppers on the croquet lawn.

But he didn't need to worry. Not only was Mrs. Banks barely dressed herself — she was in the same faded nightgown as the prior evening — she wasn't paying attention. She was too occupied with going through Mia's bag.

"Can I help you find something?" Hollis asked, coming down and pulling on jeans, along with one of the clean, expensive tees Mia had bought the day before.

"I need the clicker," she said.

"You mean the remote control? For the TV?"

She pulled out pants, socks, a clear bag full of lotion and womanly things Hollis couldn't place.

"Henry had it last," she said, arthritic hands still searching.

"Who's Henry?"

"You know who Henry is. Stop foolin'!"

But Hollis didn't, of course.

"I don't think the clicker's in there, ma'am."

"Don't tell me where it's at! I know I seen it in here."

"But Mrs. Banks ... that's Mia's bag."

"I don't know no Mia."

Hollis took her hand. The old woman looked up at him, her eyes almost cobalt.

"Brendan?"

"No, ma'am. I'm Hollis."

"You work with my Brendan at the shake shop?"

Maybe Brendan had worked at a shake shop in his past and maybe he hadn't. But unless she meant Shake Shack, the burger place, the chances were slim. To Hollis's knowledge, bona-fide shake shops hadn't been mainstream since the 1950's.

"Yes, ma'am. I work with Brendan."

"What's your name?"

"Hollis, ma'am."

"I'm Mary. You should call me Mary. 'Mrs. Banks' is my mother."

If he had to guess, she'd had Brendan late in life, and he was no spring chicken. If the elder Mrs. Banks was still living, she was a record-breaker for sure.

"It's wonderful to meet you, Mary."

"Is supper ready?"

She wobbled as she turned toward the hallway and the kitchen at its end. Hollis managed to catch her, then held the old woman with one hand around the back and another holding her hand.

"Easy now. No supper yet, but I definitely smell breakfast."

"Well, that's fine."

She'd taken her hands out of the bag. Their transaction in the bedroom seemed to be over, so Hollis started walking her to the kitchen. She put her hands on a walker with tennis balls over the bottoms stationed in an alcove on the way. After making sure she had her footing, Hollis left her.

He found Brendan in the kitchen, wearing real clothes and the same hat. He stood over the stove with his back to the door. Bacon popped in a cast-iron skillet.

"Hey." Mia was to one side, leaning against the counter

with a chipped cup of coffee. Cradling it with both hands, either uncharacteristically comfy or trying to get warm.

Hollis met her gaze and, for a few seconds, said nothing. He felt suddenly awkward, unsure what to say.

He settled on, "Hey, yourself."

"You slept a long time."

"Well, this here's a fancy spot." He looked at Brendan, who'd turned, noticed Hollis, and returned to cooking. "You two just chatting it up, or what?"

"She was making coffee when I got up," Brendan explained. Although it wasn't an explanation.

"I found the coffee," Mia added. Also no help. "It was under the sink with the cleaning products."

"Lucky I had some," Brendan said. "It tastes like piss to me, and I don't much like having visitors."

"Well, thank you for making an exception," Mia said.

Hollis leaned against the island, trying to be as casual as Mia and Brendan. He couldn't manage it. They'd woke in a maniac's home, ready to stake a devil's gambit. And yet here Mia was, as comfortable as she might be wrapped in her grandmother's afghan.

Mia trailed her fingers along Hollis's sleeve and the side of his chest.

"What?"

"This one of the new shirts?"

"Yeah."

"I guessed right. It fits pretty well."

Hollis made a face. "What's up with you?"

"What do you mean?"

"You're all ..." He waved vague gestures, presumably to indicate her satisfaction with the general situation.

"What? I finally got some sleep and feel a whole lot better. But if you want, I can get all weird and edgy like you.

Just give me a second." She began to feign discomfort, over the top.

Brendan dumped the bacon onto a paper-towel-lined plate, then set it on the table. There were already scrambled eggs, and the table was set for three. Whether that'd been Mia or Brendan, Hollis had no idea.

"Sit," Brendan said.

He sat, and was still.

"Now ... *eat*. What, is this your first morning?"

"Do you want to call your mother?"

Brendan waved a hand. "Ma's been up since four. She's already had two breakfasts." He popped a strip of bacon into his mouth, fixing Hollis with a stare. "Now. Let's talk."

He looked at Mia. They all looked at each other.

"Shit, Hollis. You suck. Maybe I should'a shot you."

"I'm sorry. I just wasn't expecting ..."

"What? Hospitality? This is Texas, boy. You spend a night in my house, I'm gonna make you breakfast."

"But you're usually ..."

"An asshole? A guy who wants to tear your intestines out of your stomach, then use them to string you up by the balls while your ripped-out colon shits on your toes? I'm still all those things. I'm whatcha call a renaissance man." He finished his bacon, then grabbed another strip.

After a moment, Mia said, "I told him about the case."

"You mean, you told him what's in it?"

"Not yet. I know a thing or two about negotiations."

Brendan pointed a piece of bacon at Mia. Between last night and now, he seemed to have gained some respect for Thomas's wife.

"This one," he said of Mia, "has a hell of a lot better head on her than you do. I got to thinking, maybe she and I should partner up. Then I cut you open and feed you to my kitties. Because really, Hollis. I've got money to spend and Mia's got something to sell. What are you bringing to the party?"

"I brought the case."

"Whoopity fuckin' do. Mia brought the same thing. Difference is, she can actually open it. I'm just trying to find my motivation to cut you in."

"Now wait just a—"

"Relax, Hollis. I told him we're a package."

"Right," Brendan said. "What I can't figure out is why. Tell the lady the truth: If you already had a way to open the case, you'da left her by the side of the road a long time ago, right?"

"No," Hollis said.

"Oh, that's right. Because you gotta fuck her first."

"Hey," said Mia.

Brendan turned to Mia. "What? You don't think it's true?" Then more bacon pointing in Hollis's direction. "Tell her, Hoss. Tell her how you treat ladies. Or partners, for that matter."

Hollis's gaze ticked around. He was unsure how to proceed.

"Anyway," Brendan said when nobody replied. "I guess it's to business. Are we ready to talk about what you got?"

"Are you ready to show us what *you* got?" Mia asked.

"How much I got to spend depends on what you got to offer. Ask Hollis. He'll tell you. I'm fair. I'm fucked-up and I got all sorts of unpopular opinions and my house looks like it cost fifteen bucks, but if I say I have the money, I have it. And if I say I'll pay what's fair, I will. Tell her, Hollis."

"He's fair."

"But you *don't* have the money," Mia said.

Apparently, this was a conversation already in progress. Damn his slow internal clock.

"I don't have it here. Nobody keeps millions upon millions in cash just laying around. I got some in the normal bank, some in special banks. There's been some issues with the financial institutions, as you've probably heard. But I'll get it, don't you worry."

"No money, no deal."

"Money's only part of the deal," Brendan countered.

"Well, then show us that."

"Now?"

Mia shrugged.

Brendan stood, and Mia followed. Then Hollis, unsure of what was going on, rose slowly to his feet.

"Hollis, grab a handful of bacon. Go on now, don't be shy."

He did.

Then Brendan said, "C'mon."

18

Brendan took them to the home's far end, then kicked open a screen door that was approximately one thousand years old. It banged against the house before rebounding. Hollis caught it, but the force tore the tattered screen a bit more away from the frame. The entire place, inside and out, was a shithole. Wherever Brendan was spending his money, it wasn't on home improvement.

"Perimeter cameras." He pointed to a small lens on the home's corner, ringed by infrared LEDs. "There's an inner ring, an outer ring, and a bunch scattered through the middle. Friend of mine rigged a simple AI that reliably separates animals and natural movements from the kind made by humans. That's how I knew you were coming last night."

"Why not just have a gate and barbed wire?" Hollis asked.

Brendan was still eating. He spoke around his food. "Got one. I opened it for you, after the outer ring saw you."

"Why?"

"Don't matter why. I'm about to make millions of dollars off that decision. When you're the one with the fortress that some piece of shit wants protection inside of, you can make those calls. Until now, let's just settle on, *I'm smarter than you.*"

Hollis kept his mouth shut. They walked on.

"Guns up high." Brendan moved them into the woods and pointed up at concealed, deadly devices. "I got all sorts of booby traps. If I hadn't turned them off, you would've arrived at my door looking like a shredded document. Nobody's getting in here without us letting them. That make you feel better, Buttercup?"

Mia nodded. She seemed to have already negotiated for protection as part of their deal.

"Now, lookie here. This is one of my favorites." Brendan led them through a copse and into a second open area.

"Jesus," Hollis said.

"I know, right? It's like a stamp collection, except my hobby can bring down helicopters." He indicated several howitzers, another antiaircraft battery, and a multi-tube rocket launcher mounted to a heavy steel deck. Off to one side, seeming too cool to look their way, was a massive Sherman tank.

"How is this legal?" Mia asked.

"*Ain't* legal. But shit, my neighbors got stuff half as big. Everyone around here looks the other way. You ask me, the second amendment gives us the right to hunt rabbits and protect ourselves from the King of England. You gonna tell me how I should hunt?"

He pointed at the tank. "That there's an M4. 1944. War vintage. It weighs 66,000 pounds, has armor three inches thick, and fires a 75-millimeter shell. If that won't hunt the shit out of a rabbit, then we're talking about rabbits I sure hope *I* never run into. C'mon. There's more."

They moved through more trees, into more open space.

Three more tanks and five helicopters. Not tourist helicopters. Armed ones.

He pointed at the tanks one by one. "M1 Abrams, T-90, Merkava 4. That's an Israeli model. And that bitch right there?" He aimed his finger at one of the copters. "Apache AH-64. Not state of the art anymore, but it keeps the teenagers from throwing rocks over the fence."

"Are all of these operational?" Hollis asked.

"Course. Wouldn't be much good if they weren't."

"What's all this for?"

"Target practice."

"The news says you're working with Governor Garrett."

Brendan shrugged. "He wishes. We're still figuring it out. See, the thing is, I was always on Garrett's side. We've been tied to US policy for way too long. Now we're a republic, and that's dandy. But if I side with him too hard, then I move from hobbyist to military collaborator. It's quite the dilemma. With enough guys like me, Garrett can fight off a whole lot of Army, should the US decide to engage, which they'd be stupid to do with all these bigger fish to fry. But then what? I'm a loyalist. I'm a patriot. But I'm still sizing up whether Garrett really is. Might be, he's secretly a coward. Might be he wants power for the sake of power."

"So ...?" Mia asked.

"So I'm acting like the belle of the ball. I'm not gonna give it up easy, to the first suitor that comes calling. I'm weighing options."

"What options?"

"We've got a really nice local militia just outside of town. They came in before the borders closed. Now, a lot of those fellows are still measuring dicks, and until they've got a central rallying point, they'll keep their rulers out. Maybe I want to be that rallying point. Or maybe I'll stick with Garrett, I don't know."

"What about McCafferty?" Mia asked.

Brendan scoffed. "The actor? No thanks. That's not an army. That's a bunch of people who want to hold hands and sing, hope it all gets better. The minute someone gets too close, he'll back off because his safe space is being invaded."

"According to the news," Hollis said, "McCafferty's got some firepower on his side, too. He says they plan to defend the city, no matter what it takes."

Brendan laughed. "What, with all the fags and spics? Good luck." He spat. "You ask me, this city's overdue for a clean sweep."

Mia, unseen, gripped Hollis by the wrist. Her hold was tighter than he would have expected, and for a long moment she wouldn't let go. Hollis shook her away.

"C'mere. Let me show you the incendiaries."

Mia dragged Hollis back, letting Brendan get ahead. Then she said, "No."

"No what?"

"I don't want to make a deal with him."

It took Hollis a minute. "Why, because he's politically incorrect?"

"That thing about a clean sweep? That's something Hitler would say."

"Honey, I told you this guy was off his rocker. What did you expect? He's got tanks. Four of them, and that's just so far. He's got tigers sleeping in his house. It's really bigotry that's the deal-breaker for you here?"

"I don't like it."

"Of course you don't. This was always a deal with the devil. But he's also the only guy in town with the kind of money we need. With the kind of *protection* we need."

Mia was shaking her head. "I don't think I want his protection. He'll turn on us."

"I told you. If Brendan's one thing, he's fair."

"To straight white people."

"Yeah, well ..."

"You comin'?" Brendan was ahead, at a low building, like a reinforced foxhole, maybe a bomb bunker. He waved big, up high.

"We need to go."

Hollis took a big breath. "Look. Mia. I'm being honest with you right now."

She met his eyes, waiting.

"We can either be with him or fight him. You see what he's got. Which side do you want to be on?"

"No side. It'll just be us."

"And when the aliens come and the food runs out and gangs start raking through the suburbs?"

"You don't know that'll happen."

"It will if the borders stay closed. If Austin becomes a police state. If it's that guy" — he indicated Brendan — "at the official governor's side. I'm sorry. I mean, at the side of the president of Texas, or the king of Texas, or whatever Garrett declares himself."

Texas, pronounced old-style, as if with a Mexican J. *Tay-haas*.

"Get your asses over here, unless you don't want to see what it's like to throw a grenade."

Hollis looked up, waved, then took Mia by the shoulder. He looked deep into her eyes. "Four days, then everything goes to shit. This is the real world now. If you want to survive, it's time to grow up."

Hollis stood straight and walked forward, toward Brandon.

Away from Mia, and a discordant feeling he was trying his damnedest to ignore.

19

Mia realized, with some shock, that Brendan was handsome. At first, he'd been too threatening, then too redneck, then too big of an unlikable fuckwit. According to Hollis, Brendan's various illegal enterprises made him one of the richest people in Texas, but he'd grown up poor and hadn't learned how to spend on anything that normal people would have, and narrow-mindedness must have come along for the ride.

But now that they'd spent most of a day with him and he'd become familiar, Mia had to admit, yes, the guy was technically attractive. It was disarming, since her appreciation of what lay beneath his skin had been in a downhill slide since their decent start earlier this morning.

She thought this while staring at him, as he returned the AK-47 to the gun vault. Basically a closet.

"What?" Brendan asked.

"Nothing."

"I got something on my face?"

"No. Sorry."

He looked sideways at her for anther few seconds, then gave Hollis a look seeming to suggest that Hollis keep his woman in line. Mia didn't know where to begin with how wrong that was.

He flopped onto a couch on the screened-in porch. A puff of something rose into the air along with a whiff of mildew.

"Sit," he said to Hollis. Then he gestured to Mia. "Go get your prize, honey."

She didn't know what he meant.

"The case," Brendan elaborated.

She still didn't move. The men were sitting, and apparently she was supposed to run off and fetch whatever they needed. She wanted to sit and ignore Brendan on principle, but the situation was dicey enough.

So, she got the case. On her way back from the tiger room, she passed Mrs. Banks in one of the rooms along the hallway. The old woman was watching a game show and asked Mia for a glass of water. That, Mia didn't mind fetching.

By the time she returned to the screened-in porch, Brendan had already lit a cigar.

"Sit," he said, speaking around it.

Mia glanced at Hollis, who gave a tiny nod which she read as, *Save your refusals for things that matter.* Then she sat.

"So," Brendan said. "You've seen what I got. What I didn't show you was the east ten, where I've got barracks."

"'Barracks'?"

"Ever since Garrett closed the borders, I've been getting a steady stream of citizen's militia type guys. Part of it is contingency — plans I made with these folks years ago, just in case. Plenty are folks that Garrett sent."

"So, you *are* working with him," Hollis said.

"A republic needs an army," Brendan told them, "and an army needs a home. It needs bunks and arms and a way to train. I got a guy who's running all that for me. Like a sergeant. Me and Garrett, we got a deal. We speak to the same cause."

He shifted, leaned forward, and touched the attaché case.

"Frankly, I've kind of got my hands full. So, now's your chance. Convince me I want to buy this off you in exchange for money and shelter from the storm."

Mia almost asked if they could get a better rate on the money, if they didn't want his sanctuary. She didn't want to sleep with the tigers again or wake to Brendan's bacon. They could live under a bridge instead. Hang with the homeless.

Hollis looked at her.

"What?"

"Open the case, Mia."

She sat back. "Let's talk first."

"Yeah, let's," Brendan said. "About whether I want what's in the case."

"Do you?" Mia asked.

"Depends what's in it. Impress me."

The walls closing were closing in. Too late to run for the fences? Maybe he'd let her go. Or release the dogs or drones or bombs and end this quickly.

Mia shook her head. "Buy it blind."

Brendan laughed, then stopped when she didn't continue. He looked at Hollis, who turned helplessly to Mia.

"Be serious," Hollis said.

"I am being serious." She turned to Brandon. "We don't know if we can trust you. If I open that case right now, what's to stop you from taking it?"

"Because that's not the kind of person I am. Didn't Hollis tell you?"

"He told me some things. The rest I'm figuring out for myself."

"Mia," Hollis warned.

"What's that supposed to mean?"

"Look. You two have done whatever dirty dealing in the past. I'm new to this, but I'm not an idiot. You aren't friends. All that's holding you together is the promise of mutual benefit. So, tell me ..." Mia met Brendan's gaze. "I open it, and we supposedly make our deal. But after that, we're still in your house, inside your little compound. I'm not seeing what protects our profits."

"Fairness protects you. As does my word." His voice was even, but Mia could tell he was getting agitated. Banks struck her as a vial of nitroglycerine: calm at first, but inches from flipping to deadly at all times.

"Come on, Mia." Hollis flicked between Mia and Brendan, seconds ticking too quickly. "This was our deal. This is what we agreed to."

She waited, arms crossed.

"All right," Brendan said, leaning in. "Then how about you tell me what we do now? I heard from some self-important lady that you aren't stupid. So how exactly do you see this shaking out? Do you honestly imagine I'm just going to smile and say yeah, that's fair, makes sense? Then keep right on giving you lodging, but not making you head out to the barracks to earn your keep like the rest of the folks here? *You* came to *me* and said, 'We got something you'll want bad enough to pay for.' Don't you want that anymore? Or do you *seriously* think I'm going to buy it blind?"

"Mia," Hollis said. "Seriously."

She stood, thinking fast. Something had flipped while

they'd been walking the heavily-armed grounds with the compound's owner, and now more than anything she wanted to run. It wasn't entirely logical. There was a feeling beneath her skin, and it'd come on like lightning.

"Bonds," she said.

"Excuse me?"

"That's what's inside. Negotiable bonds."

"Uh-huh," Brendan said. "Show me."

"If I show you, you'll take them."

"I won't. I promise."

"No offense, but that's not a risk I'm willing to take."

Mia's back was to the men, but she could feel them trading glances. She could feel Hollis's acute discomfort.

"You got a phone. Take the case out into the woods if you want, open it, then snap a picture. But if you think I'm just going to call my bank and get you money for something I haven't even seen, you're stupider than you think."

Mia said nothing.

Behind her back, Brendan said, "What the hell, Hollis? *This* is the deal you bring me?"

"I ... I'm sorry."

"Maybe we should go," Mia said.

"Nuh-uh. You owe me one night's room and board, at least. And, shit. I gave you the tour. What's to say you won't go blabbing to people about what we're building here?"

Mia turned, arms still crossed.

"That's not the kind of person I am. Didn't Hollis tell you?"

Brendan turned to Hollis. "What the fuck."

"Mia, stop screwing around," Hollis said.

"I'm just trying to negotiate."

"*Negotiate!*" Brendan said, laughing. "Bitch, you got nothing to negotiate *with*!"

He seemed to make a decision and stood. He'd been wearing a semiautomatic pistol on his belt all day, and now drew it from its holster and pointed it at Mia's head.

"Tell you what, hot stuff. Since you like hypotheticals so much, I've got one for you. What if I just kill you both right here? Or maybe *wound* you both, then feed you to my cats while you're still breathing. Not only will that put me right back where I was before your stupid asses showed up yesterday, I'll also be up one mysterious case."

"You'll never get it open." Her heart was pounding. She'd never had a gun trained so steadily on her, and it was nearly impossible to hold her nerves.

"Who gives a shit? It's probably empty!"

"It's not empty."

"Prove it!"

Mia didn't reply. Her legs were already shaking, and her vision was starting to haze.

"All right," Brendan said. "Step outside, will ya? I don't really want blood all over my porch."

"MIA!" Hollis blurted. "Stop fucking around!"

"See, Hollis?" Brendan said. "She's full of shit. Just trying to play us. *Both* of us."

He pushed the muzzle against Mia's head. Against all of her will, a whimper escaped.

"Last chance," Brendan said.

"Wait! Mia, tell him about the other thing."

"What other thing?" Brendan asked Mia.

Mia's lips were pressed.

But she said nothing. Wouldn't have known what to say if she could.

"What other thing?" Brendan now asked Hollis, weapon still on Mia.

"There's a list in there. Weapons. More than you've got here."

"Really. Thought you didn't know what was inside."

"I lied. I told Mia I'd let her lead the negotiations. We opened it together last night."

Brendan's eyes flicked between them. "Bullshit."

"I'm serious. There was a Russian guy, used to come by Thomas's house all the time. They were negotiating something. Something big. It stalled because the Russian couldn't convince Thomas that whatever he was up to would happen outside US borders, and that was really important given all the weapons on the line. Right before the Astral thing happened, they were about to finally close the deal." Hollis swallowed, then nodded at the case. "It's full of bonds, like she said, but that's really just half of it. Lists. Maps. Access codes. It's a DIY kit for enough firepower to take over a small nation."

"*Double* bullshit. Davies wasn't in to arms dealing."

"That's why he was working so hard to move it. He *didn't* want to get involved, but one of his connections gave him an impossible offer. He wanted it off his plate as fast as possible." Hollis gestured to the case. "And this was the solution."

"That's just dandy," Brendan said, his voice cold. "Now open it."

Hollis swallowed, caught a glance from Mia, and said, "If she doesn't want to open it yet, we wait."

Brendan swung the gun to face Hollis.

"Open it," he repeated.

"I can't. Only Mia can."

"Motherfucker, I'm tired of this Abbot and Costello routine. If you think I can't find a way to open that case without you ..."

"You can't," Mia said. "Believe me."

The gun moved to Mia, then to Hollis. Then Mia again.

Finally Brendan aimed it between them, screamed, and shot three slugs through the siding.

Then he holstered his gun and stalked out, leaving them with their ears still ringing.

20

MORNING. Three days left.

This time, Hollis woke to nothing at all.

Mia entered the room, already dressed. She'd laid out clothes for Hollis, like his mother.

"'Bout time. Get dressed."

"We goin' somewhere?" Hollis asked.

"Quickly."

He went to the bathroom, splashed water on his face, and pulled on the jeans and tee Mia had left him. She wasn't in the bedroom or hallway, but he found her outside, sitting on a rotting picnic table.

"Shoes," she said, looking down at his bare feet.

"What, are we going hiking?"

"Yes."

Hollis grabbed his boots, but Mia was already walking. He rushed to catch her.

"If you're planning to leave ..."

"Shut up, Hollis."

They walked for five minutes in silence. Finally, Hollis took Mia by the arm.

"Listen, Pixie. I'm not sure what game you're playing, but—"

"What game *I'm* playing?" she spat, turning. "Tell me about the Russian, Hollis."

"I was just trying to keep him from shooting you."

"Yeah. Well, I knew what I was doing."

"Sure you did. You were getting yourself killed. I don't know what you're playing at, but Brendan isn't the hick he appears to be. He's a survivor, first and foremost. Believe me, he's got a whole pros and cons list in his head about both of us. We're still here because he believed enough of your bullshit to think there's a chance he can get whatever's in that case. We become liabilities the second he decides he can't." Hollis pointed at the sky. "In case you haven't noticed, the world's got bigger fish to fry."

"Is that why you told him that bullshit about there being a map to an arsenal inside?"

"I had to say *something* — he thought you were fucking with him!"

"And *that's* what you made up? What exactly is he going to do if he finally does open it and finds out you were lying? We can't make a war chest out of the blue, you know!"

"We can make something up. He's got a dozen computers, and he goes out a lot during the day. We can type something up that looks convincing enough to buy us some time. Then you can just—"

"It's not that simple."

"Stop being stubborn."

"I'm not being stubborn!"

"Mia, goddammit! Shit's about to get real all over this planet, and it's about time to stop—!"

"I can't open the case, all right?"

Hollis stood. Waited.

"What."

"*Of course* I don't know the code! Why would Thomas give it to me? I can't get into his bank vault. I can't get into any of the safes in the house. I can't get into his computer. And I sure as hell can't get into the motherfucking case. He never trusted me with anything, okay? Not one thing. He was a piece of shit and I wanted to get away, but for *months* I was ready to run and he gave me nothing. I could steal his art, and maybe if I was lucky his wallet." She turned, then kicked the dirt. "Son of a *bitch!*"

Hollis took a few moments before speaking.

"This is not good. You really screwed this up."

"Oh, *fuck you,* Hollis!"

"He won't keep being put off. He's got too many irons in the fire. If he decides he'll never get what's in the case, he'll just give up. Kill us both. Then maybe he'll try to open it, or maybe he'll move on."

Mia was shaking her head, looking away.

"What's inside? Do you really not know?"

"I don't know," she admitted.

"But at the house, he said it was worth sixty million dollars."

"Who knows? It could be sixty million in antique cufflinks."

"It's paper," he said, thinking. He'd certainly shaken it enough, like a kid with a mysterious Christmas present. "And it's not too heavy. So it's either high-denomination bonds, like you bluffed, or it's part of a deal he was planning to make with someone, and the *deal* was worth sixty million. Like, someone was going to pay him that much." Hollis rubbed his chin. "Maybe someone would still be willing."

"What's it matter? You told him what was inside, and there's no way it'll match."

Hollis was trying to think. "Yeah. But Brendan's a pragmatist. He won't hold that particular grudge, if he likes what's in there. We have to get it open."

"I told you, we can't."

"You lived with Thomas for years. You must have some idea. The code is only four digits. Maybe we could try all the combinations. How many could there be?"

"Ten thousand if the options are numbers."

"Oh."

"But you can use letters, too. Upper- and lower-case. And 12 special characters."

"And that makes it worse?"

"Twenty-four million combinations."

"That's worse," Hollis said. "And there's no way to force the thing or pry it open?"

"Shoot it with one of Brendan's tanks. Of course, that'd destroy whatever's inside."

"Maybe it wouldn't."

"Remember, the case itself will destroy the contents either way."

"Oh."

The morning was cool. Hollis wished he'd pulled on a sweatshirt. The air smelled like fall, despite it being May. They were in the woods within the city limits, and the soundscape was empty, despite the coming chaos. The world, from end to end, was somehow upside-down.

"We have to leave," Mia said.

"It's going to get bad out there. We're safer in here."

"We can run. Get outside of his fences on foot, then steal a car. Haul ass for Dripping Springs, like you wanted all along."

"The borders are closed."

"Texas is too big. There aren't enough hands to watch

the entire border. We can get out of the state once the city's behind us."

Hollis was thinking, weighing odds and possibilities. Mia seemed tough, but she hadn't spent his years on society's underbelly. However bad she thought it might get, it would get worse. When the aliens arrived, whatever new normal Austin had settled into would be tossed in the air again. The best bet was to take their bird in-hand, not go off chasing a pair in the bush.

They could reassess when the ships came in another seventy-two hours.

"No," he said.

"No? Just like that?"

"Go off on your own, if you don't like it," Hollis told her.

Mia said nothing.

"If you knew you couldn't open the case, why didn't you just tell me?"

Mia's lips firmed. But Hollis knew. She didn't *want* to be on her own.

"We should go," she said.

"It's too risky."

Mia closed her eyes and sighed. Then she opened them and took Hollis by the arm.

"What?"

"Just come on."

They'd been cresting a rise when he'd stopped her. She continued to drag him.

When they reached the top of the hill two minutes later, Hollis almost gasped.

The rest of Brendan's property sprawled below, separated by a double row of fences. He called it his "east ten," but to Hollis's eyes it looked a lot larger than ten acres.

Rows and rows and rows of ad-hoc barracks stuffed with milling men and women, just like a real army.

"Jesus," Hollis said.

"Something bugged me when Brendan told us about the people the governor was sending his way, so I came out here before you woke up. I followed the sunrise, figuring that heading east would be good enough to find what he'd been talking about. There are thousands of soldiers down there, Hollis. *Thousands*."

"I wouldn'ta thought there were this many militants in Austin."

"That's half of what bugs me. I found a pair of binoculars and watched them. There's no way that settlement was set up within the last three days, and it sure looks to me like the people have been there for a while. The invasion didn't start it. Brendan did that on his own."

"Why?"

"Some of these guys don't like that Texas ever joined the Union. Some don't like that they lost the Civil War."

Hollis rolled onto his back, trying to assimilate all he'd seen.

"We have to go," Mia said for the third time, "unless you want to be in the middle when Brendan unleashes his people."

But Hollis wasn't so sure. "I'm staying."

"Hollis ..."

"I'm staying. I'll buy us time. *Somehow*. Maybe we can get him to buy the case blind, like you said. If we ever do go off on our own, we'll need whatever we can get."

He stood.

"Hollis!"

But he was already walking down the hill, away from brewing trouble, and into the literal tigers' den.

21

THE DAY PASSED in high tension.

The mood around the house was sour, held taut by a curious species of detente. For now at least, Brendan seemed willing to let Mia's gambit play out — to not force the question of the case, and instead let everything settle. As Hollis said, Brendan had plenty of other things to do. He vanished for long periods, maybe to oil his tanks.

"Don't try to leave. I'll know if you do."

And then he vanished again, and Hollis wondered just how seriously he should take it. Very, probably. He'd gotten the tiniest peek at Brendan's security room, and it was clean and high-tech enough to make the rest of his house look like the hovel it was.

"He wouldn't care if we left, if he didn't think we could open the case," Hollis argued.

Mia wasn't so sure. She reminded Hollis that Brendan didn't want his many highly armed secrets getting out, and that might be another reason they weren't supposed to go.

But Hollis had an idea and took it to Brendan that night.

"Of course she knows how to open it. If she didn't know the code, she would have tried to run."

Mia was visible, but out of earshot, her stone face on. Just by existing, she made Hollis's point for him.

"I can get it out of her," Hollis said.

Brendan mumbled.

The next morning, Hollis gave Brendan a fake update. Mia was cracking. He was persuading her in more ways than one. A woman's lips loosened when she got all aflutter.

Brendan remarked that Mia, who no longer talked to either of the men when they were all together, didn't exactly look aflutter to him. Hollis said she was melting behind closed doors. He was persuading her both logically and romantically. What did she think — that Brendan would keep letting them stay without any benefit? He might start thinking Mia didn't have the code at all and kill her!

"He's really starting to think you don't have the code at all," Hollis told Mia that night, after a long day of stalking the property like cats. "He's going to kill you."

"Just me?"

"Hey," Hollis said, "I'm making friends."

"Gonna go burn some crosses together?"

"I'm just using all the tricks I can to keep us alive, honeybunch."

Mia wasn't exactly happy with Hollis either, nor his cute nicknames. She became a black box. He had to play interference between two immovable objects, neither of which gave an inch of themselves away. Mia was stolid, but so was Brendan. She wanted to run and he wanted to resolve the open loop they and the case represented and get on with things.

By the next day, the official Astral clock showed less than twenty-four hours before arrival. Brendan was running ragged, meeting with general-types that Hollis only ever saw from a distance, carrying machine parts to lawn trailers then pulling the trailers across his grounds using a riding lawnmower. What exactly he was doing, Hollis and Mia hadn't a clue. They were on house arrest. There was nothing to do, so they played a lot of gin with Mrs. Banks. She didn't know how and kept wanting to make bids of so many spades or diamonds, or ask Mia if she had any fours. *Go fish*.

Around noon, Brendan returned to the house covered in sweat and grease. He smelled like a conveyor belt. He was also wild-eyed, harried, and breathing hard. Hollis was about to ask if he was okay, but then five men pulled up in a Jeep to join him, their vehicle spattered in red.

"Who are those guys, Brendan?" Hollis asked, not expecting a response.

"They're new."

"And I guess they drove through a paint factory?"

"Bit of a scuffle down on campus."

They'd heard something about that. Officially, there was no TV — other than Mrs. Bank's set — and no news in the house, but they still had Mia's phone and checked the websites between games of gin/bridge with Mrs. Banks. Riots, Hollis seemed to recall. Demonstrations gone very bad.

"What's ... ?" Hollis stopped when he saw a line of identical Jeeps through the trees, heading vaguely east. New recruits for the grinder.

"Give me the case," Brendan said.

There was no question of refusing. Mia was closest to the thing. She handed it to Hollis, who passed it to Brendan, who gave it to his five new escorts, who made it disappear.

"Don't leave. Don't move."

Hollis felt a chill. Brendan's voice hadn't had quite that same timbre before.

Four hours later, Brendan returned alone.

"Hey. How's it—?"

He slammed the case into Hollis's chest, making him wobble on his feet. It was dented, scratched, beaten, blackened, the edges where it sealed curled like Elvis's lip. But even the worst of the damage was superficial, the heart of the thing intact.

Brendan crossed the room and took Mia by the wrist. She protested the first time he pulled, then yelled the second.

"Hey, hey. Take it easy," Hollis said.

Brendan yanked Mia hard enough to cause a stagger, then took her shoulders and practically bent her over the case, which Hollis had dropped onto the couch.

"Open it."

It was a simple request, impatient but not shouted. It was, Hollis thought, the most down-to-business tone he'd ever heard from anyone. There was no debate, no question, no anything at all. Nothing but the expectation of compliance.

"No."

Brendan whipped Mia around, hit her hard across the face.

"Hey!"

Hollis didn't have a chance. Brendan had him by the collar in half a second, and slammed against the brick fireplace a half-second after that. He pinned Hollis with his left arm, then reached down with his right and removed an enormous serrated hunting knife from a sheath on his thigh.

He held it up to Hollis's eye. "I have been patient enough."

"Hey, hey, Brendan ... Let's talk about this like men."

"I'm through talking." He looked at the case, Mia still on the floor beside it, hand over a reddening bruise. "Either it opens, or you die."

"Brendan ..."

"I think you're lying. Both of you. I don't think there's anything in there — nothing worth a shit, anyway. I think you came here, thinking I was stupid enough to pay you for nothing. I think you slept in my house and ate my food and shared the couch with my Ma and accepted my hospitality, and never planned on giving me anything in return. I think you're trying to pull something, and I don't fucking appreciate being played a fool. And you know what else? I don't think you *can* open it. I think you're trying some stupid fucking bluff, and the fact that you think I'll keep falling for it, day after day, is just ..."

He lost words, now twisting the knife point so close to Hollis's eye, he could see its scratches.

"I know it must be frustrating," Hollis managed to say.

"... *disappointing,*" Brendan finished.

He threw Hollis to the ground, where he tripped over Mia and racked his head on the coffee table. Then Brendan sheathed the knife and drew his gun. This time, it didn't look like an empty threat.

"Who's first?" he asked, moving it between them.

"Brendan!" Hollis blurted.

"You, I guess. Let her see what will happen to her if she doesn't get it open."

He centered the gun, holding it steady.

"If you kill us," Mia said carefully, "you'll never get it open."

"It's been days, sweetheart. I've already given up on getting it open."

He fired. They both jumped, but instead of hitting

Hollis's chest, it broke a huge splinter off the coffee table. He was far too close to miss on accident, but it made his point.

"Pussy," Mia said between gritted teeth.

Hollis, knowing he had virtually nothing to lose, scrambled upright. He rushed to Brendan too fast, sure once he was underway that Brendan would simply blow him out of his boots and be done with it. But Brendan didn't fire, even as Hollis struck the gun with his chest, even as he leveled the weapon on his own heart. *"I can get it out of her."*

"Like you've gotten it out of her so far?"

"She knows you're serious. She knows this is it." Hollis looked up, around. "Tomorrow, the ships come, and time is up." He swallowed. "For both of us."

"You mean you and her," Brendan said.

"Yes."

"Because speaking for myself, I plan to survive."

"Of course. You're a warrior. But a warrior could always use more firepower."

Brendan pushed Hollis away with the gun. He glanced between him and Mia.

"I don't need this shit right now. You, or your fucking case."

Hollis gave him his most serious, earnest stare. Eye to eye. Heart in his throat. "Let me talk to her, one last time."

A long moment passed. Then Brendan said, "You can't run. You can't leave. You know my cameras will spot you. You know the drones will make what I'd do to you look like a nicety."

Hollis swallowed, then nodded.

"Have it open by 9:00 a.m., or I'll torture her until she gives it up, then cut you apart while you're still breathing."

22

At first, Brendan's timeframe — especially considering how angrily he'd entered the room — seemed unnecessarily generous. It was barely six by the time everything settled and Brendan again went out (presumably to meet again with his generals, maybe rally his thousands of troops), and that gave them fifteen hours to plot and plan. More than enough, Mia thought, to figure a way to get the hell out. Because finally, for once, Hollis seemed to agree that was the wisest course of action.

But Hollis threw cold water over that family of ideas after heading outside for fresh air.

"I think he was being literal about us not leaving the house," he told Mia less than a minute later.

"Why?"

"Because there are at least ten drones parked outside the front door."

Mia looked. Except she went to the back door first, where there were another five or six. All on the ground or perched atop electrical transformers. A ring around the house. Even windows were guarded.

"Maybe they're just watching," Mia said. "Maybe we can outrun them."

So Hollis threw an orange from the fruit bowl in the kitchen out onto the lawn. The drones lifted off immediately, turning on it, and blew it to pulp. They were big heavy models armed with guns — small-caliber enough that the kick didn't knock them off course, but rapid-fire so persistence accounted for their smaller impact.

Suddenly, fifteen hours didn't seem generous. It felt torturous. If Brendan was going to kill them as soon as their time expired, Mia wished for a shorter deadline. Less time to wait and freak out.

"Maybe we can hit them with bats," Hollis suggested.

"Dozens of them."

"Okay ... then we can cover ourselves with some sort of armor. Hold makeshift shields."

"In every direction at once, And against machine-gun fire."

"Well, what's *your* brilliant idea?"

Mia didn't have one. She'd run through the possibilities. Even if they could get into the security room, it seemed to be for surveillance rather than attack. The drones might be controlled from anywhere, or were autonomous AI that didn't require control. They couldn't run without being shredded, had no glider or balloon with which to fly, and couldn't make themselves impervious enough to survive so many drones following them with such persistence.

Even if they could make it to the Charger, its windows were plain glass. And that assumed the driveway wasn't mined or that there weren't anti-tank ordinances at the gate, neither of which she would put past a guy who lived with three full-sized tigers.

"Don't suppose you have an EMP weapon on you?" Mia asked.

"What?"

"Never mind."

At ten, they wrestled the bedroom TV away from Mrs. Banks. Mia plied her with cookies, which she'd made specifically for the purpose. Hollis kept asking what she'd say if Brendan came back from the barracks and asked why she was baking. Mia said that at this point, she was dead anyway. So who cared?

And they watched the news, feeling desperation sink deeper.

The world was not doing well.

They'd missed most of the worst, having been limited in their updates by the lack of a television and Brendan's watching eye. There'd been a massive traffic jam outside Chicago that devolved into an all-hands fight. Las Vegas had been set ablaze, and authorities, handicapped by gangs in the city and general apathy, had been unable to put it out. The government of the US was splintered and, for the most part, had stopped talking about Texas secession. Half of congress had simply vanished — presumed deserted, but possibly murdered by those who'd decided they'd had enough of the people in charge.

The president was still on duty, issuing proclamations that didn't strike Mia as remotely optimistic.

And bombs.

And killings.

And looting, and theft, and gangs, and guns.

All that, and their extraterrestrial visitors hadn't even arrived. It was ironic that the mere *thought* of alien visitors had done so much damage already. What did it say about humanity, that even if the aliens turned around right now and never visited Earth, they might well have destroyed it?

Worst of all was the local news.

Forest McCafferty, aware that his group had a reputation as a bunch of pacifist hipsters, managed to merge his growing *let's-not-call-it-an-army* with a group of well-armed Austinites whose beliefs walked the political line between right and left. Socially liberal, conservative when it came to the right to bear abundant arms. Then, when Camp Mabry fell apart after being severed from US military command, McCafferty's people were the first to raid it. Now *they* had a machine gun, too — *ho, ho, ho.*

Days ago, while Mia and Hollis had been distracted worrying about what Brendan was up to, the city started splintering into factions. When there'd still been five days left until the aliens' arrival, there'd been two big camps and a lot of outliers, pacifists, and independents. But now, with *one* day left, those two camps were pretty much all there was, having polarized the population down the middle.

To hear Governor Garrett speak, you were *"either with us, or enemies of the state."*

But McCafferty said, you were *"either with us, or part of the totalitarian regime threatening to take us over."*

There was a silver lining on the splitting of Austin. Violence between the parties, despite their heavy armament, had been light, with only a few scattered skirmishes. Both McCafferty and the governor seemed to fancy themselves figureheads, both of whom were officially above empty gang-type warfare. If they were to clash, the implication went, it'd be tantamount to a declaration of war. Despite cross-group tensions rising to a fever pitch, that declaration hadn't come.

"For now," Hollis said.

The news ended. They sat in Mrs. Banks's bedroom with the screen gone to commercials for things the world would soon never care about again, the impervious attaché case sitting on the bedspread between them.

Mia didn't remember Hollis going to fetch it while they'd been watching Austin's downward spiral. It was as if it had walked into the room on its own, to remind them how fucked they were — how little anything they could possibly do even mattered.

Beyond the windows, every so often, there were headlights. They'd shine bright, threaten to pierce the windows, then turn. It became a pattern, roughly every twenty minutes. They couldn't leave to see where the cars were coming from or where they were going, but Mia was sure she knew. New arrivals came faster and faster, growing the army just beyond the hills.

Governor Garrett's fighting force, gaining recruits with every passing hour.

Ready to do battle with McCafferty's lesser-trained but perhaps even better-armed crew, headquartered somewhere within the city limits.

Although, Mia thought, what did it matter?

They couldn't escape this stinking house and would be dead by morning.

Hollis turned the television off. Mrs. Banks, at some point, had come back into the bedroom and fallen asleep in a chair. He stood, crossed to the old woman, tucked a blanket around her, and propped a pillow behind her head.

Mia looked at Hollis, asking without words, *What now?*

Aloud, Hollis said, "Let's get drunk."

23

3:00 a.m.

Time wasn't exactly flying by, nor was it going slow. Brendan hadn't returned. He was too busy with his soldiers, playing G.I. Joe. Hollis had moved Mrs. Banks to the bed a few hours back and tucked her in.

Mia and Hollis were in the living room, the detritus of their long night a miniature dump around them. There'd been beers — Hollis had stacked them atop the attaché case like a monument to defeat. The floor was strewn with little bags of Doritos and Cheetos, as well as some of the actual chips, ground into the worn carpet. The littering wouldn't anger Brendan. It wasn't that they'd found and raided his liquor cabinet, nor the way they'd eaten through most of his snacks — and besides, the bastard surely had an apocalypse's worth of canned food in a bunker somewhere.

He wouldn't torture and kill them because they'd made a mess of his living room. So, in the grand scheme of things, there was no reason not to be lazy, filthy assholes.

After many shots of girly liquors — laughably, Brendan had both butterscotch schnapps and Bailey's Irish Cream, which, when combined, Mia declared to be "like snorting candy" before laughing hard enough to pee her pants — Mia discovered a hidden panel behind the paneling in the living room. Brendan, it seemed, had a secret TV. There was a switch on the wall that when pressed moved the paneling aside in a reveal Hollis declared to be "worthy of Scooby-Doo" — an observation that had seemed ridiculously funny at the time.

And Brendan also had a juke, the remote to which was also behind the paneling. The thing was stuffed with movies — fortunate, because the Internet was failing more often than working, serving mostly to update the Astral app with photos of ships close and detailed enough to chill their bones.

Mia took the lead, handily drunk by midnight and shit-faced an hour later, scrolling through Brendan's movies until she found an Ivan Reitman folder.

That's where she stopped, hit play, and began the night's amusement. First up, *Animal House*. Then *Stripes*. They had plenty of comedy to watch, either until they died of alcohol poisoning or by Brendan's hand.

Right around the time Sergeant Hulka was getting blown off his perch by a stray mortar shell, Hollis found his state mellowing, coming to equilibrium. The heady build-up and perception-shifting of *getting* drunk was over, along with the first wave of disorientation and euphoria. This, Hollis decided as he mellowed, was just how he'd be from now on.

Hazy.

Happy.

A little sick.

Definitely unable to do complex math problems. Or simple ones.

And, it seemed, with Mia's head in his lap.

He looked down at her contented, glazed-over expression and decided she was pretty. He'd known that before now, of course. It was something he'd been very aware of that night when they'd been alone in the far wing of Thomas's mansion and he'd torn off her clothes, or maybe it was the other way around. He couldn't remember which way things had gone. It hadn't been precisely an act of passion. More an act of aggression. He remembered thinking she was using him ... and he may have announced, using actual words, that he was using her, too. That sounded like something Hollis Palmer would do.

He recalled getting off, but then feeling afterward that instead of afterglow, the correct post-coital response might have been to stand up and boast, *That's what I THOUGHT!* while stalking away. He hadn't had a chance, because Mia did it first, warning him that he'd better not say a thing or she'd have her husband cut his dick off.

Just that one time, then never again. There'd been tension worthy of a trashy romance novel ever since. Minus the romance, of course.

But right now, gone was the snootiness, the bitchiness, the attitude that said she was superior enough to shit a pile of diamonds.

She had been conning Thomas all along, same as Hollis.

"What?" Mia asked, looking up.

"Nothing."

Something came over her face. An expression of curiosity. She shifted position, squinting. "Do you have a hard-on?"

"No," Hollis told her.

She half sat up. "You do. You have a boner."

"No, I don't." He looked down. "That's just the way my jeans are folding."

"So, if I were to poke that," she said, indicating his lap, "the fabric would collapse."

"You're just looking for an excuse to grope me."

Mia looked him in the eye, for a long time. Then she said, "You're drunk."

"You're drunk."

"I'm not drunk."

"You're *stupid* levels of drunk, Pixie."

"Don't call me Pixie."

"Not a fan of nicknames?"

Mia rolled away. There was a bottle of Grey Goose on the coffee table, near where Brendan had shot off the corner instead of murdering them. *Ah, good times*.

She filled a Las Vegas shot glass. No need for snorting candy now. This was an aggressive drunkenness, in need of advanced treatment.

"Thomas called me nicknames," Mia said.

"And that's a bad thing?"

"Well, seeing as he's a thieving, murdering bastard ..."

"You married him," Hollis said.

"It was an investment."

"You never loved him?"

Mia shrugged. "What *is* love." She said it like a koan, not an inquiry.

"I guess you're not going to answer the question."

Mia shrugged again. She'd already poured a second shot after downing the first.

"Chicken," Hollis said.

"Oh. I see. I guess this is the part where we each lower our defenses and reveal our past wounds." She fired down the second shot. "Fuck you, Hollis."

"I'll bet you didn't get along with your daddy."

She glared at him. Then she laughed. Hard. Hollis, too. It went on for thirty seconds and felt like forever.

"Yes," she said.

"Yes what?"

"Once upon a time, I think I loved Thomas. Just a little. I targeted him first and never stopped planning to take my alimony one way or the other. But I'm human. Even a marriage of convenience is a marriage. He could be sweet when he wasn't being an asshole."

"Thomas Davies. Sweet."

"From time to time. Surprised?"

"I don't believe it." Hollis turned away. He didn't actually have a goal in doing so, and diverted to the bottle as an afterthought.

Mia giggled when he hesitated. "Are you jealous?"

Hollis laughed.

"You're jealous!"

"How, exactly?"

"I don't know," she said. "Go look in the mirror and find out."

"There are five dozen reasons that doesn't make a lick of sense," Hollis told her.

"Uh-huh. Five dozen. Is that a number now?"

"Yeah. It's sixty."

"That's oddly specific."

"Fuck off, Mia."

"You wish," Hollis said. But that didn't make sense, so they laughed again.

Mia rolled onto her back, and Hollis stayed with his ass on the floor, back against the couch.

Time passed.

"He was embarrassing," Mia said.

Hollis had been sliding into a sleepy stupor, fatigue finally catching up with him. He lifted his head and said, "Huh?"

"Thomas. He got all ... *infatuated*. It was cute at first, then gross."

"How so?" Hollis asked, more interested than he felt like admitting.

"Well, the nicknames. Plus, he got a car with vanity plates. *Mia.*"

"That's adorable." He looked again at the ceiling.

"He had a painting done of me."

"No, he didn't."

"He did."

"Loser."

"Oh, come on. That's not sweet?"

Hollis shrugged.

"He got a tattoo. My name. Here." She touched her arm, near the shoulder.

Hollis laughed.

"What, you never did anything dumb to declare your love for someone?"

Sure, he had. Once, in middle school, before he'd been awesome, Hollis developed an intense crush on a girl named Sarah. Not long after, he'd created an account on an online forum and chosen the username "SarahLover." Hard to think about without wanting to inflict self-harm, and nothing he'd admit under torture. He certainly wasn't going to confess it now.

Hollis slid sideways, drunker than he'd realized, and found his cheek crunched against a stray Dorito. His eyes closed. Every day since the Astral announcement had been at least forty-eight hard hours long.

He needed sleep.

But then his eyes opened. Something was bugging him. Something was wrong.

He sat up.

Mia straightened. "What?"

But Hollis didn't answer. He went to the sculpture they'd named Ode to Defeat, still on the coffee table, and knocked all the beer cans to the floor. Now it was a dumb briefcase with scorch marks and dents.

Heart beating, he tapped the miniature touchscreens that comprised the case's code panel.

He stopped when it read, *Mia*.

Not enough letters. The code was four digits.

So: *MiaD*.

He tried the latch. The case didn't open.

Mia couldn't see. She shifted position, moving over.

"What're you doing?" Her voice slurred, but not as much as he would have thought.

He ignored her. "What's your maiden name?"

She sat beside him, warm by his side.

"Reid."

He entered: *MiaR*.

"Try lower case."

So he tried all the combinations: *Miad, Miar, miaD, miaR, miad,* and *miar*. Even *Reid* and *reid* and *REID*. Nothing.

Hollis sighed. What, had he really thought it'd be that simple?

"Worth a shot," she shrugged. "If it makes you feel better, I actually did catch him using my name as a password once."

"Pathetic," SarahLover said.

"You're drunk, anyway."

"Yeah. I heard that somewhere. From some drunk girl who ..."

Something still wasn't right.

"Go to bed. I am." She stood.

Hollis stayed where he was.

Mia looked down at him, and all he could do was to look up, feeling strange intuition.

"Shit, Hollis. *What?*"

"You said he gave you nicknames."

"Yeah?"

"What were they?"

"Sweetheart. Darling.'"

Hollis's nose wrinkled. He didn't like hearing about this side of bloodthirsty Thomas Davies. So undignified. "Those aren't nicknames. You said he gave you *nicknames.*"

Mia looked conflicted. Then she reddened a little. "*Killer.*"

"Killer?"

"Because he said I had a killer body." Her eyes ticked away. "Shut up. You asked."

Hollis chuckled a little, but returned his attention to the lock. It was too long of a word, but he tried anyway: *Kilr, kllr,* and a few other variants. Nothing.

His shoulders sagged. "Is that it?"

Pause. "Yes."

"Why did you hesitate?"

"I didn't."

"You hesitated. Just now, before saying *yes*."

"I don't know what to tell you, Hollis."

Kneeling on the floor with his hands on the case, he looked up at Mia, still standing above him.

"This is important. For all the marbles."

"You're not going to guess his code," Mia said.

"It's not a guess, if he's done it before."

"It won't work anyway."

"So he *did* call you something else."

She reddened.

"Dammit, Mia ..."

"*Tits.*"

"Seriously?"

"Oh, fuck you! If you're really just trying to get me to—!"

Hollis held up a finger. His heart was beating faster. What were the chances? It was even four letters.

He entered: *tits*.

Nothing.

Then *Tits*, mixed case.

And still nothing.

He sighed even harder this time. He'd felt a cosmic spark before trying, sure that'd been the answer.

When he looked back up at Mia, she was so red, she looked like someone hung upside-down. She couldn't meet his eye. She'd looked at the combination, then resolutely away.

"Mia?"

She cleared her throat. Then, very small, she muttered, "With a Z."

Hollis changed the last letter: *Titz*.

Depressed the latch.

Then, with a click, everything changed.

24

Brendan returned with a machete. Its edge had the sloppy, blurry silver look that comes from hand-sharpening. Not that it was easy to see — the edge was almost entirely covered in blood. Not entirely dried.

"Come on," Brendan said, beckoning them toward the front door. He'd opened it, and outside was a green electric utility vehicle, its engine keyed, still running. They'd seen him ferrying cargo and equipment around the estate in its rear, open like a pickup truck. Brendan called the thing his "Gator," and right now, there were two heavy tarps laid in the back, spread, one atop the other. As if he expected to transport something messy.

Hollis had entirely sobered. The case was in his hand, with Mia beside him. He'd prepared a speech, but seeing Brendan with the machete and tarps caused it to fall out of his brain.

"Come on, Hollis. Let's do this with some dignity."

Hollis stepped forward, fatigue making him obedient. He hadn't slept. He and Mia had spent their first two hours after opening the case struggling to think straight by force of will alone. They'd brewed coffee, eaten the most decent food they could find — fruit and bread, as Brendan's fridge wasn't all bacon and eggs — and spent the next four hours poring over the case's contents.

None of it made any sense. It didn't contain bonds or instructions to a cache of money or weapons or gold or anything of value. There were technical specifications — code and computer-type instructions that neither of them could make heads or tails of.

Still waiting, Brendan laughed. "Oh. Right." He pulled out his phone and touched something, then there was a whirring of the drones powering down. Hollis spied one beyond Brendan, descending to the soil.

"Come on. They won't hurt you." Brendan gestured again, with the machete.

They won't hurt you. Only I will.

Hollis said, "We got it open."

"Got what open?"

"This." He hefted the case, now closed.

"Did you now? Show me."

"First," Mia said, "we want some guarantees."

"No guarantees," Brendan said.

"We want a promise that you won't hurt us."

"No promises, neither."

"And we want safe passage off the grounds. We'll take our bags and everything we came with, and leave in the Charger. We want the gun, too. I'll take the clip and Hollis can take the weapon unloaded, if you're worried we'll try to use it, but that's part of the package."

Brendan frowned. He looked up, into the brightening sky. His head cocked. "You really got it open?"

"That's right," Hollis said.

"Well, let's see it."

"Put down the machete."

Brendan took a moment, then shrugged. He took his time circling the Gator, setting the machete in the rear. Then he held up his hands in mock surrender.

"All right. I'm unarmed."

Hollis considered telling Brendan to come in, but the situation's precariousness seemed to warrant more room to maneuver. So, with the killer drones deactivated, they both came forward.

"Where?" Hollis asked.

"Step into my office," Brendan said, indicating the flat roof of the running Gator.

"I need your word that you'll let us go."

"Friend, you give me what I want and you're free to go wherever you want. Dumb to leave my protection, but that's your call."

"And we have your word."

"Yeah."

"Both of us. With all our stuff."

"I said yes, didn't I?"

Hollis came to the Gator's front, eyeing Brendan, instructing him without words to give them room. He entered the code with his back turned. It vanished once the clasps were open. Brendan must have thought Hollis was bluffing, because his eyes widened when he raised the lid ... then, after a slight hesitation, turned it to let Brendan see.

Brendan picked up the sheet of paper on top. Then the one under. He looked through a sheaf, pausing here and there to unfold larger sheets that looked to Hollis like electrical schematics. There were all sorts of interesting but seemingly useless items inside. There were little business-card-sized sleeves with cards inside, and on them ran alphanumeric codes, two lines long. There were what looked to Hollis like ancient electronic components — transistors, capacitors, something like that, but from the seventies — and several sets of plain old metal keys.

"What the hell is this?" Brendan asked.

"It has something to do with the Astral app." Mia knew that much. They'd read all they could in the interim.

"I see that. What of it?"

"The data center is here in town," Mia added.

"And?"

"Well ..." Hollis said. Because that had been their reaction, too.

Brendan was leafing through the remainder of what was in the case. Lots of paperwork an engineer might understand but that nobody around the Gator could make hide nor hair of.

"I don't get it," Brendan said. "What, is this instructions on how to build an app of my own?"

"Not just an app," Hollis said. "That's got the blueprints to the facility, which seems to stand on its own and share data with—"

"Who gives a shit?"

Hollis closed his mouth.

"Give me the punchline, Hollis. You're a smart guy. You had all night to look through this. Boil it down for me. Finish this sentence. *Brendan Banks cares about the architecture for some stupid computer shit because ...?*"

"I ..."

Brendan seemed to be growing agitated. He probably hadn't slept either. There were bags under his eyes. "Spit it out, Hollis. Tell me why, for the past week, we've all been rubbing our dicks over this stupid fucking case that's full of nerd plans for building bullshit I don't give the slightest shit about."

"Well, it's ..."

Brendan rummaged through the papers, crumpling them, mussing the edges. "I believe you told me about a weapons cache. I think you said there were bonds inside. Where's my treasure map, telling me where to find my guns? *Where's my fucking money*? Where's anything but this ... this ...!"

As words failed him, Brendan gave Hollis an animal growl, shoved his fistful of papers back into the case, then slammed it shut. The case locked, now with papers pinched in the edges, rumpled and torn. He picked the thing up, seemed to consider hurling it into the bushes, then threw it at Hollis instead.

He caught it with both hands, barely avoiding a corner in the eye.

"Stay there," Brendan said, moving toward Hollis and Mia, between them, toward the Gator's rear.

"What? We had a deal?"

"I got a deal for you," Brendan said, retrieving the machete. "*Keep* the fucking case. For the rest of your life." He hefted the blade. "Now stand real still, will you? Try to act like steak."

"Now wait just a goddamn—!"

A sound stopped him. It was a nearly silent whoosh, more experienced than heard. Hollis felt the very air move around him, as if it had been nudged aside. The world went dim, like an eclipse. There was a rip of static, his hair rising from his scalp.

They looked up. As they did, Mia backed up a step. Brendan's machete lowered.

Overhead was an enormous polished silver sphere, blotting out the sun.

"Holy fucking sh—" Brendan began.

But Hollis's survival instinct had kicked in. He pried his eyes from the unreal sight of the alien ship and, using his only advantage, took the attaché case by its handle and swung it hard at Brendan's head.

He reacted just enough to save his life — or at least his consciousness — raising the machete arm to deflect the blow. The deflection was incomplete, barely slowing the arc.

It knocked the machete askew then aside, crashing with only slightly diminished momentum into Brendan's nose. Even through the mass, Hollis felt the man's nose break. It went like a stepped-on Dorito — a thought that Hollis, if adrenaline had given him time to think, might have found sickening after his night of no sleep, plenty of alcohol, and an embarrassing litter of snacks.

Brendan, now empty-handed, staggered back and grabbed his face. It was gushing blood, already staining his shirt in the artificially dim morning.

Mia was spellbound. She'd seen Hollis's hit, but her eyes were still skyward. The huge ship had blotted the sky, drifting toward downtown.

Hollis grabbed her arm and pulled.

Into the Gator. It would have to do. The Charger was faster, more powerful, and would surely go farther. But the keys were inside with the rest of their stuff — all their clothes and belongings, not to mention Mia's gun.

Into the seats, kicking Brendan away as he tried to rally, stepping on the gas.

The thing had surprising pickup. After a moment wherein it seemed Brendan might hang on, they were quickly free. Hollis guessed it topped out at thirty or so, but that was faster than Brendan on foot.

The wind whipped by. They rattled back the way they'd come days ago, down the pitted dirt driveway. There'd been a fence then, but it'd been open. Hollis could see it, and of course it was closed.

They'd hear the drones any moment.

"Hang on!" Hollis shouted.

They both did, bracing for impact. But it wasn't like in the movies — fences didn't so easily yield. It stopped them dead, bruising hands and spraining wrists, banging Hollis's forehead against the plastic steering wheel.

They piled out. "We have to climb!"

"It's electric," Mia said. "It'll be electric!"

No time to consider. Hollis ripped the Band-Aid, grabbing the fence with both hands. If it was going to fry him, so be it. An alien mothership had coasted overhead and there was a guy with a machete and machine-gun drones at their heels. Electrocution, all things considered, might not be a bad way to go.

Hollis looked back the way they'd come, to the house, then at the fence and its top of razor wire. To Mia, he said, "Take off your shirt."

"Fuck you!"

Time was ticking. Hollis had two layers; he could cover them both. He took off his sweatshirt and threw it to her, then peeled off his shirt and bit it between his teeth. Mia looked at him stupidly, but understood after he threw the case over and started to climb. She wrapped the sweatshirt over her shoulders and scrambled over as well, on the other side of the crashed Gator.

Hollis reached the top first, then slung his shirt over the razor wire. Mia, looking over, followed using the sweatshirt. The thin shirt wasn't enough, though, and halfway over Hollis felt one of the razors slice his arm at the biceps.

He yanked his arm away, realized that was a terrible

idea, and tried to put it back. But gravity was in charge, and seconds later he swayed, fell, and hit the ground hard.

Mia fared better — also falling, cut on the ball of one palm, but dropping a lesser distance for a neater fall to the ground. She rushed over to Hollis and put her hands on him, saying his name. He was shirtless and cold. Everything felt broken.

"Get up. *GET UP!*"

An engine, behind the fence. Before they saw its source, the gate began to rattle open. But the Gator warped the tracks with its impact, and it stalled with only six inches of daylight down the middle.

"Move your ass, Palmer!"

She dragged him upright. And shockingly ... nothing seemed to be broken. His feet were bruised and his ankles twisted, but he was able to limp up and follow Mia's lead.

Beyond the gate was a road. A culvert across it. That wouldn't help them if Brendan wanted them badly enough. But it was all Hollis could manage, and they were out of vehicles, supplies, and options.

They climbed inside, ducking low.

Then, from within their circle of darkness, they peered out and watched the massive silver mothership settle above the skyscrapers of downtown Austin.

25

MIA WAITED IN THE CULVERT, watching as Brendan reached the gate, then shook it, trying to get it to open past the damage inflicted by the Gator. She thought of running, but there was little point. The road outside his property was open, and the land, not far down, gave way to a strip mall.

He'd see them if they ran. He might have guns, or decide he wanted them badly enough to climb. Either way, Brendan might be able to squeeze through the gap, and they'd spent long enough with him to know they didn't care to trifle.

Still, as she watched Brendan rant and swear, Mia considered dragging Hollis away. They couldn't be safe here. If Brendan came through, process of elimination would suggest their hiding place. There was no way through the culvert — a grate blocked it not far in. Maybe it was worth taking the chance. Get to the mall, find other people or a good piece of lumber to swing as a weapon.

Hollis made the decision for her. He passed out, presumably from the pain.

You *can still run, girl*. Your *feet are fine*.

But even as Mia considered it — even as she felt her muscles flex, meaning to rise and sprint — she kept seeing Hollis throwing her his sweatshirt. Now shivering and bleeding in his uneasy sleep.

Brendan doesn't want you. He wants Hollis. Go on. He'd leave you.

Maybe it made her a sucker, but Mia wasn't so sure.

So, she watched the ship as it moved above the tower that looked like an old-school USB drive, then stopped. She waited while Brendan rattled the fence. For what, Mia had no idea. Would the ship discharge a massive energy weapon on the city, like in that old movie? Would it try to land?

But it did nothing. For a second, she thought she saw something fly out of it — a smaller ship, perhaps — but it was an optical illusion.

Brendan, also watching the ship, didn't persist. He had other things to do, with the visitors here. What those things might be, Mia didn't know. Fight with the hipster army? Or battle the aliens?

That was a laugh. The ship blanketed downtown.

The fence stopped rattling. Brendan got back in the Jeep and drove away, turning toward the barracks. The troops would need a leader, now that the enemy — one of them — had staked its position.

"Pixie?" Hollis muttered a few minutes later, coming around.

"Can you walk?"

"I walked here, didn't I?"

"Come on." She peeked out. "There's a car coming."

"And you want someone in a car?"

"Better than dying in a ditch."

"Get the case." Hollis pointed.

"Why?"

"It's worth sixty million dollars."

"Hollis. It's not worth anything."

"Hey. I almost got a machete to the face over that thing. Then it saved my life."

While Mia went after the case, Hollis clambered up the embankment and onto the edge of the road. He looked like hell — shirtless, pants shredded, hair mussed and full of twigs, covered in blood. There wasn't a chance that car would stop for sensible hitchhikers — especially not with aliens in town — let alone for Hollis's walking dead.

"Hollis! Let me—"

He collapsed at the edge of the road. Face-first on the concrete.

"Hollis!"

The car couldn't swerve around him. It was coming too fast, and Hollis — over six feet tall — had managed to sprawl his entire length across the road's center. On one side, swerving would send them into Brendan's gate. The other would tip them into the ditch.

Mia, who'd been most of the way to the attaché case, ran. *Hard.* She waved both hands overhead, trying to flag them down. They must have seen her, because someone inside hit the brakes. She reached Hollis just as their rubber stopped burning, frozen at the end of a pair of matching black skid marks.

Hollis lifted his head.

"I got them to stop."

"You did this *on purpose?*"

Hollis grinned. It looked painful, but still all him.

"You *shit!*"

She'd cradled his head when he'd raised it. Now she dropped it, and fuck his fresh concussion.

"Is he okay, man?" came a voice.

Mia looked to the stopped car, which she'd somehow managed to forget. A bearded man in a yellow knit stocking cap stood in the open driver's-side door. There was also a passenger — a girl in what looked like a hemp pullover, hair in dreads. Both appeared mid-twenties, and neither seemed as preoccupied by the giant sphere hovering over the city than any normal people should be.

"Get the case," Hollis croaked.

"He's fine," she told them.

26

The boy was named Ricky, and the girl Ember. They were students at UT, but embarrassed by their involvement in an institution so mainstream and rich with conformity. Mia only guessed they were students because when she'd asked about a first-aid kit, Ember pointed to the glove compartment. Inside were two student IDs, each showing a younger and more groomed version of the car's driver and occupant. The old photos, according to Ricky, were embarrassing, too.

"There's a lot you can learn that's actually a little enlightened," Ember explained, as if trying to talk her way out of trouble. "They have agriculture classes."

"My mom made me go," Ricky added.

Mia was willing to forgive them both, mainly because they busied themselves explaining while Mia was still trying to administer first aid. There'd been a kit, in the rear of what turned out to be an SUV packed with food, water, and weed — just the essentials. It wasn't a great kit, but it had antibacterial ointment and bandages. It had an ACE bandage, with which she wrapped Hollis's wrist. They had ice in a cooler, which she applied to his head and both ankles, and a shirt.

Across the chest, it read, WOKE TO THE FUTURE. Ricky told Hollis he could have it. Hollis said, "Do I have to?"

Mia thanked them. Then she asked where they were going.

"Dunno, man," Ricky said.

"Green belt?" Ember suggested. Apparently, this was the first they'd seriously had the discussion.

That made Mia think of all the camping gear they'd bought. Well, stolen. Fat lot of good that'd done them, two cars and one invasion ago.

"Do you wanna come with?" Ricky asked.

"You don't mind?" Mia asked.

"No way. We gotta look out for each other. We were trying to hook up with some friends."

Hollis and Mia exchanged a glance.

"It's cool," Ember said to Mia. "You and your husband can come, too."

"He's not my husband."

"You boyfriend, I mean."

"He's not my boyfriend either."

"Well, whatever you two are."

"He kidnapped me."

"Right on."

As they got into the rear, Ricky closed his door. Before moving the car into autodrive, he looked at Mia and Hollis then the attaché case.

"That all you got?"

"Yeah," Hollis grunted. "We're traveling light."

Wasn't *that* the understatement of the year? They had a case full of worthless crap. All of their earthly belongings were back inside Brendan's house, including their gun, money, and even the phone.

They drove for fifteen or twenty minutes. Mia lost track.

But they were away from Brendan and his army, and that was what mattered. Although she couldn't help thinking of Hollis's opinion on that from earlier.

Wasn't it better to be inside the army than against it?

That became moot when Brendan decided to kill them.

Mia sat low, Hollis stretched on the rear seat with his head in her lap — the opposite of last night. Eventually, he napped. She must have, too, because the car's stopping stirred her. Mia blinked and looked around.

They were on one of two narrow streets that forked away from a larger throughway, subtly winding into a residential area. It seemed to be on the edge of a small, quirky business district. Mia, looking around, spied a used clothing store and a record shop that still sold vinyl. Food trucks (Tex-Mex and Greek) were on a lot off the corner.

"You live here?" Mia asked.

"Nah, man," Ricky said. "We *work* here."

Mia was about to ask an irrelevant question — "Both of you?" — but Ricky and Ember exited the car before she could. Hollis sat up and she looked at him, surprised by his sudden movement. "You're feeling better?"

"I never really felt bad." Then Hollis opened his door and got out, barely limping.

She got out and took him by the arm. "I thought you were hurt."

"I dug you taking care of me. Pretending to care, anyway."

"You're a son of a bitch."

"Yeah, but I'm still pretty." He grinned again. "Ain't that right, Titz?"

"Let's stick with Pixie."

"Knew you'd come around."

The place they'd stopped was a small brick building

with ornate lettering across the front that read *Spider House Ballroom*. It didn't seem nearly large enough to be a ballroom.

"Um ..." Mia said, "you aren't actually *going to work,* are you?"

"Oh, no. We work at the music shop around the corner. This is just where we all hang out."

Hollis gave Mia a look that said, *Of course. This all makes sense.* Brendan was a murderer and a bastard, but at least his preparations were logical.

"C'mon," Ricky said. "I'll introduce you around."

"I thought you said we were going to the green belt?" Mia asked.

"Yeah," Ember said, coming alongside. "I'm going to be honest with you. I'm still really high right now."

Ricky entered the ballroom. Nobody followed. Mia, keeping her feet planted beside Hollis, took in the surroundings. There'd been virtually no traffic on the way here. Apparently, everyone had gotten to where they wanted to go and were staying put.

The light was wrong.

Then, all at once, Mia remembered something her mind must have blocked out.

She looked at Hollis, but Hollis was already looking up.

Mia did the same. And saw that they were now *under the ship.* It was blocking the sunlight, filling the sunny day with shade.

"Wish I could call my mama," Hollis said. "She always told me I'd amount to nothin', and here I am standing under a spaceship."

"That doesn't mean you didn't amount to nothing."

"Still."

Ricky had gone inside, but Ember was still beside them,

turning their twosome into a threesome. She pulled a cell phone from her pocket.

"You wanna call? Here you go."

"I was being facetious," Hollis said. But he took the phone anyway. Mia could read the look on his face. If Ember got distracted enough in the next handful of minutes, he probably meant to keep it.

"Check the news," Mia said.

"I already know the top story."

"Right. But how are people reacting?"

"Honey, I'm not sure I'd trust the reporting of anyone dumb enough to be on the job at this point."

But he started tapping around anyway. It wasn't long before he sighed and allowed his arms to drop.

"It's out. No service."

Ember took the phone. "What? It had service a minute ago." She tapped around, then brought up the phone app and tried to make a call. "That's funny."

Hollis nodded at the ballroom. "So. Shall we?"

Mia shrugged. Ember brightened then followed them.

Inside, the structure was cute but unimpressive. To Mia, it was a dark series of open but not-large rooms, totally unlike what she'd expect from a ballroom. Straight through the door was a bar, and off to the left was a door into a room full of chairs aimed at a stage. Fifteen feet square at the most, raised only by a pair of steps, projecting into the room like a peninsula. It looked like everyone was still expecting a performance.

Ricky appeared at Mia's side. He gestured at the bar, for everyone's benefit.

"Help yourself. The owner split town five days ago."

Two young men brushed by holding hands. Hollis watched them while Mia watched the bar's few-dozen other occupants. All seemed to be in their twenties, except for one older couple who'd overdressed for the occasion, both in business attire.

"Have you just been living here?" Hollis asked.

"I guess. I actually live down the street, but I brought a bunch of shit here so we could all crash together. Ember's on campus, so she's been staying here with everyone else. Me, too, actually. My parents were out of town when the announcement came, and with the borders closed, I don't think they're coming back soon. It's kinda been a *Lord of the Flies* situation, y'know?"

Ricky smiled and Mia smiled back, but she wondered if he'd finished the book. Isolated boys' clubs were all fun and games until the rapes and murders began.

"Why were you way out east, just driving around?"

"Gotta go somewhere," Ricky said.

Mia had questions, but the answers didn't matter. Ricky and Ember looked like they'd been seeking a home, when in fact they'd had one already. Their SUV was fully stocked for what sounded like a pointless day trip. *Gotta go somewhere.* Mia decided this would all be a lot easier if she stopped trying to figure it out.

Hollis, making himself at home, moved behind the bar, grabbed a glass, and after a few pulls on empty taps was able to get himself a beer.

"Want one? There's still some IPAs left."

Mia walked away. She entered the makeshift auditorium, then discovered a television on around the corner with a single woman sitting before it. Unlike the others, she didn't precisely look like she belonged in the Spider House. She was forty or so and looked absolutely terrified, like she hadn't slept in days.

"Mind if I sit?" Mia asked.

The woman adjusted the chair, bringing it closer. "Please do."

"I'm Mia."

"Carol."

Mia indicated the screen, showing a high-up shot of the state capital. "What's going on?"

Carol told her.

27

THE NATIONAL NEWS network was still up, working like the electricity, staffed — despite Hollis's jaded opinion — with eager-beavers who'd stayed dutifully at their posts. Rather than being shaken, most of the talking heads Mia and Carol saw seemed fully in their element. Talking about the alien invasion made the newspeople *more* calm. If Mia's degree in armchair psychology was worth anything, she would have guessed they were all dissociating as they gave their reports. Comforted by telling the world facts because deep down, their brains had convinced themselves it was only happening to everyone else.

Carol told Mia she'd been at the ballroom for three days. She lived in Round Rock and commuted downtown. To avoid the panicked crowds, she'd slept in her office while waiting for the streets to clear, then found her choice backfiring when Governor Garrett closed borders. She'd walked, used a scooter, and eventually found a car on the sidewalk with keys still inside. She'd stopped at Zilker Park, which was even thicker with street prophets than when Hollis and

Mia had left it, then fell in with a crew of college students who knew "a place they could hang."

Carol laughed, obviously at herself, and ran a hand through her prematurely grey hair. "I hope I don't stink. Everyone's been 'taking showers' in the bathroom sink using hand soap, but I only have this one set of clothes."

She gestured at the screen. It no longer showed Austin. The shot was of Chicago, with the ship hovering what looked like mere feet above the antennae on the top of the Sears Tower.

"What are they doing?" she asked, sounding frustrated. "More importantly, what are they going to do? They didn't all show up at the same time. Chicago's ship was a few hours before ours. Same for Los Angeles and Denver. Colorado's ship isn't really even over Denver. It keeps cheating toward Vail, then back. None of the others are doing that, at least that I've seen. So why Vail?"

"Are they all over big cities?" Mia asked.

"There's one over in Wyoming, currently over part of Yellowstone. Another's been moving slowly across the more remote parts of Canada. Mainly over water. What's that about? Oh, and you want to see a real mindfuck?"

Carol picked up the remote and clicked, mumbling that someone must be showing it. When she finally stopped, Mia couldn't help gasping.

An enormous silver sphere hovered above the Great Pyramid in Giza, Egypt, the Sphinx visible in the foreground.

"Not over Giza proper, you understand," Carol said, noting Mia's startled expression. "Over the *pyramids*. How's that for a conspiracy theory come to life?"

Mia had no idea what to say.

"There's one over Moab, Utah. And Boise. Who knew the aliens would come to *Boise?*"

"Lot of interesting things in Boise," Mia said, speaking in a trance.

Carol was shaking her head, eyes on the screen, a pained expression on her face.

"But what are they *doing?* A few people have reported seeing smaller spheres, like shuttles to the mothership, but nothing's been substantiated. Crackpots, probably. You know how everything goes foggy when something this big happens."

"Nothing this big has ever happened."

"You got that right," Carol said.

Mia sighed, sinking in. She was exhausted. She'd been running on adrenaline, forgetting until now that she hadn't slept and was still fighting a vicious hangover.

"You look like hell," Carol said.

"Thanks."

"It's okay. We all do. Where were you bunking down until now?"

Mia told her the story. There was probably no reason for subterfuge, and she didn't have the energy. Carol accepted it all without judgment. Hollis's theft, Mia's plans, their unsteady partnership, the mysterious case, Brendan's compound, his army and their narrow escape.

Thanks, aliens ... saved by the bell.

Carol seemed particularly interested in the sixty-million-dollar case — not because of its supposed value, but because of its contents.

"I think I know the place you're talking about," she said.

"Brendan's compound?"

"No. The data center. It's off 360, if it's what I think it is.

Did the paperwork say *Applied Algorithmics* anywhere on it, do you remember?"

Mia slowly nodded. "Maybe. Yeah, that sounds familiar."

"And you said it seemed to have something to do with the Astral app?"

"That, plus a lot more. Other apps and stats on some really big databases, other companies. Like ... Hyperion? Although Hollis said that's a science fiction novel."

"Probably HDS. Hyperion Dynamic Systems. That one's not in Austin. Remember hearing about the data breach there?"

"No."

"Well, I guess it wasn't a breach. More like a vulnerability."

"You seem to know a lot about this stuff."

"I'm a network engineer," Carol said. "I do a lot of work in cybersecurity."

"Oh. Well. I know dick about that kind of thing. It sure didn't look like sixty million dollars to me."

"Data itself isn't worth anything. It's only got value depending on how you plan use it. Was there any indication of what your husband meant to do with whatever he had on those apps and databases? Hyperion's database is massive, but I can't see how it'd be useful to anyone except for advertising ... maybe. I don't suppose there were any statistical analysis reports? Or any degree of frequency analysis, in terms of—?"

Mia held up a hand. "Stop. Please." She smiled to soften her words. "I'm hung over and way below your pay grade. And I was almost killed this morning. And these jeans?" She indicated her leg, where razor wire had shredded but thankfully spared her flesh. "I *really liked* these jeans."

Carol laughed. She patted Mia's shoulder. "All right. I

guess it's understandable that you look like hell. Do you want something to drink? The kids made coffee."

"Coffee would be nice. Thank you."

Carol rose. The second she did, Mia's eyes found a plush booth at the room's edge. The idea of laying down instead of sitting in hard plastic felt flat-out erotic. She started toward it, then stopped. Now upright, she had an idea.

Mia peeked into the bar's other room, then into a couple of alcoves. Eventually she found Hollis crashed in a dogpile with a bunch of twenty-somethings on the floor. Like a litter, huddled together for warmth.

"Hollis," she whispered.

But he was out. Gone. Dead to the world.

Mia looked around, eyes searching, then heavily sighed. What she'd been looking for was under Hollis's head, used as a pillow.

"Stupid ass." She crouched before him, carefully lifted his head, then slid the attaché case out from under him. He didn't remotely stir, nor did any of the kids. The group had the look of a long party's end — crashed more than voluntarily sleeping.

Mia reached for someone's discarded hoodie, wadded it up, then slipped it between Hollis's head and the concrete floor. Then she returned to the booth and opened the case's latch.

Carol came back and put two cups of coffee on the table.

"Is that it?" Carol seemed surprised. Mia's story might have implied they hadn't been able to escape with it, that they'd had to leave it behind.

She sipped, and the warmth and comfort of something so familiar as coffee was soothing. "Yeah."

Carol sat. Mia set the coffee back on the table and, deciding proper decorum was a thing of the distant past, stretched out on the cushion's red velour. Now she couldn't even see Carol, the news, the table top, or the case she'd set on its top.

Her eyes closed of their own accord. Each concession she gave to fatigue made it deeper.

"I need to close my eyes for a bit. If you're bored, have a look. Let me know what you think."

Above her, unseen, the sound of pages turning.

"Jesus," Carol said.

It was the last thing Mia heard for several hours.

28

MIA WOKE to the sound of low voices.

She opened her eyes, took a moment to remember where she was, then sat up slowly.

Carol was away from the booth and back in one of the wooden chairs. She'd pulled a round table from somewhere and had the case open on its top and off to the side. She was working on a laptop. Hollis sat opposite her, awake and looking a hundred times better.

They stopped speaking when Hollis noticed Mia.

"Oh, sorry, Pixie. Did we wake you?"

Mia rubbed her head. She was dying of thirst, though her headache seemed to be gone. The coffee was still in front of her, now ice cold. She sipped anyway.

"What time is it?" Mia asked.

"Six."

That couldn't be right. *"PM?"*

"Well, we were still at Hotel Banks at 6:00 a.m., so ... yeah."

Mia put both palms to her face, rubbing the haze away. She'd slept almost an entire night's worth on what, now that she wasn't so exhausted, was revealing itself to be a somewhat uncomfortable restaurant booth.

"Holy crap."

"Feeling any better?" Carol asked.

"I think so. Give me a minute." She sipped the cold coffee again, blinking, running a hand through her hair. She got up, stretched, and decided she'd end up paying for that much time in a booth. But her head was clearing and the relentless oppressive fog from the morning had mostly left. She felt like a person again. A small price to pay for some bodily aches.

She moved to the table, pulling up a third chair.

"I got up, and some smartass had replaced my prize with a pillow, so I came out here and saw Carol riffling through our shit. I think she mickey'd you to get a look."

Carol chuckled, returning her attention to the screen. If it was dinnertime, she'd probably already endured several hours of Hollis. More than enough time to learn to love to hate him.

"Anything?" Mia asked.

"Lots of things."

"Anything good?"

"Not so much," Hollis said. "The ships are still just sitting there, but they've been sending out baby ships. There. Like that one." He pointed at the screen where Carol had been watching the news. It was still on, and Mia saw shaky footage, probably from a helicopter, of a much smaller silver sphere exiting the large one through an opening that closed the minute the little one was away.

The little ship moved like a hummingbird. Jetted to a stop just past the big ship's wall, hung suspended in space for several seconds, then shot off like a bullet. The camera tried to follow, but captured nothing.

"Are they landing?"

"Nobody knows," Carol said. "The Internet is in and out, but the big social media sites never came back. Maybe that's intentional and maybe someone's asleep at the switch. Either way, it's hard to get cogent firsthand accounts of what might be happening with the ships, with the aliens ... any of it. The news is only reporting rumors. Nothing official."

"And the rumors?" Mia asked.

"You don't want to know," Hollis said.

Carol picked up the ball. "Might as well be vapor. Entire towns are losing their minds and the crackpots all seem to be getting on soap boxes and saying, *See? I was right!* All we know for sure is that there's still a big ship sitting above Austin, not doing anything. No communication, no contact ... nothing.

"Have little ships left the Austin mothership?"

"Yeah," Hollis said. "And people are saying they're taking prisoners."

"Wait. Do you mean ... abductions?"

Hollis shrugged.

"Rumors," Carol said. "Same for rumors that they're landing, or setting up patrols. There was an interview with some lady who's heading one of the 'reception' groups down at Zilker. She said she saw one of them unloading crew. But she said the aliens looked like big, powder-white beings. Like oversized humans. Doesn't that seem awfully coincidental? Next thing, we'll be hearing about short gray guys with black, almond-shaped eyes."

"Why is that coincidental?"

"What, the aliens look just like us?"

"Not all of them," Hollis said.

"You can't put stock in what anyone is saying right now, Mia," she said, brushing Hollis's comment aside. "Seeing is believing. People are saying all kinds of stuff. Like alien foot patrols have already surrounded UT, but we *know* that's not true because we're close and a group went out to see. So yeah, wackos are all over these shuttles leaving the motherships, saying they're full of powder-white men and giant insects. And saying people are being abducted — sucked right up with energy beams. I guess someone told the wrong people a theater outside of town was an alien base in disguise, and some stupid asses burned it down. You have to watch this stuff with a filter. It's easy to get sucked into mob mentality."

Mia looked around the room, leaning to get a peek into the bar. "Doesn't look like there's a lot of mob mentality here."

"Yeah, well, don't go outside. I think your buddy Brendan let out his army because a few thousand people with guns marched on downtown not long ago. Unfortunately, McCafferty's group is also back downtown, after consolidating what they took from Mabry."

"Has there been fighting?"

"Little stuff," Hollis said. "Scraps and whatnot. Lots of chest-beating because each side's got newspeople with 'em. But give 'em time. Who needs aliens to do anything? Wait long enough, and we'll kill *ourselves* off."

The conversation chilled Mia, returning her hopelessness from before. She turned to the case, gesturing for Carol to see. "Does any of this make sense to you?"

"Oh, yes. You said your husband said it was worth sixty million dollars?"

"It's not?"

"No. It's worth a whole lot more. He probably *priced* it at sixty million, for a buyer. For the right person, who could use what's in here, it's worth hundreds of millions."

"Use it how?" Mia asked.

Carol shrugged, leaning back, hands behind her head. "Well, it's data. Tons and tons and tons of personal data, like one of those big breaches you hear about. But in this case, identity theft is the tip of the iceberg. The bigger fish is statistics."

"Statistics?"

"Network usage. Frequency analysis of known and unknown variables." She put her hand, fingers tented, atop a stack of papers. "What you've got here is essentially an instruction booklet and access codes to crack into just about any complex system we've got."

"How? Thomas wasn't into—"

"He was into the Astral app. Hollis tells me he was one of the first investors?"

Mia nodded, not understanding.

"Without getting too geeky," Carol said, "users can log into the Astral app through a bunch of third-party authentication protocols. Whoever programmed the app built in a way to reach back through those third-party services and harvest ungodly amounts of information on how people behave online."

Mia considered asking how that was possible, how nobody noticed, or how Thomas even got involved, but that would surely get "too geeky."

"With that much data across so many fields, you can figure out a lot of things that shouldn't be possible to easily understand. I don't suppose you heard of a book called *The Chaos Code*?"

Mia and Hollis both shook their heads.

"It's about finding order in chaotic systems. Or rather, systems that *seem* chaotic. There's no amount of data that would help anyone pick lottery numbers because it's truly random, but other things we think are more or less random are actually subject to an enormous number of influences. Stock prices, for instance. Or the outcome of televised championship poker games."

"Are you saying that with what's in that case ...?"

Carol nodded. "Yeah. Someone with the right understanding and access could short the stock market right before a crash. Or buy a crappy stock with no potential just before a random event causes it to explode. Place insider bets on all kinds of sports, and be right maybe seventy-five percent of the time."

Mia sat back. Yeah. That was worth more than sixty million bucks.

"I'll tell you this." Carol patted the case. "I'm glad you stole it. This is a vehicle for someone to make repeated killings at a lot of other people's expense. Eventually, whoever used this information would have destabilized the market."

She shifted, then indicated the laptop. "It got me right in, as promised, but there's not a lot I can do because I don't have nearly enough computing power. It can't be done on the public cloud, so someone would need banks of servers to make a dent. But the right person? Welcome back, Great Depression."

Mia exhaled, unaware she'd been holding her breath.

"It's just that ..." Carol trailed off, looking at her computer's screen.

"What?"

"I don't know. Some of this activity? It's ... strange."

"Strange how?"

Carol sighed and rubbed her eyes, now looking like the tired one. "I don't know. Do you mind if I keep poking around? I could use something to keep my mind occupied, as long as the Internet sticks around."

"Well ..." Hollis said.

Mia turned to him. "You can't *possibly* be thinking of selling it, after what she just said."

"What she *just said* is that without a damn warehouse full of computers, ain't nobody gonna be able to do shit to hurt anyone."

"It could leak, Hollis. To someone who could use it."

Hollis rolled his eyes. "Shit, Mia. You been watching the news. Happen to catch the stock report? This case here ain't what's gonna destabilize the market. Last I heard, the Dow's at an all-time through-the-toilet low. As in, it don't motherfucking *exist* anymore."

Mia sighed and looked to Carol. "Yes. Of course. Poke all you want."

From behind them, someone said, *"Holy shit!"* A chair fell, as if the person who'd spoken had knocked it over in shock.

They all looked. Three of the college kids had come in from the bar, all holding drinks. Well, *two* holding drinks. The one in the middle, who looked the most startled, had lost his to the concrete.

They followed everyone's eyes to the TV screen.

It showed a suburban street, where one of the small spheres had settled a few feet above the pavement. Then the shot changed, presumably repeating what had already been shown.

The sphere was slowly lowering to the ground. It looked like cell phone footage, wobbling as the person holding it shook with nerves. There was whispering on the footage — a group of people with the camera operator, perhaps. Every once in a while, the edge of something green showed to one side. A dumpster, Mia thought, where the group was hiding to take its shot.

Without sound, the sphere reached the ground and stopped, braking with two feet to go. With cars nearby for comparison, Mia could guess the thing was about as wide through the center as a school bus cut in half.

A door slid open.

A short ramp descended.

Then, from the dark rectangle in the sphere's side, a spiny black thing, like a stick, protruded.

The stick reached the ground, and was joined by another.

Not sticks. *Legs.*

A super over the bottom quarter of the TV read, *First contact?*

Onscreen, the rest of the thing's body emerged. It was something like a black grasshopper, only when it opened its mouth — emitting a sound Mia could only think of as a *purr* — she saw that it had several concentric rings of pointed teeth. And in its throat, a blue spark throbbed like a miniature star.

The legs of another chair squealed behind them. Something heavy hit the ground. Mia did not turn.

Once outside the ship, the alien looked left, then right.

Then it scuttled away, and the camera could not follow.

The thing didn't run.

It *scuttled*, with a sound like clacking high heels.

Mia's hand covered her open, screaming mouth.

29

THINGS WENT DOWNHILL FROM THERE. Though he kept his outward calm, Hollis hadn't slept nearly as well as Mia, had taken more of a beating, and hence found himself having a hard time hanging on. He wanted to lose every morsel of his shit — after that first amateur video of the planet's visitors, then an official-news video of a shuttle over a two-story house using an energy beam to suck some poor bastard right through the roof.

Night fell. Several times throughout the dark hours, unknown noises shook the building. Some sounded human and conventional. Big, Brendan-style guns firing, or maybe bombs going off in the city center not far away. Others were decidedly alien — either literally, or earthly and peculiar.

There was a low whoosh around midnight, after Hollis had laid down to sleep but had woken again — something passing overhead like a whistle. Three or four times, he heard a sound like the clacking of heels and that low, bone-shaking purr that the alien had made on video.

In the shadows, he thought he saw moving shapes. But nothing came.

In the dark bar-slash-ballroom, the lights were off. Austin, still obeying its laws against light pollution, was mostly dark. The cocktail made it simple to see passing lights through the windows. Greens, oranges, reds, blues. Some moved at speed and others were slow. Once, there was only a glow, as if a bright light had been turned on just beyond the window's view, and only for a handful of seconds.

Someone being taken? Hollis had no idea.

All night, he fell into and out of sleep. Dreams melded with reality. By the wee hours he was unsure if he was actually seeing lights through the windows or merely dreaming. He imagined Mia waking, walking to the window, and watching for long minutes. Once, he saw a beam of light pierce the roof and pull her through it. That, at least, had been a dream. He moved to where she'd laid down, found her, and stayed close. He told himself it was to protect her. In truth, the move was more about him.

Morning came hard. Based on what they'd seen and heard, nighttime was no more dangerous than the day, but at least in the light you could see what might be coming. Hollis was awake well before dawn and looked outside to see a hint of blush teasing the eastern horizon, just above the neighborhood trees. He watched it, begging it to hurry. Red became orange. The blush spread, like a bruise. Behind him, others stirred. Came to the window. Silently waited. Silently preyed.

Everyone was groggy. Carol, who seemed most intact, used the big industrial pot behind the bar to make coffee. A half-hour later, she made another.

At just before 8:00 a.m., the news reported one of the little ships was hovering over a town outside of Budapest, where daylight was in full swing. It hovered before being noticed because a massive, town-wide riot had erupted, splitting the hamlet into factions — which sounded awfully familiar — and in the morning local time, those two sides had finally had enough of each other. Authorities estimated three hundred dead and ten percent of the village burned by the time the alien shuttle arrived.

The news camera watched as the belly of the shuttle — a larger one than they'd seen last night — opened. Suspended in a short beam of light was something about the size of a car crushed into a cube. It went dark and the heavy cube dropped, hard, shattering a fountain in the middle of the warring town.

Then there was a new shot of the thing, one corner of its cube-like mass buried in concrete. A display on its front came alive — not with a digital screen, but through a shuffling of mechanical parts. At first, Hollis thought the thing might be shifting a lock mechanism, preparing to open. But the front-facing edge kept crunching through permutations, running through the same set of fixed configurations over and over again.

The people stopped fighting. Immediately. And gathered around the cube, waiting to see what might happen, what might emerge. But nothing happened. Nothing emerged.

Just that shifting face, clicking over and over through its set of symbols.

After a while, the screen changed. Reporters — shaven but dull-eyed, made-up but like robot versions of real people — sat behind a desk. Graphics, video, and words gave updates.

The enormous motherships were still arriving, taking their places all around the globe.

There'd been more alien sightings. But it seemed now there were two kinds of beings, extremely different from one another. The best video of the insect things was still the amateur footage from the night before, but helicopter footage of St. Petersburg, Russia showed a chilling shot of the things swarming from above — ten or more bursting from a central origin, then darting in all directions down empty streets.

But there was a second kind of alien as well, and although good footage was hard to find — the Internet, apparently, was spotty everywhere — they appeared to be the beings Carol had mocked. Massive, all-white figures with bald heads. They looked like idealized humans, standing on legs like ours. And from all reports so far, all the second kind *did* was stand. Everywhere anyone reported seeing one — or a line of them, as it seemed they liked to form orderly, military-like lines — they simply stood in place, silent, with impassive expressions on their far-too-human faces.

The news flashed back to the cube outside of Budapest. A tag in the screen's corner declared it to be LIVE FOOTAGE, but precisely nothing had changed.

Carol, perhaps because she'd tired of the news or perhaps because she'd grown bored, returned to her laptop and the information inside the case. Watching her, Hollis felt a new fascination. He'd thought what was inside was no more than gibberish, but ... *a way to cheat the market? A key to instant riches?*

Too bad he hadn't snagged it earlier. He knew a handful of people who would have paid handsomely, and in any currency Hollis desired.

"Anything new?"

Carol took a long moment before responding to Hollis. She frowned, shaking her head. "Does anyone else have access to this, do you know?"

Hollis shrugged. "No clue. I guess whoever put that case together could get into the databases you were talking about. Thomas, maybe. Or someone he works for? I don't have any idea. Why?"

She didn't answer. Just kept right on concentrating. Hollis stood behind her, fixed to the screen, learning nothing. She seemed to be watching network activity — maybe the "someone else accessing the system" that she'd alluded to.

Yesterday, Hollis had seen the occupants of the Spider House Ballroom come and go. They'd even gone out on the streets to play Frisbee. Now, the mood was claustrophobic. Nobody left. Or even opened the doors.

The American president made an address, as did the leaders of several other nations. But nothing of substance was said. The military was still unsure how to proceed. Attack, investigate, or turn to the diplomats?

The earliest of the alien ships had been in place for over a day now and had done little more than send out shuttles. An attack would have been easier to deal with. At least then there wouldn't be this tense silence. And they'd all know what they were dealing with, even if they were doomed. An attack would fully mobilize the military — maybe get that big, ugly stack of nukes out of storage and ready for use.

But the ships didn't strike. In most cases, shuttles weren't even sent. Many cities saw nothing — no smaller ships exiting the bigger one or aliens on the ground.

Was this an invasion? An occupation?

Some pundits said the aliens were abducting citizens, and that was an act of war. It was time to act.

But nobody acted.

Governor Jefferson Garrett, who was now famous not just within Texas but nationwide, had much to say about the lack of action. *This*, he said, is why Texas had seceded — because the federal government was inept and cowardly. When Garrett gave his address from the front of the Capitol, Brendan was visible in his entourage, a bandage across his nose where Hollis had broken it. On his other side was a general Hollis swore he'd seen at the barracks, with a line of bland-faced men standing behind him.

Occasionally, the news cameras turned around to show the gathering around the governor's stage. The crowd was large — much larger, Hollis thought, than he'd expect with insectile aliens on the loose and abduction spheres in the sky. But it was a two-sided crowd, with numbers clearly displayed for a show of might.

To one side was Banks's polished, trained militia.

And on the other was the ragtag group of armed locals, Forest McCafferty front and center.

Broadcasters broke into the coverage of downtown Austin. They announced a new development in Hungary, then cut to the scene near Budapest.

Video showed the big mechanical cube, still with its corner buried in concrete near the fountain. The super on the bottom of the screen read, MOMENTS EARLIER. The face of the thing continued to shift configuration with a sound like robots marching.

Then there was a bright white flash, and the cube was gone.

Hollis held up a hand to shield his face, as if the news had lulled him into feeling present and it was blowing up right in front of him.

But the cube didn't do a thing. Once the flash was gone, the square remained as it was. Curious Hungarians were either rushing forward or freaking out behind it. But none of the animosity from before returned. They were too damn scared.

Back to the reporter, who brought it all around for those who'd been late to tune in.

"A strange object, dropped from one of the small alien ships into the town center sixty-six minutes ago, has inexplicably vanished, leaving authorities to wonder at its purpose."

Leaving Hollis to wonder the same thing as he sat in front of the TV with frightened others whose names, he now realized, he hadn't even learned.

Noon.

Carol continued to plink away on the laptop. She seemed obsessed. Hollis was jealous. Having nothing to do, no real goal, and nowhere to go was unnerving. At least Carol had a purpose, even if it was meaningless. Wasn't there something similar Hollis could do?

He couldn't remember the last time he'd been without a scheme or some angle to work. Couldn't recall the last time he'd had to wait and see what someone else might do. There had to be a con. Someone to fool or an arbitrary end to seek.

But no, the people here had nothing Hollis wanted. And flight meant maybe running into those ... *things*.

The news got into a rhythm, with the biggest stories recapped at the top of every hour. The 1:00 p.m. report of downtown Austin showed the two groups still in place, with Garrett on his grandstand promising "Texas-level action" and McCafferty now with a mic of his own, promising sane action instead of "cowboy recklessness." The two duked it out, playing a verbal game of high-stakes chicken.

Their respective groups of angry citizens were behaving, possibly because they'd been searched before being allowed onto the lawn. Only the police were armed, and they could be on either side. There weren't even fistfights, the groups staying far away from one another. Hate in the air, thick like stew.

Garrett's group referred to "disobedient factions within the city." He hinted to his followers that those factions were composed of the same wealthy people whose interests had run the state back when it'd still been one. Texas was for Texans. And hadn't so much of Austin always joked that it wasn't *really* in the state — that it was better than its fellows past the city limits? Maybe those people should just get the hell out if they didn't like it there. He'd even open the borders, exclusively for them.

And McCafferty, speaking obtusely, pretending those he represented weren't the people Garrett was talking about, said the state needed a compass. Why would anyone sensible go, if it meant leaving the Texas they loved to a bunch of brainless bullies?

Snipe.

And snipe.

2:00 p.m. Then 3:00 p.m.

At 3:45, the broadcasters cut in to announce that a new cube had been dropped in the town of Pochaiv, in western Ukraine. Then they cut to footage. The cube was the same as the one near Budapest, and as before, people were stunned and fascinated, wanting to get closer than their nerves allowed. Its appearance synced perfectly with the arrival of tanks, meant to disperse citizens who'd taken their looting too far. But the military seemed to have fractured, with separate sides sending muscle.

Now two tanks and a shitload of soldiers were around the cube, aiming at it, considering figuring out what it was the easy way — or at least making it irrelevant.

Sixty-six minutes later, that cube vanished, too.

Someone changed the channel. If you flipped through the TV long enough, you could find someone making pronouncements about anything. The cry to engage the stoic ships was louder than ever. And so, some locals flew small planes up, trying to signal. Hot air balloons launched, just to get closer. Brave men and women even got nearer to the smaller ships, but nothing happened — no opening, no sign.

Pundits started talking about preemptive attacks. Especially the Russians, who got loud on the matter.

Other pundits warned that engaging the visitors aggressively would mean the end to everything.

More footage of both kinds of aliens. Strong and silent powder-white monoliths alongside black scurrying insects. No one had any idea what they were doing, but plenty of pundits were guessing.

More rumors of abductions, including the first internationally recognized name, Mara Jabari, of Cairo.

More cubes.

Which vanished sixty-six minutes later.

Until one, without explanation, did *not* vanish.

At the sixty-six-minute mark, news cameras (unable to get close, for all the infighting and congestion) watched the cube dropped on Serpukhov from the sky. A clock ticked in the screen's corner.

Then there was a white flash, same as before, only much larger.

And when it dissipated, the town of Serpukhov was in ashes. Not burning — *in ashes*.

Completely vacant, all hands dead.

And silent.

More grandstanding. Everyone had an opinion. The UN, which had moved to an undisclosed location, called for many votes on a myriad of topics. There was no consensus. According to one source, an unnamed diplomat repeated history, removing his shoe to bang on the tabletop in anger.

The president gave another speech that said nothing and promised no specific course of action. This made politicians of all stripes very loud, but none more booming than Jefferson Garrett. And in debate with him, Forrest McCafferty was equally loud.

That's how it was, until Moscow finally scrambled fighters to approach their mothership.

And how it was when Moscow decided to launch nukes at the thing.

There was a burst of unholy fire.

The ship finally flinched.

And within seconds, all of Moscow was incinerated.

The city center. And the surrounding suburbs.

All of the estimated five million people still left in the city ... dead.

Hollis could only gape. Those around him mumbled, cried, and bargained with no one, pointing to the ship above their own city that seemed plenty capable of doing the exact same thing.

Hollis — equal parts angry, scared, and motivated — decided it was time to stop playing the victim and *do something.*

He wasn't the only one.

30

"Motherfucker, we can't just—!"

Mia looked over. That was Hollis's rascal voice, gone righteous before someone rammed him with a shoulder and stopped his talking. She'd had an eye on the news, but most of her attention had been with Carol. She'd just said that thing about how the database kept rearranging itself when something happened — something bad, that caused Hollis to make his empty declaration.

Mia caught his gaze and moved toward him but stopped when a group of men ran past the window, shouting.

Tires squealed.

Two somethings — one near, one far — seemed to either crash or blow up. The walls trembled for a millisecond, and Mia felt it in her bones — air inside telegraphing violence from the outside to her body.

The ballroom's occupants rushed to the windows.

A few went to the door, including Hollis.

Mia followed, their business unfinished. "Hollis, what's—?"

His face was hard. Angry. "They nuked Moscow. Just turned it to dust."

"What? Wait ..."

"The Russians got pushy. The aliens shoved back. Now it's time to kick some ass."

He put his hand on the knob then opened the door. Mia had to grab him by the opposite arm and reel him back, surprise alone giving her an advantage over his superior weight.

"Wait! Who knows what's going on out there?"

"Who fucking cares? I ain't gonna just sit here and wait to see what happens. I'm not exactly a sideline-sitter." He went again for the door. She held him fast.

"*Wait,* goddammit! What exactly are you planning to do?"

"I don't know!" Hollis spoke as if her question annoyed him, because the answer was so obvious.

"Well, don't you think you should know what you're going to do before you rush out into a panic?"

"Some people are thinkers, I'm a doer. I didn't think when I took that case, and Carol tells me I saved the world."

Well, that was a bit much. He'd maybe saved the US economy, which had gone to shit thanks to the aliens.

"*Stop,* dammit!" Their struggle had become comic. Hollis was practically dragging her, leading arm out with fingers spread. "Listen to yourself for a second, will you? You're pissed, but nothing's changed. Are you planning to rush downtown and start shouting up at the mothership? That'll show 'em, won't it? You don't even have a gun!"

"I'll find one."

"And do what with it?"

"Anything's better than what we're doing here."

"We're not doing *anything* here!"

"Exactly. We ain't doin' *shit* here. There's nothin' I could do that would get me less than this."

"This," Mia said. "You mean being safe, having some people to count on?"

"Like I can count on these hippies. At least with Brendan, we had a chance."

"After he killed us, you mean? What's your problem, Hollis? You know you can't do anything, so why try?"

"That's a real super attitude, Mia. Just like a hero."

"What, and you want to be a hero? Maybe you're *not* planning to fight. Maybe you're planning to run."

Hollis snatched his hand away but didn't move. He stared Mia down, his anger finding a temporary target. "So what if I want to run? Running's what we both signed on for."

"Not me." Mia shook her head. "You led. By the time I had a choice, the world was ending."

"Well, zippity-do-dah. Ain't *you* the superior one? Sorry. Guess I'm just a criminal. Not like you, with your plan to rob your husband so you could run off and fuck someone else with a fortune in your panties."

Mia hit him with small, flailing blows.

"Get off me!" he spat, shoving.

"Dammit, Hollis! Try to run now and you'll get your stupid ass killed!"

He glared. "Oh, yeah? What do you care?"

"I *don't* care! Fine! You want to go? Then go, you redneck piece of sh—!"

From beyond the walls came the rat-a-tat of an automatic weapon. Short bursts, close enough that Mia heard bullets hitting the walls. Someone shouted, and someone else screamed in pain.

Hollis tackled Mia, taking her to the floor.

One of the windows popped. A small, double-tap as two bullets struck it. Dual holes, like a deep bite from long fangs. More bullets struck glass. The real target, perhaps — maybe a car or a nearby building. Then another hit a different window — scattered fire, surely. It was more likely hooligans shooting each other than targeting the ballroom specifically.

Hollis put his hand on her head, pushing it down. Her lips kissed filthy concrete. But she hugged the floor anyway, scared into paralysis, waiting for it to end.

Outside, she heard the slam of a car door. An engine, gunned. Two sets of tires squealed away, one after the other. A crash followed, as if the drivers weren't terrible, wounded, or maybe indifferent. It was a whole new world.

Hollis let go of her head. She looked up.

"It's over. You can get up."

For some reason, that really pissed her off. *"I can get up? That's okay with you? Well thank fucking God for Hollis fucking Palmer!"*

She was hitting him as they moved to sitting. Hollis raised both hands, shielding his face.

"What's wrong with you?" he said between blows.

"What's wrong with *me? Fuck you!"*

She hit him one last time, hard, in the center of the chest. It took his breath, and Hollis had to lean against the bar and fight for recovery. By then, Mia had turned away, crying furious tears. She wiped them away, as pissed at herself as she was at Hollis.

Why was she crying? Men didn't cry when they got pissed, and they saw it as a sign of emotional break. Of weakness. She wouldn't let him see. She *would not.*

"Shit, Mia." Hollis was only a voice. Her visual world was the wall in front of the fliers for upcoming acts. She could attend a poetry slam. Watch a troupe of actors try to perform Shakespeare while one of their crew was shit-faced drunk.

"You okay?" he asked.

She still didn't turn. "Go fuck yourself."

"You kiss your mama with that mouth?"

Mia returned to the ballroom. With no idea of what to do, she climbed onto the small stage. Only, there was nothing to do up there, either. Maybe Hollis, as infuriating as he was, had a point. She wasn't used to sitting back, either, waiting to be squashed.

Hollis followed her. "I need to get out of here. You get that, right?"

Mia didn't even know what she felt. Was she more afraid or more out-of-her-mind livid? And if she was angry, who was she mad *at*? Hollis? The aliens? The posturing assholes downtown, neither of whom she found herself able to side with?

McCafferty was presumptuous and unwilling to face certain harsh, politically incorrect realities about death and the pickle his government had forced them into. Garrett was a grandstanding prick, clearly more interested in his ego and power than anyone's welfare. McCafferty's followers struck her as obnoxiously righteous. Garrett's as bullies with inferiority complexes. But how was it any different than any other day?

She'd given up listening, was done with talking to people outside of her circle. Even before the aliens, you couldn't go onto LiveLyfe without hating everyone. Every self-important post. Everyone's stupid opinion on every little thing, always in conflict with someone else's stupid opinions on the exact same subject.

On their second day, when they'd been smoking weed in the Ferrari what felt like years ago, Hollis had drunkenly said, *Fuck this world.* And Mia — at the time and now — couldn't help but agree.

You really could only count on yourself.

We were all in this thing alone, not together.

Mia turned to face him. Too late, she hadn't wiped her eyes enough and dammit ... *Yeah*, he saw.

"I get it. Go on. If you want to head off and fight the aliens or run away, you go ahead and do it."

Hollis looked like he might do exactly that.

But instead he sighed, went behind the bar, then poured himself a half-tumbler of Grey Goose. A third went down in a gulp. He wordlessly passed Mia the glass before moving into the other room.

She lost sight of him as he rounded the corner. "Don't do me any favors. Don't you even think of staying *because* ..."

She wouldn't say it.

Hollis didn't answer. Maybe he hadn't even heard her.

Mia went into the bathroom to compose herself. Beyond the walls, she could hear the popping of gunshots. It wasn't as bad as it could have been, considering all the firepower that had been at Camp Mabry and was now in Austinites' hands, all the goodies Brendan put behind the governor's might. It could have been worse by a factor of a thousand.

That, she felt sure, would come later.

Fuck this world.

She splashed water on her face then stared into her own eyes. *Maybe they should wipe us out. Maybe, in the end, the universe would be better off.*

Mia watched her reflection — a dirty, smelly, bag-eyed, bedraggled girl who once upon a time seemed to have her shit together.

"Just make it to tomorrow," she told herself. "One day at a time."

Night was coming.

Things would get worse before they got better.

31

But it wasn't like Hollis could just sit still. Maybe the streets were going to Hell, or maybe they'd been in the wrong place at the wrong time, having caught a small group of rebels with their dander up. Either way, Hollis wasn't willing to take it on faith. Containment wasn't in his DNA. None of the strands had him waiting for a storm to pass. He had to know the current lay of the land, then act.

Hollis Palmer didn't play these things blind.

He hadn't slept through the night since he'd been twenty. So, no surprise waking in the middle of it. He'd already prepared, had a small backpack containing a bottle of water, binoculars from an army surplus store down the street, and the gun he'd taken off a dead body last night after it'd gone quiet and they'd gotten bold enough to leave the building and explore. Taking a phone sounded smart, so he took one of those, too. Ricky's. There was zero chance he'd miss it.

By now, Hollis had risen in the night a dozen times since he'd been with Mia. She slept soundly, and he never disturbed her. So he made like before, tiptoeing toward the bathroom, then stopping and looking back at the door. They all slept wherever around here, having pilfered blankets and set up an indoor refugee city. Mia was one among many, but he easily picked her out. She no longer looked so troubled in the moon's azure light.

He watched her a bit too long. More and more, her cracks had been showing. Mia's problem was empathy. It was a lot easier not to be upset by the city devolving into war if you didn't care who died, so long as it wasn't you. Hollis could protect himself. Same for Mia. That should have been enough.

So why are you doing this?

Why are you sneaking out in the middle of the night and heading into the lion's den downtown?

If it's really just about you, shouldn't you point for the border, haul ass, and hope to keep getting lucky?

But the answer was obvious. Hollis was surveilling his purposes. Depending on what Hollis learned, he might decide that now was the time to jet — and because he'd have checked the state of things first, he'd have ensured a clean path of escape. Because flight, he'd decided, wasn't optional. Not with Governor Garrett and McCafferty's people about to start trading blows. If Mia didn't want to leave, she didn't have to. She'd be stupid to stay, but as Hollis was fond of saying, you couldn't fix stupid. She'd been warned.

If you think you might leave tonight, shouldn't you be taking the case?

Yes. Of course. His bargaining chip, to buy his way in when he found a place to stay. He knew its value, so now he could find a buyer.

But he hesitated. Sneaking out was one thing. Taking the case was another. He'd watched Carol continue to plink away at it well into the evening. There was something behind the data. Another unseen hand. Something that Hollis, watching, thought might have meaning.

Come on, hustler, if you want to be a man, this here's your chance.

"Can't sleep?"

Hollis almost jumped out of his skin. He'd navigated the human minefield in the ballroom and bar but had been so focused on steering clear of bodies, he hadn't so much as looked around upon reaching the door. His thoughts on returning for the attaché case went out the window, kicked out by the force of surprise.

Hollis put his hand on his chest. Carol was on the stoop, smoking a cigarette in the moonlight.

"Jesus. You scared me."

She removed a pack of smokes from her jacket and shook it toward him, one butt inching its way out.

"Do you smoke?"

"Do *you*?" They'd been here for days, and this was the first he was seeing of Carol as a smoker.

She puffed. Took her time with a long exhale.

"I quit six years ago, after my divorce. My husband turned out to have a second family. Can you believe it? That kind of thing is only supposed to happen in the movies. Messed me up. Smoking helped me cope. Then one day I was about to put one between my lips and I thought, *I'm doing this because of him. I'm ruining my health because of* him. It was like someone slapped me. I quit cold turkey. Out of spite, I suppose."

"No, thanks," Hollis said.

She returned the smokes to her pocket. "One of the dead guys we found last night had these on him. I took them when you took that gun."

"Hey, look, I was gonna—"

Carol waved a hand. "If anyone here should have a secret gun, it should probably be you. It's kind of macho bullshit, but it's sweet how you protect her."

"Protect who?"

Carol took another drag, smiling slightly.

Her eyes went to the downtown mothership, which looked ethereal and silently terrifying in the scant midnight. "Anyway. I figured it was as good a time as any to start up again. If it's cancer that kills me, I'll consider myself lucky." She nodded at Hollis's backpack. "Going somewhere?"

"No. I was just—"

Again, Carol waved his words away.

"Don't bullshit me, Hollis. I know who you are."

"You do?"

"Yeah. You're a reluctant hero. A misunderstood bad boy. I've seen the way you stalk around the ballroom." *Puff.* "Downtown?"

Hollis assumed the question referred to his destination. At least she hadn't assumed he was heading for the hills. Which he still might, if he found a way to come back for the case.

He nodded.

"You know there's no chance it'll end peacefully, don't you? The minute Garrett or McCafferty stops staring down the other, they'll have to admit what they're actually afraid of. The governor is McCafferty's way of pretending the real threat isn't right above us. He'll keep his hate where he has more control, if that buys him some time not thinking about what he can't control at all."

"I thought you were an engineer, not a head-shrinker," Hollis said.

"I'm many things."

"Look, I've gotta ..." He made vague gestures into the dark streets.

"I know. You got a car?"

"I was thinkin' I'd borrow Ricky's."

"Not a great idea. I saw on the news that they're setting up roadblocks. None are pros, though, so you'll be able to get around them on a motorcycle."

"Now if only I had a—"

Carol dangled a set of keys.

"*You? You* rode here on a motorcycle."

"Purely for practical reasons. One of my co-workers rode one to work every day, but he ran away on foot when it happened. These were in his desk."

Hollis took the keys. "You really are a surprise."

Carol shrugged, a pleased look on her face.

"It's just down there." She pointed. "You know how to ride?"

"Did you forget your assessment of my character?"

"Right. If you'd lived in the 50s, you'd have been a greaser. Be safe."

He nodded and started off.

"Hollis."

He stopped and turned. "Yeah?"

"Remember I said I could see someone else trying to access the databases? How it seemed that another user was someone parsing the zettabytes of information your case gave me access to?"

"Yeah."

"I've been thinking about it. Kept me up all night."

"Why?"

"Because I think it's them."

It was very quiet.

"Who?"

Carol pointed her cigarette at the mothership. She repeated, *"Them."*

"Why?"

"I don't know. I just know that they're going through it much faster than our best machines can, and they're rewriting it off-site. Honestly, it sort of looks a little like what I'd do if I wanted to train an AI."

"An AI? But ..."

"Or not. I just know that whoever else is in there, they're very interested in what might be Earth's biggest behavioral database. Very interested and ... *using* it somehow."

The thought gave Hollis a chill. He wasn't sure what to say.

Carol took another drag on her cigarette. "Come back in one piece, okay?"

32

Whoever else is in there, they're very interested in what might be Earth's biggest behavioral database.

Carol's words rolled inside his skull as he barreled, without a helmet, down a stretch of unfamiliar road.

This part of Austin, he didn't know. He just aimed the motorcycle's front tire at the big buildings and let the streets take him where they wanted.

Very interested and ... using it somehow.

Using it how? What good would human data be to the visitors? Why would they care to see how humans behaved, via their digital footprints through a covertly connected series of the planet's most popular apps?

Hollis saw something ahead, then stopped.

Near the entrance to the University of Texas (beneath a huge sign that read HOOK 'EM HORNS), someone had set up one of those roadblocks. It was amateur hour — rather than tanks and rows of antitank structures, there were three minivans and an embarrassingly small number of sandbags. From what Hollis could see, whoever had brought the minivans had stopped by Home Depot first and emptied the sand aisle. When spread across an entire street, they amounted to a mildly inconvenient speedbump.

He killed the engine and walked the bike closer. There were two men at the obstruction, pacing with big guns over their shoulders. Hunting rifles or automatic weapons, he couldn't see across the distance.

He took the bike down another road, to the west side of campus, and found that one blocked, as well.

"Fuckers," Hollis muttered. *"Now* you're organized?"

The third street was barred, but only by one armed woman driving a Kia. Still, *Armed.* Hollis was, too, but she had something you fired with two hands while he had a pistol he wasn't looking to shoot.

Far enough down, he finally found a clear road. The methodology was strange — and, Hollis thought, entirely ineffective. You couldn't block an area off halfway. You either did it all the way or didn't bother. It was like trying to build a swimming pool with only some of the sides in place.

Were they trying to cordon off campus? Hollis wasn't sure and didn't care. He saw no lights in that direction, whereas the area around the now-closer Capitol was lit like a Christmas tree. He supposed they were doing a fair job, all things considered. The Texas State Guard had been joined by the National Guard's Texan members, but they plus the out-of-city militia still amounted to a few thousand people, max. They'd focused most of their efforts on closing the Texas and Austin borders. *That* was where the more heroic encampments were. Impressive that they'd found the manpower to barricade anything at all.

Hollis moved a few avenues down, then kicked his cycle back to life. It was loud in the still streets, but that was okay. He could hear other engines moving around. The "soldiers" watching the streets, last week, were still average Joes and

Janes. They wouldn't come chasing him. They were doing what they thought of as their current duty, but he doubted they'd go too far above and beyond.

Taking his roundabout route, Hollis made his way toward the Capitol lawn. Closer, he found more citizen roadblocks and decided to stash the bike.

He tucked it between a dumpster and the back door to an office, then moved through the shadows until he found a building tall enough and close enough that its roof would offer a sniper's view of the Capitol.

He found one within a few minutes, then tried the front door. Wide open.

Neither of you have enough hands to secure this place, do you? The whole thing was stupid. Hollis's mind kept returning to what Carol said, about how Garrett and McCafferty and all their ardent fans were turning their anger on each other so they wouldn't have to face the horror above.

Or, Hollis thought, even on the streets of Austin.

Another chill. It'd been one thing to see those big insect-like aliens on TV, but it'd be quite another to run into them on the ground. It was enough to make him race back then close and lock the outer door. Paranoid, perhaps, but Hollis didn't want anything clacking up behind him.

He climbed the stairs, exited at the roof, then made his way to the edge. The lawn was brilliant with floodlights. It looked like the world's worst concert, where everyone just stared at those opposite and were allowed to have no fun whatsoever.

He pulled out his binoculars and had a closer look. While he couldn't see McCafferty, Banks, or Governor Garrett, Hollis could see a heap of their people. Even from here, it wasn't hard to tell them apart. None wore uniforms, of course, but their wardrobe choices told the story.

Garrett's people were dressed practically, whereas McCafferty's looked more fashionable. One side looked prepared for battle and the other ready to put on a spectacular re-creation of a skirmish. Both had weapons, search policy be damned, and so far, that kept them equal.

Hollis scanned the crowd. About half held firearms. The rest had bats and chains ... even machetes. Weapons they'd had in their garages. Almost nobody had graduated to full auto. For some reason — maybe the old search policy, who knew — even those with guns mostly had pistols. He spied no military equipment.

But still, he'd seen what he needed to see. He'd felt it, gotten right into the energy. Before he'd come down here to see it with his own eyes, there was a chance Hollis might have agreed with Mia and the others that staying in town was an option. But through the binoculars, he could see the hate and feel the heat. Brendan had tanks and Apaches and howitzers. If the locals had raided Camp Mabry, they'd have pretty much the same.

Whether anyone was trained on all that equipment or not was barely relevant. Even if you couldn't figure out how to fire a tank, you could drive it over people. Even if you couldn't fly a helicopter, you could crash it into something. Anyone could figure out how to hurl a grenade.

As if his thoughts were made manifest, a whining engine sounded from the south, near the lake. It was hard to see well from here, but someone seemed to be driving a Jeep with a top-mounted carbine along Caesar Chavez, screaming toward a roadblock in front of the Four Seasons.

The two groups at the Capitol heard it, too, as heads on both sides turned in surprise.

Shooting at the roadblock. Shots from the carbine sounded like cannon fire. Someone threw something explosive — one of those theoretical grenades, maybe — then one of the roadblock vehicles burst open, the sides blowing out in a starburst of shrapnel and a billow of white smoke like a bag of dropped flour.

There was no fiery orange explosion. Hollywood, it seemed, had lied to Hollis. But someone was screaming, and a second detonation started a series of wooden sawhorses along the roadblock's front to burning.

Then, tensions on the lawn erupted to match.

It happened in waves. Entire sections did nothing, falling short of their posturing when push came to shove. Others engaged immediately — some one-sided at first, some with both at once.

It quickly spiraled out of control.

Fuck this. If there was any doubt left that I'd stick around this shitburg to see what happens, it—

His thought was severed by a squealing like a rusty hinge from above.

The bottom of the mothership opened. Five or six of the smaller craft dropped into the air above Austin, but unlike most times the news had seen them, these shuttles moved *fast*.

One zipped toward the burning roadblock then fired a single pulse of energy, raising a cloud of dust large enough to subsume a block.

Another moved to the dead center of the Capitol lawn, causing some but not all of the combatants to look up. It began to fire small green beams with perfect precision, taking out those with the biggest guns or the hardest charges like an automated sniper.

Two of the others crash-landed on the lawn itself, half-burying themselves in the turf rather than making their usual elegant descents. The tops of both opened in a rapid spiral motion. An apple peeled from the top in a flash.

Then, with the tops off and the things looking more like cups than spheres, a handful of the bug-type aliens spilled from each. They moved like lightning, covering the lawn in seconds.

Hollis was paralyzed. He knew he should run — and *hard* — but he couldn't stop watching.

The black aliens didn't have weapons because that's what they *were*. A few times, prey spotted predator and tried to sprint away, but the aliens were far faster. They reached the running humans in a blink and tore them to shreds. It was not elegant or precise, like the sniper fire from above. They had all the delicacy of a blender's blade. Several combatants were torn in half. Many heads were simply bitten off by blue-glowing mouths full of concentric teeth. Blood coated the lawn like paintball impacts, sudden and complete. Benches got new paint jobs. Screams like Hell's chorus ripped the air.

When one of the silver spheres whooshed overhead, Hollis's paralysis broke. He shoved the binoculars into his bag, barely got it over his shoulder, then made for the stairwell. But of course, it'd locked behind him.

"Motherfucker!"

The sphere passing above paused. Curious, as if it'd heard something.

Hollis made for the side, barely checked that another building was bunkered to this one, and dropped a full floor to the tarpaper surface. His knees, still not quite recovered from his dive over Brendan's fence, whined in protest.

Hollis ran.

Past air conditioner compressors. Antenna clusters. Hook-shaped ventilation tubes.

Behind him, the sphere peeked over the roof of the building he'd jumped from.

This rooftop door was also locked. No surprise, seeing as he was in a place not meant for sightseeing.

He climbed to the next building, this time lowering himself over the edge before dropping. The impact didn't hurt as much, but he lost seconds. And that curious silver sphere was still behind him, slowly closing.

Hollis looked back. A tiny black circle opened on the thing's bottom.

With an inarticulate grunt, he ran. Hollis could still hear the chaos behind him. At the Capitol, at one or more of the roadblocks, maybe hand-to-hand in the streets.

Even if he got down, what might face him? Some of those big white guys, holding him down politely so he couldn't escape? Or the bug things, stalking with their bone-chilling purring sounds?

But the door to the third building's roof was open, and Hollis tore through it, hauling ass down the stairs then onto the street before stopping to check what he might be running into.

All was clear, though, so he ran back to where he'd parked his bike, irrationally sure it would be gone. It wasn't, so he backed it out, keyed it, then slammed his foot down hard enough on the starter to make his leg scream.

Again, with the engine's roar, he was sure they'd come for him. But they didn't — not humans from either side, not aliens on the ground nor ships in the sky. The sphere was still above him, lowering now, following his egress with interest.

Hollis, on his way back to the ballroom, didn't need to avoid any roadblocks.

Every one was burning.

33

Mia was in an earthquake.

Except, no, it was Hollis, shaking her hard enough to give her brain damage. "We have to go!"

"Hollis, what the hell?"

"Get up!"

He let go of her shoulders so suddenly that she racked the back of her head on the concrete. He moved to her pile of belongings, which he was returning to what had once been her go bag.

Had it really only been a week since she retrieved it from the W? The life for which she'd originally packed that bag felt like it'd happened to someone else, a million years ago, in a distant and unknowable land.

He was panting, out of his mind. Around them, a few people were starting to stir, but so far he'd hissed everything, overcoming the fervent emotion clearly impregnating his every fiber. By some miracle, nobody was awake.

"What are you doing?"

"I told you! *We have to go!*"

He had the bag in one hand, Mia in the other. He

dragged her through the room, stepping on a few sleepers, finally waking them, causing less of a commotion than his energy seemed to warrant. At the spot where the ballroom joined the bar, he shoved the bag's handles at Mia then used his now-free hand to close the attaché case and grab that, too.

Mia searched for Carol. She was on the room's other side, asleep. Good. She'd been working too hard, up too late. When Mia went to bed, Carol was still wide awake. It wasn't good for her to keep grinding so hard on what ultimately didn't make any difference.

Just like whatever-this-was couldn't be good for Mia. Or Hollis, for that matter.

She wasn't able to shake him off until they were outside. She broke free with momentum, barely avoiding a neck-breaking spill down the short flight of steps onto the patio below.

"What's wrong with you?" she said.

He didn't look himself. His eyes were wild, his breath short. As if he'd been running for days.

"Fighting. Downtown. Garrett and McCafferty's people ..."

Mia looked around. Listened. The night was still.

"I don't hear anything."

"I guess they stopped."

"So, they fought," Mia said. "But it's cool, because now they stopped."

"Not them. The aliens."

"You said it was Garrett and—"

He seemed to focus, to still his nerves. "It was. They're camped out around the Capitol. They've blockaded a bunch of the streets."

"Where are you getting this?"

"I went down there." He shook away her rolling eyes. "No, no, listen. Someone blew up a checkpoint, and then it all kind of spiraled out of control. Then the aliens ..." He was still distracted. Still a bit out of his mind.

She looked up. The mothership was calm, frozen, and hovering.

Hollis's gaze joined hers. "I guess they finished. I guess it's over."

"Look, Hollis. You haven't been getting enough sleep. I swear, my mind is playing tricks on me. I—"

"I'm not making this up!"

The force stopped her.

"We have to go."

"I told you," Mia said. "I'm not going anywhere."

"You think you're safe? You actually think that staying here, holed up inside this building not three miles from where I just saw—"

Mia held up a hand.

His lips clenched. He was actively pissed now. "Don't be a fucking idiot, Mia! Don't pretend you're the airhead fuck toy Thomas married you be!"

Mia took a step back, blinking. "*Excuse* me?"

"I have a motorcycle. We can get past the blockades if we go off-road. The news said a lot of the automated gas stations are still open, especially near the cities."

"Are you sure? I don't know that I can operate a pump, Hollis. I'm just an airhead fuck toy."

"Oh, *that's* what you're going to worry about right now?"

"What else should I be worried about?" She pointed toward the building. "The shelter and helpful people we're with?" She gestured downtown. "How about the silent night and *total lack of trouble?*"

"Lack of ...!" He huffed. "I just told you." He jabbed a

finger at the mothership. *"They. Do not. Come in peace!* Do you hear me? Or do you have too much cum in your ears?"

Mia smacked him so hard, it turned his face sideways. A palm print was already reddening on his cheek.

"Fuck you, Hollis."

"Hate me later. Once we're past the border." He reached for her as he shook off the slap, but she stepped back, her face set and head shaking. "Why would you want me?"

"Don't be like that."

"More to the point, why would *I* want *you?*"

"I *saved* you!"

"Oh. You did? Seems to me you've done a great job of getting me into trouble. Seems to *me*, I've saved myself. Saved *you*. I didn't want to go to Brendan's in the first place. Then, when we escaped, *I* dragged *your* ass into the ditch so he couldn't shoot you through the fence."

"Just like you let me drive us out of town like I wanted all along? If you hadn't tried that shit at the bank, we'd be singing 'O, Oklahoma' by now!"

"I was trying to get away from *you!*"

"Bullshit!" Hollis blurted. "I ain't fuckin' stupid, Mia. You told me all along you had that combination. Why didn't you just tell me you couldn't get into the case? Even when we were at Brendan's, you were still puffing hot air about it. What was that, if not you trying to *force* me to keep you around?"

"Oh. The great Hollis Palmer can't be forced into anything, can he? You kept me around because you *wanted* me around!"

"To bitch at me the whole time?"

"To help you! To keep your stupid, hillbilly ass out of trouble!"

"No way." He shook his head. "Ever since we hooked up on Thomas's bed, you've been dyin' for seconds."

She hit him, harder. Again, and again. Then she grabbed the case to take with her.

He grabbed it too, both of them holding the handle. "Oh, no, you don't. You wanna stay and get killed? Fine. I don't need the hassle. But *this* is going with me."

Mia yanked the case.

Hollis held fast.

"It's mine!"

"Bullshit, it's yours! I stole it, fair and square!"

"I earned it!" Her composure was shredding, all she had felt but hadn't said spilling at once. "I'd been planning my con for months! Who do you think left transponders in all the cars, Hollis? Who set the alarm to malfunction with the locks open, instead of locking the house down? I knew I might need to get out fast, that the alarm might end up getting triggered! Do you think I didn't plan for contingencies? Do you really think I'd go to all that trouble and leave anything to chance?"

She yanked again. Hollis yanked back, causing her to totter and almost fall.

"I thought it all out! You *screwed up* everything I'd been working on — not just for the months it took to set things up, but for the entire goddamn time I'd been married! This was my retirement, and you ruined it with your stupid, brainless *smash and grab bullshit!*"

Mia put her entire weight into one hard shove and came away holding the case.

Hollis staggered back.

Lights came on behind her. Their fight, it seemed, was waking the sleepers.

He held a hand out. "Give me the case, Mia."

"Fuck off!"

He reached, snatched, and grabbed the handle.

"Give me the case, and when Thomas comes knocking again — which he will, when what's in here makes its way into the open market — I'll tell him that you had nothing to do with it. You won't sell it, anyway. It's worthless to you. I'll tell Thomas you were innocent, and I dragged you along. You'll need that. If you plan to stay in town, he *will* find you — and I'm sure by now, your plan to rip him off has left traces."

Mia watched Hollis for a few delightful seconds. Then her cheeks puffed with bitter laughter, and she surprised Hollis by letting go. "Tell Thomas whatever you want. Go get him. Go drive right up to his door, if he's still there, and tell him all about me."

Hollis looked at the case, now in his hand, wondering what had just happened.

"If Thomas looks, he won't find traces of my plan. He'll find traces of yours."

"I didn't have a plan." But now he looked stupid, caught off guard.

"Sure, you did," Mia said.

They stared at each other. People were at the door, watching their standoff in the ballroom.

"You're not thinking clearly. I told you, Hollis. *I thought of everything.* I couldn't just run off letting Thomas think I was guilty. He'd come after me, like you said."

Clearly, he still didn't understand.

"I framed you." Mia moved closer. "Remember, that time we had sex, how *angry* it was? How I kept whispering for you to be rough, to pin me down and smack me around?"

His eyebrows drew down in confusion.

Mia whispered. "What do you think that'd look like on

the video I made? Do you think it'd look consensual ... or forced?"

All the best parts of her plan. All the scapegoat tracks she'd made in the dirt of the crime, with Hollis Palmer's marks all over them. All the little clues that, when she made her move and absconded with a whole lot of Thomas's money, would point to an abduction.

Poor Mia Davies, dragged away from her loving husband by a scoundrel.

Poor Mia, missing and presumed dead at the hands of the criminal Thomas already knew was in their midst.

"I was going to disappear. And when Thomas went looking, all signs would point to you killing me. All signs would say you stole his money, deposited it offshore until the heat died down, and took care of me. Then, because you're that stupid, you went back to work in his house, right under his nose."

Hollis's voice was dull with disbelief. "He'd never believe that."

Mia gave a hateful, biting smile. "Oh, honey ... Thomas loved me and hated you. He'd believe whatever I told him to."

34

Twelve hours to the Texas border.

Hollis stopped for gas twice after weaving his way through east Austin and, as predicted, finding a weakness in the Texas State Guard's perimeter in an open stretch of overgrown land.

There weren't enough soldiers — professional or otherwise — to watch the city border in its entirety. Using simple math, Hollis knew the Texas one would be even easier. The border was enormous. They'd settle for blocking major arteries to stop artillery and caravans, then let the rest go. In concept, Texas was now its own country. In practice, both nations had more than immigration on their minds.

But after his second refill ran dry without a functioning station in sight, he had to go on foot. Stupid cycle with its tiny tank. Hollis was either driving it inefficiently or the tank had a leak, because despite keeping his eyes always open, he didn't spot a third refill spot in time. And it's not like he'd been able to carry extra gas from the last one, with the attaché case strapped to the back.

Once on foot, he foraged for supplies. He'd reached a

little town with one gas station that'd been sucked dry, but it still had supplies in the grocery. It also had a Target where he re-acquired some of the camping supplies they'd lost after looting the first time. Hollis grabbed a large camping backpack and transferred his scant supplies inside it — some water, binoculars, the gun, and Ricky's stolen phone.

He got the smallest tent and most compact sleeping bag he could find, plus some external batteries to power the phone just in case the cellular network and Internet held out. He strapped it all to the big pack and walked out feeling like a mule. This was going to be a long-ass walk, especially having to hold the case.

He looked down at the thing before picking it up. "You'd better be worth all this, you shitter."

But it would be. He might not make it all the way to Georgia, but he'd make Louisiana eventually. There were crooks everywhere, and chances were they'd gain power in the coming days, not lose it. And now, he had something to trade. He could open the case, and help the buyer understand what was inside. A valuable cocktail, still worth something in the new world with aliens overhead.

And if Mia wanted to be an asshole and play rough? Well, then fuck Mia and her whore of a mother. More for Hollis. He could finally make his own choices rather than running everything through a goddamned committee.

He only had to hike for a half hour before finding a car with a dead occupant — victim of road rage, judging by the head wound and smashed windshield. The transponder was inside, the autodrive worked fine, and the tank was almost full. Things were starting to come up Hollis.

Hours later, before his new vehicle's gas ran dry, he found an automated station, still working. He filled the tank using one of Mia's go bag credit cards — palmed the second he had a chance — plus all the canned gas the trunk could carry. If Hollis got rear-ended, he'd go out in a blaze of glory.

His luck improved even further after that. Each time he passed a working station, Hollis topped off — but out in the sticks with lighter populations, it seemed *most* were still working, with plenty of gas in their subterranean tanks.

By noon, he'd made the border. Skirting the roadblock, even in a full-size car instead of a motorcycle, wasn't hard so long as he was willing to take it off-road and endure the splashing gas in the trunk, filling the cab with fumes and giving him a headache.

After that, he was back in the good old US of A.

And for some reason, even while crossing land under nothing but sky, Hollis saw none of the alien motherships from one horizon to the next. Last he'd seen was over Houston. Then ... nothing.

Once well inside Lousiana, Hollis returned the car to the road, then parked on a rise to rest. Something superstitious made him keep the engine running while he got out to stretch his legs, the autodrive off and manual parking set. Last thing he needed was for the thing not to start again or to take off without him. And yeah, those things were unlikely to the point of absurdity. Paranoid, even. But stranger — and worse — things had certainly happened.

Hollis scanned his mental Rolodex. Who was in the area? Who might still be around?

He could head for the Georgia islands, but they were still half a country away, and there were a lot of new sheriffs in town. He didn't know if things had gone *Deliverance* in the outskirts, but if Hollis was honest, he was as afraid of the people as he was of the aliens. Or more.

Maybe it was better to see if he knew anyone local. They didn't need to have much — just guns and money. If he'd been willing to stay in the Republic of Texas without support from what remained of the federal government, he could have found someone like that every twenty minutes.

"Guns and money" described a lot of folks in Oil Country. Another Brendan — ideally without the tigers or the bounty on Hollis's head — would do.

Someone who'd want what was in the case, yet have just enough honor not to steal it and pay him nothing. Someone who ...

"Oh, shit."

Lafayette. Where was Lafayette, Louisiana from here?

Hollis slipped Ricky's phone from his pack, where it'd been cabled to one of the charger batteries. Fully powered, unlockable without a security code either because Ricky either trusted the world or was usually too high or dumb to remember it. He opened Maps, then was halfway through typing his destination when the thing told him the Internet wasn't available.

Hollis looked around. He was kind of nowhere, but he could still spot three cell towers. The phone had almost full bars. For now, at least, the cell network was still working. The Internet, however, was not.

There was a green sign down the road. Hollis dropped the pack, fished out the binoculars, and spied it:

LAKE CHARLES 40
LAFAYETTE 114

A good enough answer. He had two hours or so, if the roads were clear and he didn't run into any Big Daddy Roth roadsters who wanted to run him into a ditch and eat his skin. As far as apocalypses went, this one wasn't living up to the clichés. Destroyed cities and shooting, sure, but no roving gangs. Chances were, as long as he didn't have to stop for gas — he shouldn't — he'd be okay, and he'd be there soon enough. The guy he was thinking of wasn't even in Lafayette proper.

Like Brendan Banks, Sonny Malone built his compound near a city but outside of its urban center. In the western outskirts. Perfect for a ne'er-do-well approaching from the Texas side.

Hollis was about to get back into the car when he had an idea. The cell network was strong, so his phone might work even if the internet didn't.

He dialed 411, found the robotic voice of directory assistance still operational, and asked for Sonny's Market in Lafayette, Louisiana.

Thirty seconds later, a number was ringing.

35

Sonny answered with his usual charm.

"Who the fuck's this?"

"Sonny. It's Hollis Palmer."

There was a long pause.

"Hollis Palmer ... I'm the guy who—"

"I know who you are. I was just wishing I could say hello with my fire ax."

"I know we didn't part on good terms. I—"

"You fucked my mom," Sonny interrupted. "Like, literally fucked the woman who raised me."

"I'm sorry about that. We—"

"In the ass. Who fucks someone's mom in the ass?"

Hollis wondered who tells their son about their anal adventures, but decided not to ask. Truth was, Terri or whatever her name was had Sonny when she'd been fourteen years old, then developed a Crossfit addiction. She'd been forty-five when Hollis met her, and still smoking hot. Going to the back had been her idea, not his. What Hollis and Ms. Malone had would have been sweet, maybe, if he hadn't stolen her purse and moved to Tulsa in the middle of the night.

"Look, Sonny ... I've come across something I think you'll—"

"And what about my statue, Hollis? Did you 'come across' the statue you stole from me?"

Oh, right. Hollis sort of remembered that. Sonny had decorated his place with all sorts of tacky statues and busts. Hollis found the one in question funny because it had fully articulated testicles. He'd stolen it while drunk, then thrown it into someone's swimming pool.

"Sonny," Hollis said, hoping to barge through the old grudges since he'd never be able to face them head-on anyway, "do you still run any gambling?"

"Why the fuck should I tell you?"

"Because I found a ..." What was the best, most compelling, easiest way to convey the case's value, even if it was technically inaccurate? "... a system predictor."

Hollis didn't even know that was a thing, but it sounded good leaving his mouth.

"Oh, yeah? What makes you think I care?"

"If you could take bets and know in advance how the wager would turn out ..."

Sonny laughed. "That's useful. Tell me, who's going to win the Broncos game next week?"

Broncos Stadium had been destroyed by some asshole's dirty bomb just last night. Hollis saw it on his news app, before the Internet crapped out.

"It predicts more than sports. Can I bring it by? I'm not far."

"Yeah. Sure. Bring it by. Tell you what. Remember the platform out back, where I hang meat to dry? Go there with your eyes closed and wait for me to show up. Oh, and if you could stop ahead of time and paint a target on your balls, that'd really help me out."

This was going poorly. Hollis would have to give Sonny something. Something that he wouldn't need Internet to find or be impressed by.

He knelt with the phone pinched between shoulder and ear, then entered Mia's embarrassing combination. For a fractional second before popping the lock, he was sure she predicted his coup and changed the code.

Hollis about leapt with joy when he saw Carol's notes. Instead of an incomprehensible mess, Hollis had a neatly organized stack of papers and a kind of Dummies guide, with a START HERE card on the top stack.

It didn't literally tell Hollis to START HERE, but there was a string of numbers and slashes Hollis took for one of those nameless Internet addresses. Below was a simple password: *carolsgame007.*

A password she'd clearly made herself, at an address he was now remembering she'd suggested she'd *made* herself. Somehow, Carol must have created whatever-this-was. A web shell on top of whatever big data the case accessed, maybe. A graphic user interface she'd built even from an end-of-the-world shelter, just to make Hollis's access card a bit simpler to use.

Oh, Carol — you magnificent person, you.

Hollis tried to remember what the shell site had looked like. Carol showed it to them both, but he, of course, wasn't paying attention.

He did remember it looking impressive.

And he knew it still needed the password to be useful.

He couldn't look on the phone because he didn't have Internet. But maybe Sonny did, making this a chance worth taking.

"Sonny, listen," Hollis said. Then he read off the numeric Internet address and told Sonny to go.

There was nothing. The other end of the phone became less snarky, more absent.

"Sonny, are you there? Did it go anywhere? Is Internet working there?"

"All right," he said, his voice now entirely different. "You've got my attention. What's the password?"

Hollis considered. He had an entire case full of information, so there was no way a single password would be all Sonny needed. It probably granted top-level access, and you'd need what was in the case to make sense of whatever the password unlocked. But still ... no. One ace wasn't enough to play with Sonny Malone.

"Are you still at the Market? Did you evacuate during the arrival?"

In a hard, even voice, Sonny said, "I'm still at the market."

"Good. I can be there in—"

"So are a few other people. Folks who pull off fingers for a living."

Hollis thought that was a strange career choice. He forced himself not to be intimidated. Until the case's lock was opened, *he* was in charge.

In an equally even voice, Hollis said, "Do you have anyone who's great with data? A hacker or two?"

"We got some nerds."

"Good. Because before we make a deal, I'd like to get some answers from them about what I have." Hollis was thinking of what had been bothering Carol. If the aliens had their insectile fingers in the data somehow, that might matter. At the very least, it made his skin crawl — in a way that felt, for some reason, strangely personal. "I think I can be there in two to four hours, depending on what's waiting between me and you."

"Fine."

Hollis was about to hang up. But then, being Hollis, found he couldn't help himself.

"How's your mom?"

36

It only took an hour and a half to reach Sonny's Market on the west side of Lafayette. It was right where Hollis vaguely thought he remembered it. Instead of needing to hunt until he stumbled across the place — the GPS still wasn't working — all he'd done was pull off the road and there it was. There'd been little traffic and no fires, blown-up buildings, gangs, or delays of any kind. He'd driven fast and straight, making spectacular time.

If only Sonny's place was somewhere he wanted to go instead of somewhere he needed to be.

He spent the entire drive playing scenarios in his mind. Sonny, unlike Brendan, couldn't be counted on to "play fair" out of some sense of honor among thieves. Hollis needed to out-maneuver him and keep the best cards close until the perfect time to play them.

He'd already ruled out the idea of staying with Sonny, though he'd flirted with it at first. Best to make his deal, get paid, then get the hell out of town. If that meant he had to be on his own, fine. Hollis was used to that.

Although ... he'd be damned if it didn't feel strange

being by himself after spending the world's longest week with Mia Davies.

He looked at the empty passenger seat. "Fuck you."

Good thing he'd gnawed his way out of that bear trap. He'd never trusted Mia, though even his suspicion had been misplaced. Hollis always thought her a sexual manipulator because the entire time he'd been living as one of her husband's henchmen, she'd been writhing around him like a serpent. A rich man's wife with an itch, looking to act out and have fun. That's what he'd figured at first, and he'd continued to believe that when he'd dragged her off as a hostage. Turned out, she was a fellow crook, underhanded as he was — and if Hollis hadn't discovered that when he had, who knew what perfectly opportune moment she'd have chosen to throw him to the wolves?

Imagine if I'd taken her to Sonny's?

She'd have "helped" him work out his scenarios, planting escape valves for herself in every one while making Hollis think they were all his idea. She'd probably have changed the combination and stoked Sonny's hatred of Hollis to the breaking point.

It was damn good that things happened this way. Scenarios were easier to plan with only himself and Sonny to consider.

He'd need to show Sonny what the information in the case could do from an arm's length, while holding back one important key. They'd need to agree on a price — cash would be best, as it was the most liquid and still had value — hand over what was due, then get away without being shot in the back.

So far, Hollis's favorite way of handling that involved him holding onto a password then phoning Sonny with it once back on the road and hauling ass toward Georgia. *If* Sonny would go for it, of course.

But Hollis could insist. He was bringing the deal and could thus dictate the terms.

He sat up taller. Yes. That was how it'd go down. He had to be confident, not let Sonny bust his balls.

Hollis arrived and was raising his fist to the door when he stopped at the cocking of a weapon behind him.

"Set it down, asshole," Sonny said.

"Just once, I'd like to go and visit someone without getting a gun pointed at the back of my head."

"Who else have you been visiting?"

"Brendan Banks. You remember Brendan. I think he fucked your mom, too. I mean, who hasn't?"

Something hit Hollis. He saw nothing for a while.

He woke up inside Sonny's Market, lying atop a meat-cutting table stained with what he hoped was cow blood. There was a rolling cart on one wall filled with both traditional and non-traditional butchering paraphernalia. A man in a red-smeared apron was orbiting it, but the real activity was on his other side. Hollis found he was able to turn his head, but it wasn't easy. A heavy strap bound him at the shoulders. Others held his wrists and ankles, and a sixth circled his waist. The sides of beef, in this butcher shop, must sometimes wiggle.

Sonny saw him moving and came forward. There was a third man with him, this one in a black rubber apron that made him look like the Gimp's personal chef. This other also wore a mask over his nose and mouth and was holding a huge, two-handed cleaver. Behind them both, on a table, was the attaché case. Closed, of course.

"How do I open it?" Sonny said.

"No *hello*?"

Sonny hit him.

"Well, hello to you, too," Hollis said.

"What's the combination?"

"I'd rather not say."

"Maybe I cut off one of your hands."

"Come on, Sonny. We worked together. Don't you have any nostalgia for our shared past?"

"Heinz, cut off his hand."

The man in the apron stepped forward. Fortunately — and depressingly — Hollis predicted at least some of this. The butchery was new but brutality expected. Hollis knew Sonny well, and thought it a risk worth taking. Above all else, Sonny was a pragmatist and never saw the need to do get messy in light of a simpler way.

Still, Hollis was human, and so was his hammering heart. "I'll tell you if you let me up."

"How about you tell me, *so that* I'll let you up?"

"There's a few more passwords and combinations, even after the case is open."

"Okay. Tell me them, too."

"Sonny. I know you, and I came anyway. You know why?"

"Why?"

"Because I wanted to make a deal. I *wanted* to. I mean, shit ... there are aliens everywhere!"

"I know. There's a mothership over New Orleans." He said it as *Naawlins*. "Those fucking little ships are all over the place. Head into town, why don'tcha? Streets are filled with bugs."

That was interesting. Hollis had never heard of anywhere "filled with" on-the-ground aliens. What had happened in Louisiana to merit it? What was different here?

"I'm not looking to pull a scam. I'm not looking to rip you off. Why would I? There's no time. I've got places to go."

"Back to Brendan?"

"Brendan and I didn't see eye to eye."

"Where, then?"

"With all respect, Sonny, I'd rather not say."

No one spoke for a beat. Then Sonny said, "Heinz?"

The man with the cleaver came forward, clearly grinning from behind his mask.

"Look," Hollis said, trying to smile, thinking fast. "I came here 'cause I got something of value. I coulda gone to anyone with it, but I chose you. Even knowing you wouldn't exactly welcome me with open arms, I came here because I think you're a reasonable guy at the end of the day and are smart enough to put benefit before petty grudges. So, was I right or was I wrong? Do you want to do things *this* way, where you don't get anything and I don't walk away lookin' pretty ... or do you want me to open that case for you, take a look at what we got together, and maybe make a deal where everyone wins before E.T. comes knockin'?"

Sonny met Hollis's gaze for what felt like a full minute. Then he sighed to the man in black rubber and said, "Let him up."

37

Carol put her hand on Mia's shoulder.

She jumped, then turned with an apology on her face. She was being so silly.

"Are you okay?" Carol asked.

"I'm fine."

"You don't seem fine."

"The Duke's messenger set me on edge, is all. I'm okay."

"*The Duke?*" Carol repeated.

"The guy who left the note reminded me of the creepy messenger for the Duke in *Escape from New York*. The hissing guy who brought the president's finger." Carol didn't understand, so Mia tried again. "Snake Plisken?"

"He reminded you of a snake?"

"Never mind." Explaining pop culture references to people on whom they didn't land was a bummer. Hollis would have gotten it.

Mia looked around the mostly empty ballroom then through the window at the popped hatches of a row of SUVs and minivans, stuffed full of the ballroom's supplies. Where they were going, nobody was sure. For now, *away* was a good enough location.

"We're almost ready to go," Carol said. "Are you coming with?"

Mia nodded. She'd be stupid to say no. In a weird way, Mia was the reason the Spider House crew was changing headquarters. It'd be rude to let them all move, then stay put herself. Well ... either rude or appropriate. The others might be safe if Mia stayed behind, seeing as Hollis had already fled.

"Yeah. How long 'til we head out?"

Carol shrugged. "Ten minutes?"

"I'll be out in five."

Carol gave Mia a thin little almost-smile. She probably didn't mean to convey pity, but Mia saw it anyway. There was no reason for her to spend another second inside, seeing as her scant supplies, stuffed back into what was once her go bag, had already been put on the curb with the others. This wasn't home and never had been. It wasn't like she had to grab her toothbrush from the bathroom or ponder whether or not to take an heirloom clock. The fact that she needed a moment alone filled her with self-loathing. Carol's understanding filled her with embarrassment.

She unfolded the note the creepy, spike-haired messenger guy had given Ember when he'd come to the ballroom's door. The note had gone from Ember to Carol, then from Carol to Mia. Only the three of them knew exactly what it said. Carol told everyone else that one of the warring factions downtown was headed this way and they needed to leave before they arrived. Nobody questioned her. A few days inside, and Carol had become their reluctant den mother.

The note said:

**Send Hollis to the Capitol
with the case
at noon tomorrow
or everyone dies.**

It was written on official State of Texas stationery, from the Governor's office.

There was no question as to who had written, dictated, or otherwise authorized the note.

Mia didn't know how Brendan had found them, nor why he hadn't come himself instead of sending the messenger with the big bulging eyes. She had no idea why Hollis was being given a deadline instead of getting abducted.

Maybe Brendan was too busy running the de facto Republic of Texas military. Maybe he needed to make appointments to wrangle his hectic schedule. *12:00 p.m. – Kill Hollis Palmer. 1:00 p.m. – Lunch with the Queen*. Maybe Brendan had slipped some sort of high-tech tracker into the case before Hollis hit him and ran.

Brendan struck Mia as a guy with delusions of grandeur. No harm in letting Hollis know he was a wanted man. His army controlled the city. Well, the joke was on them — Hollis had already hauled ass. And judging by what Find My iPhone told Ricky when he'd discovered it missing, a thief who had to be Hollis was halfway to Louisiana, well beyond the barricade.

It didn't matter. Hollis was gone with the case. Brendan was nuts. And Mia was holding the bag.

Thanks a lot, asshole, she'd thought more than once.

Maybe it was a bluff. Maybe Brendan had sent his messenger and summoned Hollis because he couldn't spare the troops to pursue him. Maybe, when noon passed, nothing would happen.

Or maybe it wasn't a bluff and some of the arsenal Mia saw on the tiger farm would have reduced the ballroom to dust.

There were a lot of unknowns but none mattered. They needed to leave. It was possible Brendan would find them again, but Mia couldn't see how. If he was tracking anything, it'd be the case — which Hollis, fuck his heart with a pitchfork, had taken.

Right now, Mia was the only thing left in town that might lead Brendan to the case that he hadn't lost his lust for. She had to make herself scarce because when Brendan learned the object of his affection was no longer nearby, he might decide to vent his frustration on the nearest party. Or the one he deemed responsible.

You let him go, she could imagine Brendan saying.

And Mia, given the opportunity, could only agree.

Yeah. I let him go. I told him to go. Fuck Hollis. He was always just a means to an end.

So why all the nerves? Why this curious unsettled sense, of things unfinished?

"Mia?" Carol said, snapping Mia out of her reverie.

"Yes?"

"We're heading out. Last call."

"I thought you said ten minutes?"

"Honey. It's been fifteen." Carol's voice dripped with pity.

Mia wanted to protest. It couldn't have been more than two. There was no way she'd spent more than 120 seconds on this bullshit. On this latest pickle that Hollis and his selfishness had gotten them into. If he'd stayed, he could have gone and left the rest of them safe. If he tried to refuse, Mia herself would have bound and gagged him. They'd have stuck him in one of the cars, set the autodrive for the Capitol building, and washed their problems away.

And why not? She certainly didn't care about the attaché case anymore. Carol already told her she'd gotten most of what she could out of it. She was a network engineer, not a database architect. A user, not a hacker. Without the Brendan Bankses of the world to buy or bargain with, what use was a bunch of stupid paperwork and IP addresses?

But no, Carol's expression said that it had been at least fifteen minutes. Probably more.

"I'm coming," Mia told her.

38

The hacker was a thin black man who wouldn't have stood out in any crowd. He didn't just look like an office worker. He looked like the mold from which all other office workers were cast. Sitting next to him, looking up at Sonny with his stern face and head of tight brown curls, Hollis felt surreal. It was like training at a rather boring temp agency, except if you failed the skills assessment, the agency's owner shot you.

"I'd really like to see the rest of what you have," the hacker said. "For context."

Hollis looked up at Sonny. His eyebrows raised because of course that lined up exactly with what he had been saying — *Give me everything, or else*. But Hollis didn't flinch. It'd be easy, in a situation like this, to forget he held the cards. But now that Sonny's interest in Carol's discovery had been piqued, his word was gold.

They'd already discussed the impervious briefcase. Hollis hinted at all the further layers of depth and security on carefully marked cards inside. He'd opened it far from the others, slipping only the first card — IP address and password — out before locking it again.

This was a tightrope, but fortunately it seemed that they all finally understood each other. As long as Hollis played fair, Sonny had no reason to cross him. And as long as he wasn't crossed, Hollis had no reason not to play fair. A perfect Cold War.

"Do what you can with just this," Hollis said. "Are the aliens accessing it?"

The hacker — *Socrates* — sighed and pushed up his black-frame glasses. He was wearing a white shirt that looked and smelled starched. It was as if he'd found a dry cleaner still open. His style was left over from a world that was at least temporarily dead, and it was strange to see it here, in Sonny's back room.

"Is it valuable," Sonny said. A clarification, rather than a question. The hacker's job was assessing Hollis's bounty as an asset. Secondarily, if there was time, he could answer his questions.

Socrates loaded another window onscreen. Then another. What he was doing in them, Hollis hadn't a clue. He typed. Hollis waited.

"Well, *someone* is snooping," Socrates said. "I'd need the full access logs to be sure, but based on the imported partials, I see a distinct third-party access point that's been used a lot over the past few days. Maybe two, depending on how you're counting."

"What do you mean, 'depending on how you're counting'?"

"It's complicated."

"No, it ain't. Here's how *I* count. One, two."

Socrates typed again. "One is read and write," he said,

pointing at something that meant nothing to Hollis." More keys. "But this? See this?"

"No," Sonny said, leaning over.

Socrates looked harder, as if seeing something new in the gobbledygook. Then he tapped the screen with a fingernail. "If you'd kept doing what you were doing at your old spot, that could have become a problem."

"What? Why?"

"Well ..." He seemed to think. "It's not getting database access. There's an authentication issue, of course. But ..." More typing, some clicking. "Ah. See?"

"Again, no."

Socrates turned in his chair to face Sonny. "Some older systems, when accessed via public wireless, were vulnerable to data snooping. It's a way of literally picking certain kinds of data out of the air." He turned to Hollis. "When your person was working on this, was she working from something like a company connection or open Wi-Fi?"

Hollis shrugged. He only knew that Carol had worked, not how, or to what end. "I guess."

"Was it a newer Wi-Fi setup, or an older one?"

"I have no idea."

"Well, what was the place itself like. Was it new and fancy or older? The kind of place where other technology hadn't been kept up?"

Hollis considered the Spider House. It wasn't exactly fancy, and to his knowledge *had* no other technology.

"It could have been older," Hollis said.

"There you go," Socrates said.

"Jesus, Socrates," Sonny said, exasperated.

Socrates took a breath. "There are still some 802.11 Wi-Fi systems in use out there. Back in the zeroes and tens, there was a big freak-out about packet theft over insecure Wi-Fi systems. If that kind of system was used to work on this stuff and was never updated, it's possible that someone was spying on anything sent over that connection, even if the sites themselves were fine. The insecure Wi-Fi *makes* it insecure. Make sense?"

"I guess," Sonny said. "So, what ... Someone's been spying on the information we're looking at now?"

"Sort of. They can't get access, but they can see anything sent back and forth. It'd be like listening to two people reading sentences from a book back and forth over the phone. You'd know those sentences, but not the entire book."

"Is it a problem?"

"I doubt it. Our system here is locked down. In fact ..."

Socrates typed, clicked, typed.

"Okay. That's what I thought," he said, reading the screen. "Whatever was snooping isn't here. I just unlocked our system, then locked it back up. Nothing tried to ping in. The snooping device must have been at the actual location."

"Are you saying there was some sort of spy device where I was last, in Austin?"

"Looks that way."

That was interesting. It might be a total coincidence — something left at the Spider House weeks or months ago and forgotten — or it might not be a coincidence at all. Someone might have planted a device meant to spy on activity around the briefcase alone. Now, who would have technology like that? And reason to use it?

"What about the other thing?" Hollis asked. "You said it was 'read and write.' What's that mean?"

"That there's someone else with the codes. They can get at the information same as we are, but they can also add to, edit, or delete it. Maybe the Astral app's creators, though this doesn't look like admin access to me. Look at all this brute-force trial-and-error. It's like a hacker's pirate signal."

"So someone found out about this information and tried to hack into it," Sonny said.

"Yeah. But this doesn't look like any access attempt I'd try. It seems like it was easy for them to get. Like they decrypted it without the key."

"And?"

"Well, that's impossible." He looked at each of them in turn. "Or at least, it's impossible *for us.*"

They all looked up. At the ceiling. At the sky beyond — which, over Lafayette, didn't boast a mothership, but still the implication was clear.

"Cut to the chase," Sonny said. "Is it worth what he says it is?"

"Oh, I think so. Once we've got full access, anyway. I'm no expert in predictive algorithms or chaos theory, but I can say that if you know what the data here predicts, you could be a very rich man."

"The guy I got it from said it was worth sixty million dollars. I'll sell it for thirty."

"You'd make that back in a month," Socrates said. "Assuming the currently exploitable economic systems hold that long."

"Five million," Sonny told Hollis. "Pending review of whatever's still behind the curtain."

"He just said you'd make *thirty* back in a month," Hollis protested.

"*... assuming the systems hold.* The aliens might nuke the world before I get my return on investment."

"Oh, come on."

"Take it or leave it," Sonny said.

But Socrates was holding up his hand. "Now, hang on

just a second. There's still the matter of this alien access, assuming that's what's happening. I can't keep them out."

"Comes with the package," Hollis said. Then he echoed, "Take it or leave it."

"It's not the fact that someone else has access that's the problem, it's ..."

"What?" Sonny asked.

Socrates squinted, frowned, slowly shook his head.

"They're ... *doing* something with it," he said, puzzled.

"My lady said it looked a little like training an AI."

"Maybe. But it's more than that. And there's ... something else."

"What else?" Sonny looked closer, as though that might help.

"I'm not sure. Give me a few hours. Is that okay?"

Sonny looked at Hollis.

"I ain't goin' nowhere," he said.

39

Hollis and Sonny were in the small apartment off the market, watching a series of horrible sitcoms saved on Sonny's juke, when Socrates entered the room, slapped a slim stack of papers onto the coffee table, and said, "You need to see this."

They both looked up, not at the papers. Socrates seemed worn thin, his shirt collar no longer stiff and his face all sweaty.

"Okay," Sonny said, unimpressed with the urgency. He was on the opposite end of the couch, holding a pistol. Even without any aim, the implication was obvious. And poor Hollis had his in the car, if it hadn't been searched.

"First," Socrates said, coming around to kneel in front of the coffee table, "I'm now confident that the third-party access is coming from the aliens. It's more advanced than any technology I've ever seen. I'll be able to tell more once I see the full database ..."

He looked at Hollis, who was shaking his head. They were still walking the tightrope. He'd sneaked a few more addresses and passwords and instructions from the case for Socrates to work with, but he was still holding plenty back. He'd call with the combination, once he was paid and safely away.

"Anyway, the first thing I'd guess is that your tech was half right. I wouldn't say they're using the data to train an AI, but it's similar. There is a type of neural network involved."

"Why's anyone making a neural whatsit?" Hollis asked Socrates.

"It's not clear, but that's not really the problem. They're copying it all off-site. I can't tell where or exactly what's happening, but based on the logged transfer rates — which are mercifully limited by our piddly Earth-bound network — eventually they won't need this dataset. They'll have their own, which I'm guessing will be rearranged to fit whatever purpose they have in mind."

"Which is?" Sonny rephrased what Hollis already asked and Socrates hadn't known.

"No clue. But I have to wonder, why would they go to all the trouble to replicate such a large set of human data unless they planned to use it? You could train an AI with all they're taking, but ... hell, they might be able to make an aggregate human brain. The intelligence that'd be inside us all if we considered humanity as a single collective organism."

Sonny, in a moment of social weakness, turned to Hollis like an equal. "Did that make any sense to you?"

"Nope."

"All I care is whether it'll win me the Powerball," Sonny told Socrates.

"The lottery, as far as I know, is no longer—"

"Figuratively, Socrates. Come on."

"Whatever the aliens are building with this data, it won't affect anything you do."

"And you're still convinced it's valuable."

"Oh, yes."

Sonny turned to Hollis with wide open arms. "Fantastic! Then I guess me and this asshole have a deal. Five million. You down?"

Hollis didn't like the discount, but the rest of his rich yet unsavory friends had probably all run for the hills. "Yeah, sure."

"There's one more thing," Socrates said.

"What?"

"Something's been bugging me about their activity, like I told you."

"I don't care, Socrates."

He pushed on, playing boss. Socrates looked to Hollis, maybe thinking he cared.

"I've been logging all the documented arrivals. I designed a news-scraping program that grabs whatever it can when the Internet's working. It's given me a decent record of all the reported alien activity around the planet. Everything the motherships have done, all reports of the smaller craft, supposed abductions, aliens on the ground — both types. I'm sure it's not comprehensive, but—"

"Get to it, Socrates," Sonny said.

"Why did they destroy Moscow?"

"Because the Russians tried to nuke the mothership."

"Maybe," Socrates said. "But was it the aggression toward the mothership that made the aliens do it, or aggression *period?*"

"What's the difference?"

"Moscow wasn't the only city where authority

approached, or even *fired on* the ships. Our best stuff doesn't make a dent. So why annihilate Moscow?"

"Because of the nuke?"

"The nuke, or the decision to *use* the nuke?"

"Oh, fuck off, Socrates," Sonny said.

Hollis must have looked interested, because Socrates continued. "St. Petersburg. What was different between St. Petersburg and Tallahassee?"

"What happened in Tallahassee?"

"Or Pochaiv. Remember Pochaiv, where they dropped the bomb?"

"Bomb?"

"The cube the aliens put right in the Pochaiv town square. Remember?"

Hollis remembered. "It vanished, though."

"But it didn't in Serpukhov. The cube destroyed that city. Why?"

Hollis didn't want to be intrigued, but there he was, leaning forward. "Okay. Shoot. Tell me why."

"Both cities were deep in riots and violence. But in Pochaiv, they stopped fighting long enough to investigate the bomb. In Serpukhov, they didn't."

Hollis found himself thinking of what he'd seen downtown. When the fighting started and the aliens loosed their shuttles. Hollis expected a night of escalation, but it stopped. Because, said the news, so had the violence.

Not between humans and aliens. But between humans and themselves.

"Are you saying the aliens don't like when we fight with each other? Why the hell would they care?"

Socrates's attention ticked toward Sonny, then back to Hollis.

"What if they see it as a sickness? Like ... a planet-wide mental illness?"

"Socrates ..."

Socrates held up a hand. "Sonny, with respect, if the aliens are taking our data and ... well ... making a *collective brain* ..."

"Humans don't have a single brain, Socrates," Sonny said.

"But what if the *aliens* do? What if they're behaving as they are because they're approaching us with false assumptions? Their movements are coordinated — non-local and real-time, without detectable signals sent between the ships. They're behaving as if *they* share a single consciousness. So maybe that's what they expect from us."

"What of it?"

"It would explain why they don't like it when humans fight among themselves. Maybe it feels to them like worldwide schizophrenia. And maybe it isn't just that the aliens *don't like* it. Maybe they fundamentally *don't understand* it."

"Why would they destroy our cities when we go to war with each other? What the hell kind of way is *that* to cure schizophrenia?"

"Ever hear of a lobotomy?" Socrates asked.

"That's crazy," Hollis said.

Socrates shrugged. "Zeroing-out has always been a viable way of resetting an error. When a computer gets caught in a loop or something electronic goes on the fritz, what's the first thing you try? Turn it off, then on again. Pull the plug, then put it back in. I've shown you my data, Sonny, and the database confirms it. Gives us a lot more context. Makes me *more* confident in my analysis, not less. Beyond the abductions, the *only* times we've the aliens attack are when humans are going at each other. What if that's their attempt at electroshock therapy on our supposed malfunctioning collective mind?"

Sonny stood. "Well, this was interesting."

"I'm serious, Sonny."

"I know you are, Socrates. And it's fascinating. But I don't see why it matters. The aliens are like our nannies? There to send us to the naughty spot when we act out against our playmates? Okay, wonderful. That affects my life not at all."

Socrates looked from one of them to the other, still at opposite ends of the couch, though Sonny was upright.

"Haven't you been watching the news?"

"No, we've been watching *The Nanny*," Sonny said. "*MAN* is that a bad show."

"So, you don't know about Texas?"

"I was raised in Texas," Hollis said. "In school, they taught us every fucking little thing about it."

Socrates reached for the remote. It took him a few tries, but he was finally able to switch the input and turn on the news. The anchors, every time Hollis saw a broadcast, were increasingly disheveled, as if they'd gone days without grooming.

And today, they were talking about the top story, which for once wasn't the alien occupation. They reported on the United States and the most recent state to leave its union.

A banner across the bottom read, *NUCLEAR THREAT?*

Hollis listened. Heard. And started to fear.

When it was over, Socrates filled in the blanks.

"Despite Moscow, your governor wants to make a nuclear strike on the aliens. Only, he doesn't have control over a launch site. But he *does* have the Pantex plant near Amarillo. It's the only location in the US — or *formerly* in the US — where old nuclear weapons can be dismantled or refurbished. Rumor says he's about to make a dirty bomb with that old stockpile then send it up with conventional rockets."

"Brendan," Hollis said.

"But that's not even the problem," Socrates said. "The president's not planning to allow it, and his patience is gone."

"You think the president wants to nuke Texas?" Hollis said, though of course that was absurd.

"It doesn't matter what *I* think." Socrates pointed at the TV. "But I'm wondering what *they* will think, if they can see our broadcasts?"

Oh, shit.

Hollis patted his pockets. He needed his phone. He had to call someone. Anyone. Brendan, to get him to knock it off. Mia, to tell her to get out. Or Ghostbusters. Weren't they always who you were supposed to call?

He was considering his exit when the Austin mothership, visible on TV, began glowing white. There was a pulse, and an energy wave shot outward.

The lights, in Sonny's Market, went out.

As did every electronic thing from Austin to Lafayette, and who knew how far beyond.

"Think they'll stop bickering now?" Socrates's voice said in the dark.

But to that, Hollis knew the answer already.

40

All the lights went out. In every building, along every road, and especially inside the cab.

The moon had been out, but now it was down. Stars offered the only illumination, and an eerie yellow glow radiating from the underbelly of the mothership. The moon, now set, reflected on its silver surface from below the horizon.

Carol gripped Mia's arm, though it was hard to see her

Lights weren't the problem. The car seemed to have blinked to full-manual — and, Mia was quickly discovering, that meant *full* manual.

She grabbed the wheel, but it got heavy once their speed dropped. Which didn't happen fast enough. The brakes, which she wedged her full weight onto, were stubborn and thick.

"*Shiii ...!*"

But Mia could barely hear Carol yelling. She was trying hard not to panic, to steer the suddenly dead vehicle away from the roadside street lamps, all them dark. Seeing them was her primary concern, and avoiding them second.

She hit a wooden bus bench and annihilated it, moments later they were breathing heavy on the lawn of the Long Center.

"You okay?" Mia asked.

"Did you see that flash? From the mothership?"

"*Carol*. Are you okay?"

They were trying to find each other in the dark, without much luck. Carol let go of her arm, but Mia wished she'd kept it. The crash was only the most immediate threat. There was another to come, and by now it had to be quickly approaching.

She could hear an engine, not far off.

"I'm okay. I'm coming around." Carol sounded banged up. They'd been hauling down Barton Springs Road at a decent clip, barely paying attention, when all the electronics had gone inexplicably down. Good thing Mia was sitting up front, or she'd never have been able to navigate their crash.

The engine was louder.

"Good. Because you'll need your legs. Come on."

Still, Mia practically had to yank Carol out and onto the lawn. She was either more hurt than she was admitting or in shock. She hoped for the latter. The mothership had blacked out the city at an inopportune time. Mia had been playing chicken with the truck behind them, trying to subtly evade it while not letting the driver know he'd been spotted. But it's not like the guys were fooling anyone.

Between the barricades and the soldiers now constantly walking the streets, vehicle traffic was almost nonexistent. Mia had been hoping to pass for two gals heading out for a gallon of milk or something, then find a good spot to ditch their pursuers. They were in the quietest vehicle — a dinky, fully electric model that barely left a footprint. It'd made sense until the aliens killed all electronics, and they found themselves wrestling manual steering and brakes in a car designed to rarely if ever use either.

The assholes behind them were still burning gas, and might be willing to shoot in the dark to stop them.

"Where are we going?" Carol asked as they started running. Shambling. Mia was setting the course, heading for the blackest spot in the barely-lit landscape — a darkness she hoped would mean water. Carol was luggage behind her. And yeah, she sounded dazed. The crash was hard, and the airbags hadn't deployed. Seemed you needed circuits for that. Mia had somehow avoided a concussion, but Carol might've hit the dash.

"You know, I've lived in this city all my life and have never checked out the statue of Stevie Ray Vaughn."

"Are you serious?"

Mia was focused on hauling ass and didn't answer. Running through the dark was like a trust fall. Her eyes were adjusting, and she could sort of see shapes in the gloom, courtesy of the moon's dim reflection on the mothership's gleaming silver skin.

They heard and almost saw the pursuing truck mount the curb behind them — and, conveniently, strike their pathetic little car. At least their superior engine hadn't given them superior mobility. Or headlights.

"Come on, Carol. Don't wuss out on me now."

"Slow down!"

"Tell that to the guys chasing us through the dark," Mia huffed. "See? This is why they tell women to run in pairs."

"Are you seriously making jokes?"

"It's how I cope."

Like Hollis.

Once around the back and into the open, Mia ran faster,

now sprinting blind. She had seen the statue and was hoping her memory of the lawn beyond it was correct.

They made it to the bike-and-run path, which crunched underfoot. The dark shapes of trees and brush loomed ahead and beyond that, the broad expanse of Ladybird Lake. Mia ignored Carol's protests, dragging her to the right, past a parking area, then nearly impaling them on a bike rack.

Once they were near the 1st Street bridge, Mia dragged them down and they stopped, in a crouch, breathing through a series of heavy exhales. A fair hiding place, out of sight unless their pursuers saw them stop and take cover. Doubtful. They might not have even left their crashed truck.

"Oh, shit," Mia said.

"What?"

"My bag is in the car." All Mia's worldly possessions, save the clothes on her back and the few small things in her pocket. Even her phone was in there — not that it was worth crap now. But in the moment, she didn't care about the phone or her spare jeans or anything else. What she wanted — and wished she'd had the foresight to grab — was the gun.

They stayed put, squatted low.

"Who are they?" Carol asked.

"The same guys who showed up at the campus rec center before we did. The same guys who were at the YMCA."

"I still don't understand why they were at the YMCA."

"Well, it's fun to stay at the YMCA."

"Will you please stop joking?"

Mia took a deep breath. So far, she saw no one in pursuit, but it felt like too much to hope for. Ever since the two of them had left the Y, they'd been playing their game of high-stakes chicken. There'd been no doubt — in Mia's mind, at least — that the men had been following them. *Preguessing* them, almost. Their group left the Spider House to evade whoever the Duke's messenger represented, but strange men had shown up at their new home anyway. Three times now.

The YMCA had been the last straw. When the same truck full of men with guns appeared, Mia decided she didn't feel like organizing yet another mass move. Like Hollis, Mia was best on her own. She packed to leave, then went. Unfortunately, Carol spotted her and came along. And wouldn't you know it — those assholes chased *them* instead of sticking around like shit on the shoe of their group.

"How do they keep finding us?" Carol asked.

From the Spider House to the graffiti park. From the graffiti park to the rec center. From the rec center to the Y. Each time, they'd thought they were getting away clean before the same assholes were right there behind them.

Mia didn't answer. She cared less about how and more about why. They wanted Hollis. She got the message, they all did. They'd left the Spider House to avoid being punished for his bullshit, but if the pursuers were so smart, why didn't they understand he wasn't with their group?

How were they supposed to comply with the messenger's demand? Hollis was gone. He'd absconded, abandoned them. Flown the fucking coop. The way the men in the truck kept chasing them felt abjectly unfair.

They were still, crouched beneath the pedestrian bridge, trembling in the dark. Mia tried to breathe low, sure the men would hear them. But the men didn't come. Maybe she and Carol had gotten away.

Then there was a great plume of fire not far away, as if from a dragon's mouth.

Two trees nearby were suddenly on fire ... and *now* they could see.

Four men, all carrying what looked like rifles. Or, in one case, a motherfucking flamethrower.

A hundred yards off, maybe less.

"Holy shit," Carol said.

Mia was more practical.

"*RUN!*"

41

When Sonny's emergency lights ticked on, Hollis had one hand on the attaché case and another on the doorknob. Shadows were harsh, the world now turned into noir.

Sonny was pointing a gun directly at his face, aiming blind. "See, this is disappointing."

"Put the gun down, Sonny. I was just making sure where it was."

"Uh-huh. And the doorknob?"

"I was groping. Socrates's lucky I didn't grab his dick."

"Lucky."

"Well, you know. If I turned it like a doorknob."

Sonny flicked the safety off his pistol.

"Come on, Sonny. We were making a deal."

"I know. So maybe you should put down my property."

"Where's my money?"

"Are you kidding me? That fucking thing" — he indicated the TV, which was of course dead — "just hit us with an EMP. I can't get at my money right now."

"I don't think it was an EMP," Socrates said.

Both Hollis and Sonny stared at him in the sharp light and shadow.

"I'd guess an EMP would have knocked out the electronics in the emergency lights," Socrates said in a smaller voice.

"Well, then what the fuck was it?" Sonny demanded.

"I don't know. It seems to have a lot of the characteristics of an EMP."

"Thanks, Socrates," Hollis said. "You're immensely helpful."

"Hey, fuckwit," Sonny said, the gun still aimed. "This is about you."

"Oh, come on. Let's pile on Socrates."

"Socrates, relieve Hollis of his luggage."

Socrates took the handle, then after a few yanks, to which Hollis was stubbornly resistant, the case finally came free. Sonny made *gimmie* gestures with his free hand, and Socrates set it at the boss's feet.

"Good doggy," Hollis said.

"Tell me one reason why I shouldn't shoot your ass right now," Sonny said.

"Because I'd have to turn around."

"Socrates, hit him with something."

Hollis's hands were up. He glared at Socrates, nonverbally letting him know that he should take Sonny's suggestion as sarcastic, lest Hollis beat his ass and damn the consequences.

"Come on, guys," Hollis said. "Sixty seconds ago, we were all in agreement. Five million for one case."

"I like this deal. Where I kill you and take it."

"You don't have the combination."

"He's right, Sonny. I really need the rest of what's in there."

"Shut up, Socrates."

"I'm not seeing the problem. Just give me my money, and I'll be on my way."

"Two million," Sonny said.

"We agreed on five."

"Yeah, well. Shit happens. Things change."

"Two isn't enough."

"Then there's really no reason to stop myself from shooting you."

Hollis, hands in the air, felt himself sweating. "All right. Fine. Two million."

Sonny looked around and found a flashlight in a drawer, but it was dead. For some reason the emergency lights survived but the flashlight was fried. Maybe it was hit and miss due to the distance.

Finally, Sonny found a roll of duct tape and threw it to Socrates.

"Do his hands."

"Oh, come on," Hollis said. "You're not taping my wrists."

"Hmm. Explain this theory to me."

"I don't want to stick around anyway. I just need a car."

"Oh," Sonny told Socrates. "Now he needs a car."

"Mine will be fried. I know you have that Chevelle."

"You want to take my classic? Fuck you! I should shoot you for suggesting it."

Hollis tried to take the wiseass down a notch. He wasn't trying to be unreasonable. He just needed a ride back to Austin, and fast. Someone had to tell them what Socrates discovered about the need to put a lid on the fighting. The national issue would ultimately boil down to a local one. This wasn't about the president and the governor, or even the USA and Texas. In the end, it'd be about Brendan's ability to make the missile Governor Garrett wanted versus the City Defense Force's attempts to stop him.

Everyone watched the news, and right now McCafferty's group — as the only anti-governor force left in town with any muscle — would be seeing themselves as the last line of defense.

The world thought McCafferty and the governor and Brendan Banks had locked horns before? They hadn't seen anything yet.

"I need to get back to Austin," Hollis said.

"What, are you crazy? Your capital is about to be a crater."

"Someone has to tell them. Someone has to stop the fighting."

"And that's gonna be you, Gandhi?"

"Respectfully, Sonny, it's none of your business."

"I guess not." Sonny shrugged. "But fuck if you're taking my baby."

"Any modern car will have an electronic ignition. I can pop the clutch on something older. I need a car that's—"

"1.5 million."

"Your Chevelle isn't worth five hundred grand, Sonny."

"1.5 million and you keep your testicles." He lowered the gun, sighting on Hollis's balls.

"Fine! Fuck you, fine!"

Thirty seconds passed. Nobody moved.

"I need the keys, Sonny," Hollis said.

"What, you want to go *now*?"

"What were we just talking about?"

"I told you. I can't get the money now."

"Why not?"

"My safe is designed to be inaccessible when the power goes out. Someone cuts the juice, they probably mean to ..."

Sonny, seeming to tire mid-sentence aimed the gun at Hollis's chest. "What the fuck. Are you a security consultant now? You've gotta wait until the power comes back on."

Inside his mind, Hollis could see a giant clock ticking. He could make the trip in eight hours, if conditions were perfect. Maybe seven if there were no obstructions, if he could pass the borders quickly and easily, if the gas he brought with him, duly transferred to the Chevelle's trunk, would get him there without stopping, and if he pissed in bottles along the way.

Seven hours was a long time when balls were already bristling. He could practically feel the heat coming off McCafferty's smug, woke, goatee'd chin. Same for Brendan's redneck chest. Felt them both, all the way in Louisiana.

Every minute he waited was another one for someone to do something stupid. Nukes didn't need to be involved. Tensions had to be sky-high in Austin, and spitting in the wrong direction could cause a war.

And, soon after the declaration of inter-city battle, an alien apocalypse.

Hollis had seen what the aliens could do in Austin the other night, and they'd been getting warmed up.

He thought of Moscow and Serpukhov.

Seven long hours at the least, and Sonny was telling him to wait.

"I need to leave. I need to get back."

"Why, shit? You're safe enough. The Moscow suburbs still exist, and we're way the hell out here. Even if the president nukes 'em, we should be fine. I got cans and a manual opener. We're gonna have a party."

"I'm sorry. Deal's off, Sonny." Hollis shook his head, stepping forward to take the case before anyone could react.

Sonny cocked his head, as if in disappointment. Then he

raised the gun, eying the case and Hollis's grip on the handle. "Now, *that,* I *know* we just talked about."

"Who knows how long the power will be off? I don't have time to wait for your safe to open."

"Then maybe you make a donation. Leave the case for me."

"Why would I do that?"

Sonny wagged the gun.

"You know you can't open it without me."

"Maybe I'm an optimistic sort of fella."

"It's not possible unless you have the combination, Sonny. Believe me, I tried. *Brendan* tried."

"A *really* optimistic sort of fella," Sonny said.

"You going to shoot me?" Hollis asked from his side of the stalemate.

"I'd rather make the deal."

"I don't have time for the deal."

"Then, yeah. I'm gonna shoot you."

Still, nobody moved. Until finally, Hollis set down the case and kicked it toward Sonny with the tip of his alligator-booted toe.

"1.5 million bucks. You really just gonna leave, champ? Where're we goin' here?"

Hollis thought. Then his eyes met Sonny's and he said, "You may all go to hell. I'll go to Texas."

42

Sonny was reasonable in the end. He must have felt he'd get value from the case even if Hollis refused to play ball, so he gave him the keys to his Chevelle, which Hollis cranked from a push start by popping the clutch.

The motor was running after that, so Hollis decided to be reasonable, too. He found a bag of tennis balls in the garage and used a utility knife to cut one partly open. Then he wrote a word on a slip of paper, shoved it inside the ball, and surprised Sonny at the last minute by throwing it hard across the nighttime lawn and yelling "Fetch!"

When daylight came, the ball would be easy to find, with the combination on the slip inside.

Except Hollis hadn't written the real password. He kept thinking of what Carol had said, about how the information inside, in the wrong hands, had the power to collapse an economy — and Sonny's hands were very much the wrong ones.

Back when Hollis was first researching the case — back when he and Mia were new, and she'd been pretending to know the code — he'd learned something interesting about this particular model. Not only would forcing the case open destroy the contents, you could enter a panic combo to incinerate the interior.

Tomorrow morning, Sonny would enter that combination.

And afterward, Hollis would need to stay away from Sonny Malone, and his rather large grudge.

On the way out of town, he stopped at the dropbox trash can to retrieve his phone and gun. The first would be toast, but the second would work fine.

But to Hollis's shock, the phone was perfectly functional. No service, but that was neither new nor unexpected. The rest seemed okay.

He looked at the trash can.

It was metal. The lid had been tightly fastened, and the paranoid owner had staked it to the ground with a metal chain. His bag had been atop some plastic bags, not touching the sides. That particular constellation of circumstances, Hollis seemed to recall from a paranoid friend, might have caused the can to serve as a Faraday cage. There'd be no magnetic fields inside such a thing ... and hence, no electromagnetic pulse, if that was what the mothership had sent out to zilch the rest of the town's gadgets and power.

Fascinated — and grateful — Hollis stuck the phone back in his pocket before tossing the gun onto the passenger seat. Even without service, he'd been counting on the thing.

He took to the road. The dark was ominous and peaceful. Hollis had all he needed. Water, his gun, and most interestingly, Ricky's phone. It might be usable if the networks returned. He'd found it unharmed beneath the seat of his old ride, without a signal but miraculously still functional. The seat mechanism was heavy, the front and rear protected by interwoven metal. It too must have acted as a Faraday cage — a thing Hollis didn't understand but Socrates had verbally longed for after the EMP, but before it was too late. Somehow, the clunky car seat had shielded it.

A phone without signal meant little. Except, Hollis thought, it might end up meaning everything.

He drove on.

His nerves didn't settle. After two hours, now nearly one in the morning, Hollis found himself agitated enough that he had to stop and rest. Not only was his mind on fire and in desperate need of sleep, he'd also expended considerable focus to drive. The effort didn't hit Hollis until his eyes were finally given a break, but by then he realized how substantial it'd been.

The roads were clear so far, but he'd been traveling at seventy, which was as fast as he'd dared given the circumstances. He improvised headlights (one of Sonny's emergency lights, duct taped to the grill with the spots pointing forward), but they lacked the candlepower of genuine headlamps. The drive so far had been a screaming roller coaster, full of prayers not to crash.

Cities he passed, like the sprawl of Houston, dead husks filled only with darkness.

"Gotta go, gotta go," Hollis told himself.

He might already be too late.

"I SEE HIM," Carol said.

They were under the Congress Street Bridge at the walk-and-bike trail, near the walkup to the pedestrian overpass. The air was accented with the cornmeal odor of bat guano. Above, when there was quiet, they could hear the bats themselves. Soon, they'd start their nightly pilgrimages, emerging *en masse* at dusk. For now, they were bunkered under the bridge, and Mia couldn't help a nihilistic thought.

In a few months, when summer arrived and their nightly hunts began, would there still be humans around to see them?

But Carol's question jarred Mia from her reverie. It'd been a long night. Nearly three hours after the first blast from the flamethrower, they had managed to move less than a mile. The best escape paths led them into the open. Across one of the bridges, along one of the downtown streets, through the center of the trail itself. It had felt safer to lay low, after they'd run from those burning trees.

They'd quickly realized that the men were shooting blind — that while all four of *them* had been clearly visible from where Carol and Mia had been squatting, the women probably never had been. They'd been meaning to scare them, hoping to flush them out. It'd almost worked. Mia shouted to run and they had, but then Carol pulled them into the bushes. The men passed while they held their breath.

It'd been high-stakes game hide n' seek ever since.

The man Carol was referring to — the one carrying the flamethrower — Mia nicknamed "Burning Man." *Get it?* she'd said. Carol, again, hadn't found it amusing.

Burning Man — and, Mia now saw, his three buddies — were still a few hundred feet away.

"We should move," Mia whispered. "He could burn all the grass, and us with it."

But Carol, now past the initial shock, finally had her head back. It was the middle of the night, but she was morning-coffee sharp.

"No. If they had any idea we were here, he'd have

burned it already. The only reason not to hose the entire area is because he thinks we might have escaped."

The men were coming closer.

"Somehow, they're tracking us," Mia said. "They'll figure it out."

There had been a long period, almost an hour ago now, when it seemed that their pursuers had finally given up. They'd been crouched by the lake in a fairly comfortable spot, and they had themselves a palaver. The men's ability to pre-guess the movements of the Spider House crew — not to mention the way they'd found Mia and Carol even after they'd left the crew solo — suggested they were somehow being tailed. But since that flash from the mothership, their movements stopped being purposeful. If they'd once had a way to watch the women's every movement, it was gone. They were six ordinary people downtown in the dark.

From thirty feet or so away, Mia saw a blue flash, like a miniature fire. It was between them and the men, but not at their location.

Was someone else out here? Someone walking the path for reasons unknown, carrying a lantern?

But the blue flame vanished, and Mia could see only the darkness. Could only hear the footsteps of deer, which had intermittently dressed the soundscape since they'd entered this part of the trail.

"Did you see that?"

"What?"

Mia checked the men's position. They'd gone around a corner, out of sight. She'd given up on their surrender, but at least she could rise safely from her crouch. Stretch her legs. Look for their savior, carrying the strange blue lantern.

Something hissed. Or purred. Almost like a large snake, or an ailing bobcat.

"And did you hear that?"

"That, I heard." Carol's voice was uneven. Nerves frayed. It was impossible to stay on high alert for that long, so choked on adrenaline.

Mia squinted into the distance. Where were the deer? By the lake? She peered, trying to see. But the water was black, no longer accented by reflected lunar light. The moon had set too far, and they were enveloped in ebony. Only the subtle adjustment of their eyes allowed them to see anything, and even that was scant.

"It sounded like—"

Mia backed up. She'd struck something, and yet they'd been crouching in tall grass. There were no stanchions nearby.

She turned. Behind her, still and wearing an expression of vague contentment, was one of the muscular white-skinned aliens. Just standing there. Waiting for nothing at all.

Mia's mouth tried to make sounds. She managed to tap Carol, who began to step backward.

Then they heard the sound again.

Not a hiss, but a choking purr.

They were all around, black bodies invisible in the night.

The bug like aliens chattered their ugly song.

Mouths opened, revealing that churning blue spark.

The men with guns, it seemed, were no longer the problem.

―――

Hollis was behind the wheel again, speeding, blinking.

He'd been uneasy for hours, filled with certainty that he was racing a cruel and unforgiving clock — that it'd let him arrive in time to watch the city fall to ashes. It had the feel of rushing for a train destined to depart without him. Futility was his copilot, and unease his straitjacket.

But this was different.

And beyond the windows, outside in the gloom, Hollis thought he saw shapes.

Not aliens, not people, not ships, not buildings, and not cars.

No. These looked like rocks.

Giant, out-of-place, standing rocks. Maybe seven feet tall, standing on edge, arranged in unending lines like a forever march of power-line stanchions into the distance.

He'd traveled this same road, in the opposite direction, to reach Louisiana. He was back in Texas, the border's defenses a joke now that whatever was happening in Austin had drawn the guards' attention. He didn't remember passing the line so much as *having passed* it, wondering at an abandoned Jeep and some raw materials that, given support, might one day become a blockade. But there was nothing. Had it only taken a blackout to scatter the roaches?

And now, these strange rocks that he was sure hadn't been here before.

Once past the line, the red-hot panic was replaced by the steady worry that'd dogged him since leaving Lafayette.

But for a minute there, he'd been sure of immediate danger.

Or ... not really *him*, right? *Hollis* hadn't precisely felt in danger so much as the danger out there to be had. Like déjà vu. The sense that something wasn't quite right, and might never be again.

It was gone, leaving only the stain of memory.

He thought of the city ahead. Of the mothership and what it might be planning. Of what Socrates had said, about the aliens maybe being surprised that humanity didn't share a mind and singular consciousness.

Fighting others was fighting ourselves.

War meant breakdown. Internal dissonance in the blended humanity of their reckoning. A schism, not conflict with something outside. It was disease. Failure, from the inside out.

Hollis was nowhere near enough to see the Austin mothership, but he willed the people beneath it to hold on. To clench their hostilities — to wait, and let the venom settle.

Don't fight, he thought at all those imagined people. *Keep your shit together, for once in your life.*

He looked at his watch. Manual. Still ticking, driven by springs and Swiss precision.

He'd probably arrive around 7:00 a.m., if nothing new arose and the Austin border didn't present a problem.

Four hours left. Hollis kept driving, cold from his sweat.

"Shit. Shit."

Mia, too startled to speak, said nothing.

She glanced over. Carol was having a hard time keeping it together. So was Mia, of course, but trying to keep Carol calm was strangely relaxing. Taking care of someone else projected Mia out of her own. A new sensation, but still she clung to it like a raft in choppy seas.

The tall, bald alien was still watching them, as if amused by their befuddlement. Mia could see, by the light of the aliens' sparks, that there was an enormous stone not far behind him. One she was sure hadn't been there before — and behind him, a stack of the same lying horizontal.

A voice in Mia's head — her own, she supposed— said, *Don't fight. Keep your shit together, for once in your life.*

"Stay where you are," Mia whispered.

By the light of the spark, she could see Carol's eyes judging the distance between the white alien and the others. She was going to run, and take her chances.

"Carol!"

Carol looked back, a spell broken.

"Don't move. Just ... stay where you are."

Unsure why she was saying it. Unsure why, all of a sudden, she very much believed that was the right course of action.

Carol licked her lips, nerves showing. She blinked, still eyeing the gap.

"Trust me," Mia said.

The bald alien met her gaze. Mia probably imagined it, but it seemed as if his subtle smile grew ever so slightly wider.

A noise came from farther down the path. Now that the women were standing, the men with guns had finally seen them.

"Hey!"

Guns pointed. Marching toward them, seeing only what they wanted to see.

"Down on the ground!"

The white alien was shielded by the rock, invisible to the hunters.

"DOWN!"

Now close, still unseeing, the lead man struck Mia in the gut with the butt of his rifle. She kept her breath but fell to her knees, gripping herself in immediate agony.

"LAY DOWN ON THE—!"

The first man stopped shouting, the others' faces contorted in confusion.

He saw. But they did not.

Midnight black aliens crackling in blue, surrounding them all.

Mouths open.

Purrs escaping.

The men raised their weapons and fired. The air filled with zings and the ricocheting of bullets. There was too much movement after that to be sure, but as much as she was able to tell in the flash of muzzle fire and tearing limbs, Mia didn't see a single alien falter or fall. They were armored, covered in a thick exoskeleton. Tiny human bullets didn't appear to so much as scratch them.

The men fought. And shot. And kicked. And screamed unholy terror.

In the middle of it all, as blood and gore rained, Carol took her by the hand.

Mia raised her head as a severed arm fell to the ground beside her.

Carol nodded. Tugged.

And slowly, without protest, without running or raising a hand or a weapon, they crawled through the grass. To the bridge over Ladybird Lake, above the nesting bats' collective home.

Up here, there was light.

Blue light.

From the mouths of the thousand-alien army to the south, lined up like soldiers interrupted mid-siege.

"Walk," Mia said.

There was only one way to go. From the mouth of one beast into another.

They crossed the bridge, away from the alien regiment.

Toward the humans that had already laid siege to downtown north of the river, entrenched along Caesar Chavez.

Midway across, Mia seriously thought about jumping, but the fall would break her.

Below was death. Same for behind. And above, where the governor and McCafferty's armies puffed their chests behind standing weapons.

"What now?" Carol asked.

"Just keep walking," Mia said.

43

There was nothing to do but surrender to the army at the end of the bridge. It was ironic. Judging by equipment, fatigues, and manner, Mia knew immediately it was the Citizen's Army holding Caesar Chavez — the *governor's* army, generaled by none other than Brendan Banks.

Brendan, who'd sent the note demanding Hollis surrender himself at the Capitol. Brendan, whose men had been following her and Carol from place to place to place until they'd ended up becoming toothpicks for alien beings.

And so it was to Brendan that, an hour and a half later when pre-dawn came, Mia and Carol were given by the soldiers holding them.

Brendan emerged from an Army tent on a hotel lawn, stepped through the flaps in his boxers and an undershirt, stretching to greet the world, his hated form visible to Mia's eyes in a way that nothing had been since the mothership's pulse. Mirrored aviators. Cigar clamped between his teeth.

"Well, then," he said, seeing Mia. "Some dickhead woke me up in the middle of the night to say they'd found you, but I thought it was a dream."

"Maybe I can make it a nightmare," Mia said.

Brendan stopped, head tilting, assessing her anew. Mia and Carol were both in plastic zip-tie restraints, tethered to an anchored park bench. Neither had slept. But on the plus side, Mia was no longer afraid. She'd had so much terror last night, everything else was pale by comparison. If Brendan was trying to intimidate her, he'd have to try a whole lot harder. Chop something off, perhaps. She'd run from spot to spot, been shot at with a flamethrower, hidden for hours like a refugee, run into an alien nest, seen four men reduced to unseasoned meat, then done a death march into her captors' hands.

Mia had a much higher threshold these days, and a lower tolerance for macho bullshit. They hadn't captured her and Carol. She and Carol had, if anything, captured themselves.

Brendan stepped forward, stretched again, then glanced back across the bridge. The aliens were gone, their unknown work finally finished. They'd never advanced. It was possible, Mia thought with regret, that if they'd remained passive, they could have walked right through them.

Probably not, but escaping — or, for that matter, being vivisected — might be better than dealing with Brendan's morning breath, pathetic morning wood visible in his filthy stained boxers.

He knelt, then came so close to Mia that she thought for a bizarre second he might try to kiss her.

"You're tough. I get it. Saw that when I was your gracious host."

"Gracious until you tried to kill us."

"Yeah. Well. Make an omelet, break some eggs."

Carol was watching this. Looking from one to the other, she said to Mia, "You know this guy?"

"Know her," Brendan said to Carol, "and her boyfriend."

"He's not my boyfriend."

"Oh. You had a little spat?"

"What's going on here?" Carol asked.

"Remember how I told you I knew who'd sent that guy with the note?"

"You said it was the governor."

"Not the governor. The governor's lackey. The governor's *errand boy*."

Brendan, still within inches, stared for another several seconds. Then he moved his cigar to one side of his mouth to accommodate a giant grin.

"I knew you'd run, even then. Because you're stupid. And so is Hollis. I took out insurance. A way to follow you, for as long as I could."

"How have you been following us?"

"Don't matter. Let's talk about Hollis."

"He left," Mia said.

"Bullshit, he left. I know Hollis. He wouldn't just walk away from the likes of you."

"I kicked him out."

"Why?"

"I was done with him."

Brendan gave a tiny chuckle. *"Bad ass* chick! Now tell me the truth."

"Do you have shit in your ears?"

Brendan considered, then took a small knife from his pocket and cut the tie holding Mia to the bench. He left the binding on her wrists, then marched with her halfway down the Congress Street Bridge. The light was rising fast. The sun still wasn't up, but the reds and oranges made it easy to see — particularly when, at the middle of the bridge, Brendan pushed Mia's center of mass past the railing and out over the water.

"I got no use for you," Brendan told her, his previously pleasant voice turned to a growl. "Truth is, I got no use for Hollis, either. I want that case and the combination to open it. So how 'bout you tell me where to find both?" He looked back toward the encampment. Then, realization dawning, "That lady with you. That Carol?"

"Um ..."

"Thought so. Between what you said and what I spied her computer doing, I got a pretty good idea of what's inside the case."

"You listened to us? You spied on her computer? How did—?"

Brendan shook Mia. Given her disadvantaged position, she almost slipped and fell to the water.

"I thought I wouldn't care what was in that case. Went a long way to act like I didn't after you fucked me over. But I changed my mind. See, I talked to my guys. Showed 'em what I snooped out of the air when you were all back at that shithole near campus. And you know what? I'll betcha anything one of the things your magic database can predict for me is troop behavior in a crisis. Thing is, I'm inches from what you might call a 'career-maker' of a move. Only thing holding me back is that hipster douchebag back at the Capitol."

"Forest McCafferty?" Mia asked.

He nodded. "I'd *love* to know what the folks over there are likely to do. Just a smidgen of a hint. And what's more, there's some security at this plant I need to get into in Amarillo. Got some *really neat* cargo up there I'd love to get my hands on. Betcha your fancy database could get me past *that*, too. So if you could just get me the case, I'd really appreciate it."

He pushed Mia farther, a tip from spilling.

"The Internet's out! It won't do you any good!"

"Give it time," Brendan said. "Everything saves a copy. And a big place like that, their data will be shielded plenty against whatever the ship did to everything else. *Everything's* doable, if you got the key. And anyway, my guys say the Internet don't matter. We can break in, get direct access to the data center. So, again, where's Hollis?"

Brendan looked at Carol. "Maybe I go get your friend over there. Toss *her* ass off the bridge."

"No!"

"Or maybe I give you to my officers. They'd really like you, lady."

"I don't know where he is!" Mia shrieked. "I don't know where the case is! Kill me, kill Carol — I still *don't fucking know!*"

One more shove. Her feet left the ground, and this time Brendan had to pull Mia's shirt to reel her back. The simple act — having to save her from falling, even if it was for his own purposes — seemed to have stolen her wind.

He let her settle. As soon as she found her balance, she kneed him in the testicles as hard as she could.

Brendan croaked, bent almost double, but managed to stay away from her legs and their follow-up strikes. He never let go of her and she couldn't run. It was fine. She couldn't leave Carol, anyway. The knee was more for spite, less for advantage.

"You'll pay for that," he said, dragging Mia back to camp at a limp.

44

Just after 7:00 a.m., with the sun high enough to feel like an alarm that's already gone off, Hollis arrived at an abandoned Spider House Ballroom.

"Shit."

He needed Carol, who understood what was happening more than anyone other than Socrates, and still might be able to learn more. With the right meeting of the minds, there were still nuts that Carol, here at alien ground zero, could help to crack. He and Mia hadn't left things on the best of terms, but maybe with the end of the world — or at least the city — imminent, she could be persuaded to stop being a manipulative, conniving bitch and help out instead.

In the end, that's what mattered — stopping what was about to happen in Austin. If Socrates was right, the aliens would only attack if the humans struck first, or if they attacked each other.

What if they see it as a sickness? Like a planet-wide mental illness?

The two halves of Austin, embroiled in hatred. McCafferty on one side, representing liberal Austin.

Garrett and Brendan on the other, representing conservative Austin and, honestly, the rest of Texas.

Here and now, the debate was nuclear armament. Maybe it was about secession and whether or not it'd been wise. But Hollis had been thinking for the entire drive, watching the horizon and waiting for a mushroom cloud. Truth was, the two factions had *never* gotten along. They'd *always* been at each other's throats.

Every issue, election, social program, tax hike, and new opportunity, folks like McCafferty and Garrett squared off. It'd always seemed to Hollis that both sides were wrong. And total puckering assholes. He found one group righteous, the other reactionary. They'd always been oil and water, and the only difference now was they had an excuse to kill each other.

If they did, the aliens would respond.

It's like worldwide schizophrenia. Ever hear of a lobotomy?

Hollis looked through the empty window, spying the mothership. If the aliens expected humanity to be more alike than dissimilar, they were in for a shock. If they wanted humans to sing Kumbaya, this city was more fucked than Sonny's mom.

In the quiet, Hollis thought he heard a shot. Just one, though he tensed waiting for more. A line from an old show came into his mind. *Live together or die alone.* And yeah. That about summed it up.

He searched the place, looking for clues — maybe looking for whatever device had been spying on the Spider House's Wi-Fi, per what Socrates discovered in the access logs.

He needed Carol. He needed whatever she still had on her laptop, which he had to assume she'd taken with her. He needed evidence to take ... well, shit, to *someone*. Although that was a challenge he'd thought on plenty. Who was in a mood to listen? Which, of the city's angry figureheads, was open to hearing what Hollis Palmer had to say?

In a corner, crumpled up, was a single notepad-sized piece of paper.

He opened it and found a demand for himself to be at the capitol building at noon tomorrow. Or probably noon today, assuming the note was new.

He didn't know who'd written nor received it. But he could guess who the demand had ultimately come from, and what the ballroom's occupants must have done when they'd read it, since they'd had no Hollis to deliver.

"Splendid," he told the empty ballroom. "Now what?"

―――

Mia, again zip-tied to the bench and now with a clear view of Brendan as he went on his rounds through what seemed to be a rather entrenched and organized band of folks, turned to Carol and said, "I think I can reach that razor."

Carol didn't seem to understand. Mia couldn't explain right away because Brendan had posted a man and a woman to watch them while he did whatever he was doing. It seemed her execution was on hold. Seeing as she claimed not to know where the case was and Carol, though knowledgeable, couldn't give Brendan his desired predictions, he'd apparently decided to put them on the back burner. He could only bluster so much, only go so far if he wasn't ultimately willing to deliver on his threat. If he wanted a shot at the case down the road, killing either of them would be a bad idea. Carol had the know-how. Mia had the combination. Both were necessary, and beating them up solved nothing.

So, frustrated, Brandon had returned them to the bench. Mia wondered, but didn't ask, why not use his voodoo to follow Hollis, same as he'd spied on them so far. Tensions along the lake were too high. Brendan, above and beyond it, far too volatile. One shove, and Brendan — and all those under him — might explode.

He'd mumbled with a group of his fellow war mongers about how McCafferty's people were still blocking access to the Pantax facility. Said something else about how the borders had softened. Muttered about how things would have to be done, then wandered incoherently away, leaving these two knuckleheads in charge, too close for Mia to make a move for the razor.

When they moved a bit farther away, Mia elaborated, whispering, for Carol.

"We have to distract them. Then I think I can get to that razor over there."

Carol looked. The razor was a literal straight razor, hinged in the middle. Someone had dropped the unlikely item on the lawn, five feet or so from the bench. Since the armies set up their standoff camps downtown, before the news blipped out and since, Mia got the distinct impression that at least Brendan's side had gone all Civil War.

The South had lost the first time and wouldn't lose again — and to prove it, all the men were growing beards and doing things in antiquated ways. Like using straight razors. More than once, she'd also seen someone pull an old-fashioned pocket watch from an interior pocket, then open it to check the time. They all struck her as big-boy versions of the locket around her neck — a way of playing pretend, to pass the time.

Mia had spent some time staring at the problem. She'd need to twist in her restraints, hang fully off the bench, and extend to her full length to bump the razor with her toe. She was five-eight, but she'd need every inch to reach the thing. It wouldn't be fast, or subtle.

"I could shout, 'Hey, is that General Lee?'" Carol suggested.

Mia didn't reply. She'd need longer than a blip to stretch out and make an attempt at the razor. Ideally, everyone in the vicinity would need to look away and *keep* looking away for several minutes. Unless a circus erupted near the capitol building, nothing could draw that much attention.

Mia looked over toward the capitol, where McCafferty's City Defense Force was camped — the part that wasn't blocking the Rangers' exit to Amarillo, apparently.

And suddenly, she had her idea. "Follow my lead. I think we can get them to fight."

Hollis had broken into a nearby apartment building and was standing on the roof, trying to see downtown. Last he'd heard — and there was no reason to think things had changed — that's where the armies were preparing to face off. It was where Brendan would be, and *maybe* where Carol and Mia had ended up. As good a place to start as any. Even if Brendan hadn't gotten hold of the women, trying to talk him down might still do some good. Buy them time to escape.

"Whatever you assholes do," Hollis told the skyline, "*don't start fighting.*"

"WHAT?" Brendan demanded, standing in front of the bench where Carol and Mia were restrained.

Mia reminded herself to tread carefully, lest the anger she was about to stoke boomerang on them. He seemed dejectedly pissed. If she had to guess, just talking to them now hurt his pride. He'd followed them, caught them, threatened to throw Mia off the bridge if she didn't talk. But she *hadn't* talked, and here she still was, alive and unbeaten. To Brendan — especially right now, as his opponents managed to keep him from the horrid nuclear plan the news had been discussing before the plug was pulled — she must remind him of failure. And guys like Brendan hated to fail.

"I have something I'd like to trade."

"What?"

"I want you to cut us free if I tell you."

Brendan pretended to consider. "Fine. I'll cut you free."

He didn't mean it, and she knew it. His thief's honor had gone out the window right around the time he'd lost what remained of his rational mind. That, Mia guessed, had happened somewhere between twenty-four and forty-eight hours ago, when the city's two sides stopped sniping at each other from afar and set up formal camp, big weapons and all.

"When we were at the ballroom," Mia said, reciting her internal script, "a guy came through saying he was on his way to McCafferty's camp. He said something about 'amphibious assault.' Something having to do with Camp Mabry? So I'm thinking, if you can get your hands on—"

But that's all it took. Brendan was more keyed-up than she'd realized, wound tighter than a clock spring about to break. She'd watched him stalking the front lines all morning, ranting about McCafferty's move, about the equipment they had, about how he and everyone he stood for would rather die than surrender.

Mia doubted the man even remembered what he was fighting for — if anything — because his paranoia had grown so thick. Only the enemy mattered, not either side's goals.

"They have amphibious assault vehicles?"

"Well, I ..."

"Where? How many?"

"I don't know. I was just thinking—"

He stormed past them, to the river. Looked both directions. Then rushed to what Mia decided was their command tent. Seconds later, word began to spread. The very air seemed to thicken.

"What's happening?" Carol asked.

"He's worried all of a sudden that he's exposed at the rear — that McCafferty might attack from the water."

Carol looked. "That's absurd."

And yes, it was. The whole scene along the lake had felt to Mia like boys playing with deadly toys from the start. Only a handful, on either side, were military. Those in charge very much weren't, though guys like Brendan made it a hobby. The notion that Forest McCafferty — who two weeks ago had been a rather famous actor but nothing more — was now preparing to mastermind a pincer attack on a bunkered-down armed force was ridiculous. But as Mia guessed, Brendan seemed to be deciding that safe was better than sorry.

He'd protect his flank.

He'd resolve the issue of the City Defense Force blueballing his intentions for Amarillo.

Brendan Banks, it seemed, was the kind of guy who

believed that even if fighting solved nothing, it was still better than sitting around looking like an asshole.

Troops shifted around them. Then Brendan himself was stalking toward the front line, holding a sword.

A motherfucking sword.

As the troops watched their leader move into position, Mia slid down on the bench. Her ass hit the ground, and her legs began to stretch. If anyone saw her now, the jig would be up.

There was a roar as an engine started to one side. A tank.

And, after a full minute of rushing and men playing telephone, she heard a heavy whooshing. The blades of a chopper, she guessed, starting to turn.

"If I were you," Carol said, watching Mia's quest for the razor, "I'd work faster."

Mia almost had the razor but was already wondering if this was wise. She hadn't thought much about the alien battle for a few hours, seeing as their current predicament was more dire. But now she thought of those boulders, and the strange energy she'd seemed to sense coming from them.

The voice inside her head...

Hollis.

It had been his voice — and what had *that* asshole been doing there?

Don't fight, the voice had said. *Keep your shit together, for once in your life.*

All around them, grown men and women failed to keep their shit together.

Don't fight.

And Mia thought, *Fuck off, Hollis.*

But who was she kidding?

She knew without a doubt they'd all screwed up, and now they were going to pay.

HOLLIS HEARD the first shots as he was pushing the Chevelle hard, doing his best to get as close to downtown as he could without running afoul of roadblocks. They were close. That's when he realized that not only was he hearing shots, he was actively being shot *at*. He'd driven under a roadblock on an internal park road near a kayak dock, lucking into a clear street that nobody, in this ragtag operation, had found manpower to cover.

Except with machine guns, which now rained fire on the Chevelle from above.

Apparently the mandate "maintain order" had devolved into "shoot first, ask questions later."

When a rain of bullets hit the roof and punctured the radiator, a glut of steam caused Hollis to lose his line of sight. Moments later he'd hit a pole and had been bruised by the seatbelt — no airbags in that old bitch. He scrambled from the car and held both hands up, knowing that if the shooter was more panicked than sane, he was clearly committing suicide.

"Don't shoot! I'm on your side!"

Hollis had no idea whose side the shooter was on. He'd seen roadblocks by the Governor's Ranger crew that looked intimidating and official, and some by McCafferty's people that looked rather hip and considerate of everyone's feelings. The guy with the gun could stand for anything right now and Hollis would agree. *Oh, you like to eat babies? Cool, let's grab forks!*

"What's that?" the man shouted.

Hollis could see him now, on a low bridge fifty feet back. "I said, you ain't gotta shoot me. I'm on your side!"

"No, you're not! You said *ain't*."

That didn't make sense to Hollis, but he could see now that the guy with the gun was wearing a patterned short-sleeved shirt with a collar and skinny jeans. There was a porkpie hat on the bridge's railing, as if he'd just taken it off. And Hollis thought, *Shoot. This kid's from the latte crew. Shoulda hid my accent.*

"Don't move, or I'll shoot!"

Behind the kid, silent, a silver dome slowly rising.

"Hands behind your head!"

Hollis did as he was told, but now the shuttle was all the way up. It seemed to be watching him. Waiting.

"Kid? Maybe you should put down the—"

The shooter panicked. The gun went off, probably by mistake. Shots pocked the dirt at Hollis's feet, and a second later the alien ship opened fire. It didn't just hit the shooter. The bridge sundered in two, concrete pieces falling to the ground or clinging to dangling rebar like goobers on a string of floss.

The sphere moved toward Hollis. It was perfectly smooth, nothing defining on its silver skin.

It stopped five feet away. There was a slight hum, and Hollis could feel a charge, his hair wanting to stand.

"I come in peace?" he told the thing.

Five seconds. Hollis closed his eyes, waiting to die.

But then the charge dissipated and the hum moved away.

Then Hollis opened his eyes to find himself alone and alive.

45

Instantly, Mia knew.

She wasn't sure how. Or why. She had zero evidence, zero substantiation. But whatever was about to happen along the river downtown — whatever she'd *caused* to happen, igniting bunkered tensions like tossing a match into a room full of fumes — was a bigger mistake than anyone realized.

Panicking for a few distinct reasons, she stretched for the razor with all she had. The plastic ties bit her wrists. Her shoulders ached from the contortion. For a while she was hanging on the zip ties, abrading her skin and surfacing blood. But then she managed to kick the razor toward her, wiggle her shoes off, and pick it up with her toes. Unable to accurately drop it into her hands, Mia instead foot-handed it to Carol.

She opened the thing, and thirty seconds later they were free. Carol started to run toward the bridge.

Mia grabbed her. "We have to stop it."

"What? Why?"

"Because I started it."

Carol looked at the melee, now turning hot. The shots had already started. "Honey, this started *long* ago. You just gave it a nudge."

"It's wrong."

"Of course it is. But boys will be boys, and we have to go."

Mia answered by doing the stupidest thing she could think of. She rushed into the fray rather than away from it, found Brendan, then grabbed the back of his jacket sufficient to almost bring him down.

He twisted around. Already pissed, he saw Mia and turned livid.

"Oh, for fuck's ..."

Brendan reached for the pistol in his side holster, flicking the safety off as he raised it. There would be no hesitation — no grandstanding, monologues, or final words. He would shoot her through the brain, and if that meant the end of his quest for the magic attaché case, he seemed to have decided that was fine.

But before Mia saw the black bore of the gun's muzzle, someone across the block began firing. A rogue, perhaps, not acting on orders. Heads spun. Bullets raked bodies. People fell to the curb.

Other weapons came up. More shots fired.

Brendan turned. Mia — the only one, perhaps, focused more on her mission than reacting with violence — gripped his gun hand with both of hers and pulled. He resisted. Falling atop him, she raised her elbow hard and racked his lower jaw into the upper one. The gun shook loose, and Mia grabbed him by the collar. Carol, an unknown distance behind, was shouting her name.

She saw from Brendan's eyes that he wasn't going to

listen without coercion, so she picked up the gun and pressed it to his forehead.

"You have to stop this! It's ...!"

But really, she had no idea. Whatever had been so strong within her moments ago was already gone, ephemeral, like clinging to a dream.

"What? What the hell is it?"

"I ... I don't know."

Brendan bucked. Mia lost her position. She kept the gun, but barely. She couldn't aim it successfully now, so she tried to hit him with it. But Brendan was in battle mode and not about let that happen. He parried, then struck her hand with his arm. The gun skidded away, kicked further by tromping feet.

The panic wasn't yet full-blown. Many were shooting, but not everyone. Same for running and fighting.

"You have to listen to me! I know about them!"

Brendan threw her away. She wasn't worth his time. War was brewing. He clambered to his feet.

Mia chased him. "You still have their respect! They'll listen to you!"

"I got shit to do. You wanna complain? Talk to the bureaucrat."

Governor Jefferson Garrett was not far away on a homemade grandstand surrounded by soldiers, seeming unsure what to do. In theory, what was happening had been his idea. But Brendan had quickly taken over operations, and she doubted a guy like that had asked much permission. Garrett was the figurehead, but right now he seemed torn between trying to calm the fight and egging it on.

His attention jumped between the active warzone — still just a skirmish, though that could quickly change with tanks and Apaches firing their engines — and a camp of people across a still-mostly-open expanse of lawn. McCafferty's group, Mia had to imagine.

Talk to the bureaucrat.

Well, fuck Brendan Banks. She could do that.

She pushed through the throng, hearing shots, hoping none of them hit her. Somewhere, a grenade or other explosive blew. There was a lot of shouting, many words thrown back and forth that sounded less like the current standoff, more like old issues never healed.

At the foot of the governor's stand, Mia was tackled. Brought down — luckily, it seemed, as a volley of gunshots took out three people just to the left.

"Governor Garrett!" she shouted, already unsure why she was doing this, what intuition had compelled her to move toward the mess rather than running away. *"Governor Garrett, listen to m—!"*

There was a sound, stopping Mia's mouth. Immediately half of the group went silent.

The other half followed suit, looking around confused until their eyes found the sky.

One of the spheres moved above the dead center of the fighting group.

Its bottom opened, spiraling into blackness like the iris shutter of an old-fashioned camera.

Then, a thing emerged.

A *big* thing.

It fell to the street with a mighty crash. The ship closed and moved away, leaving the people — many bloodied, most with a mixture of murder and terror in their eyes — to move slowly toward the thing three inches deep in the concrete.

A cube, with a mechanical display shifting through unknowable runes on its face.

46

Hollis spotted Brendan right where the news showed him last, camped out by one of the hotels along the lake, on the south side of Caesar Chavez. Hollis spied him with the binoculars before he stormed into the crowd of his own soldiers, and the shuffling started.

He also saw Carol. And Mia.

Hollis ran. Maybe this would be easier than he'd thought. The south side, once he got past guards distracted by the passage of the shuttle that had blown away his buddy, was more or less undefended. At first, Hollis thought he'd still have a challenge, then tensions rose and all eyes turned north.

I just have to get to Carol and Mia.

It was too late to save the city. Shit had been getting increasingly real in Austin for more than a week, what was starting now would get worse fast. The time for any sort of diplomatic solution — for any solution that relied on logic more than adrenaline — had passed.

He doubted anyone would even try to hear him, or be

able to. That part of the brain would be shut off by now, the amygdala and id given full rein.

Getting the women would have to be good enough.

But when Hollis was halfway across the bridge, Carol and Mia somehow got free. And instead of running away, Mia hauled ass after Brendan and Carol more or less followed.

"Motherfucker," Hollis said, running faster.

By the time he reached the far end, escalation had risen and stopped.

He saw the alien ship overhead and ran even faster.

MIA COULDN'T HELP BEING INAPPROPRIATELY SPELLBOUND by Forest McCafferty. He was an Austin legend, and now here he was, away from the silver screen and championing half of his city. Even if he was being kind of a dick about it.

In the quiet over the cube, McCafferty stared up at the governor and spoke in his slight drawl. "Look what you did with all your separatist bullshit."

"This isn't my fault," Garrett said.

Several of McCafferty's people were trying to form a human shield in front of him, protecting their captain from harm. He pushed them away.

"Sure, it is." He moved toward the cube, then touched it while everyone gasped. "They know you want to nuke them."

"The US wants to nuke *us!*" Garrett said.

"Only 'cause you're going to nuke the aliens."

"Then it serves them right! Washington has always dragged its feet. We need action, but they won't *take* it. That's why our great Republic seceded in the first place!"

"Uh-huh," McCafferty said. *"I* don't remember voting for secession."

"The Republic of Texas has always done best on its own."

"Then why didn't you ask the people?"

"There wasn't any time."

"Well, there's time now." He raised his voice and called to the people. "Who here wanted Texas to leave the States?"

A lot of hands went up — all of them on the south side of the battlefield.

"And who wanted to remain Americans? Who kinda felt like it was bullshit when some blowhard decided for all of us?"

The other hands rose. More than half, Mia thought.

"There ya go," McCafferty said. "Majority wins in a democracy. 'Less you plan to run a racist dictatorship, like your Confederate heroes?"

"Hey!" Someone shouted from the governor's side. "Shut your mouth!"

"Austin doesn't speak for Texas," the governor said. "Not everyone is as elitist as you and your ... *people.*"

"Really? 'Austin doesn't speak for Texas'?" McCafferty almost chuckled.

"Well? How many people in this city were born here? You sit here, complacent, and think what you think is how it should be. I'll remind you that most of the state doesn't feel like you do, all righteous atop your piles of money."

"There is is," McCafferty said. "Coward's defense."

"And there it is," Garrett countered. "Rich white privilege. And you think we're the bigots?"

McCafferty put his hand back on the cube, apparently changing the topic. There were so many hotbeds, from religion to politics. "We're not letting you take Pantax."

"Try to stop us."

"We will. We are."

"These ships," the governor said, pointing upward, "are abducting our people! And all *you* want is to 'try and understand them.' Well, *I'm* not willing to wait and see if they take my children. I say, *we fight back!*"

A great roar rose from one side of the crowd. Even some of McCafferty's people, got caught up in the moment, then realized only belatedly they'd cheered for the wrong side.

"The president wants to wait and see, not act rashly," McCafferty said.

"Not my president," Garrett said. Then he bellowed, *"This is Texas!"*

Another cheer rose from the crowd, larger this time.

McCafferty looked conflicted. He was giving the governor too many softballs, teeing him up triples and homers. He was losing the crowd. Even some on his side were starting to nod.

"I can't let you kill us all," McCafferty said.

"You *are* killing us all, with your lack of a spine."

"When this goes off" — he indicated the cube — "you'll feel different."

"What makes you think it'll go off?" The governor listed cities — some Mia hadn't heard of — by ticking points on his fingers. "In all those places, these things vanish after they drop. Only once has something exploded. You know what I think?" He frowned, feigning thought. "I think they're tests. What's the mettle of the people in the cities? Are they worthy? Or are they cowards?"

"You don't know, Garrett," McCafferty said.

"Which is why we mustn't give them a chance!"

More cheers.

"What do you plan to do? If this is their warning ..." He indicated the cube.

"Kill the host, kill the parasite." Then, with the air of a grand flourish, Garrett found Brendan in the crowd and nodded to him. "Tell them."

———

HOLLIS STRUGGLED THROUGH THE CROWD, finding them unresisting. He was in time to hear McCafferty and Garrett debate, then in time to hear Banks take the makeshift stage.

Apparently, Amarillo wasn't the only game in town.

And apparently, Brendan's men had intercepted a caravan on the way to the Pantax facility — and three warheads with it. He told the crowd he wanted more, though the rockets he'd already rigged should still do the trick.

What Moscow had done wrong, he said, Austin would do right.

The motherships weren't perfect spheres, he told the crowd. There were ports high up, where the smaller ships came and went. With proper remote guidance, small missiles could be remote-piloted through.

Like the ones that were locked, loaded, and preliminarily aimed a few miles outside of downtown.

Mia jumped when Hollis finally found her in the crowd. Anyone would have. The temperature along Ladybird Lake seemed to have dropped fifty degrees.

"We can do this," the governor said. "We *will* do this. And you can't stop us."

Mia and Hollis were grabbed from behind, thrown to the ground and bound, then roughly taken away.

47

"I HAD THIS," Mia said, inside the back of a tractor-trailer, zip-tied to a cargo handle, same as Hollis. "Don't you roll your eyes at me."

"Oh, piss off. This is what I get for trying to save you."

"What exactly were you saving me from, freedom?" Mia asked.

"That's clever. I came back to save the city."

"For a price?"

"Not everything I do is for money." He wanted to rub what had happened at Sonny's in her face — the whole abandon-the-case-and-money-to-run-hundreds-of-miles-back routine — but it wasn't worth the time. Hollis couldn't see his watch, but easily more than a half-hour had passed since the alien ship dropped the cube. He'd explained Socrates's theory. Mia had reluctantly agreed it felt right. Her only hesitation seemed to center on not wanting Hollis to have even the thinnest victory.

"Just most things," Mia said.

"Is this really how you want to die? Fighting?"

"Why not? It's how we began."

The rear door opened. Previously, their only source of light had been an oil lantern Hollis suspected might asphyxiate them. Now the daylight was bright by comparison.

There was chatter at the far end. Nobody they could identify, for the glare.

Then the doors closed again, leaving only one of the newcomers inside.

The governor, Jefferson Garrett, holding a plastic milk crate. He set it on the metal floor opposite them then sat. "So, you're Hollis Palmer."

"You know me?"

"Banks told his guys to execute you. I was curious who he wanted dead, so here I am."

"Isn't this Texas?" Hollis asked, mocking his speech from earlier. "Isn't this the land of executions?"

"And I'm the governor. I'm here to see about your pardon."

"Why?"

"Because Banks thinks first and acts rashly."

Hollis smirked. "Like seceding without a vote?"

"Like firing missiles I never authorized."

"So ... what?" Mia said. "You don't want to nuke the aliens after all?"

"Actually, this is a case where Mr. Banks and I agree. I say what I mean and mean what I say. If only Mr. McCafferty would do the same."

"He's shootin' straight," Hollis said.

The governor had one slacks-clad leg demurely folded over the other, a black loafer dangling. His smile was patient and bland. To Mia he said, "Banks told me you wanted the violence to stop. I want it to end as well, but this struck me as something more, especially when paired with your relationship to Mr. Palmer."

He picked lint off his trousers. "Have you noticed the big stones the aliens have been planting here? The more they drop, the more I find my mind open. I get ... *feelings*. Hunches. I guess It could be the stress of our current situation playing tricks with my mind, but when I knew he'd taken you two into custody, I had a strong feeling we should speak. Does that make sense?"

Mia looked at Hollis. There was something in that glance, but he wasn't sure what. But somewhere deep in his mind, he sort of knew.

"Why, after breaking free of Banks, did you chase him?" Then, before Mia could answer, he turned to Hollis. "And why, knowing Banks, did you come down here to him? He painted you both as selfish. I imagine he expected you to run. So why are you here?"

Another shared glance.

Mia spoke first. What she said surprised Hollis — more about hunches and feelings and interior voices. Strangely, what she reported "believing for no reason" were the same things Hollis spent his drive — past a lot of standing stones — intensely pondering.

Mia finished, then Hollis found himself telling the governor everything. What was the harm? The case was gone, the contents probably already destroyed by its failsafes. His theft meant nothing, nor did his many other crimes and evasions. He was bound in the back of a truck in a city that might soon cease to exist, given all the shooting and resumed violence they'd heard through the trailer's walls, and the stray bullets puncturing its metal skin like a kid poking air holes.

How much worse could it get? And besides ... wasn't that why he'd returned? It certainly wasn't for Mia, who still had a broomstick up her ass.

"You think the aliens don't like it when we fight," Garrett tried to clarify.

"That's the theory."

"But not just fighting with them. Fighting *with each other*."

He nodded.

"Forgive me, Mr. Palmer, but that sounds to me like the thinking of a pacifist in wartime, who'd rather lie down and be rolled over than stand and fight for what's right."

"It's actually that—"

The governor held up a hand. "And what's more, you don't have all the facts. You only know some of the domestic events and a few of the international ones. I don't believe there's as clear a correlation as you say between nonviolence and alien inaction. If we don't so much as fight, how can we hope to win?"

"Maybe there's nothing to win *against*, if we don't fight," Mia said.

"And you're willing to take that chance? Miss, forgive me. But citizens of all nations are being taken by these ships. They're plucking people from their beds at night. They've destroyed our cities, and these are only the things we know of. Are you suggesting that my response to an alien invasion should be to stand back and smile?"

"I don't know how it all works," Hollis said. "But at the very least, we need cohesion. If we're going to win, it won't happen by being fractured."

The governor's head bobbed, but Hollis could tell he was only trying to be polite and hear them out.

"What would you have me do?"

"Don't fire the missiles," Mia said. "Don't fight with McCafferty's people."

"It's not that simple. McCafferty's group has taken the

capitol while you've been here. They're determined to stop us. They won't listen. They're the aggressors now, not us."

Mia sighed. Hollis followed.

"I'm very sorry," Garrett said, standing. "I'm pleased to have met you ... but there's nothing I can do."

48

There was a banging, again, from the far end of the trailer's box. Someone outside, almost as if knocking. Mia's chin lifted off her chest. Against all odds, she'd been drifting into sleep.

"Go away," Hollis said. "We gave at the office."

The doors cracked, then opened just enough to let a dark shape slip inside. Mia was wondering about the covert entrance when she realized it wasn't the governor or his people come to visit.

"Carol! We thought you'd gotten away!"

"I did. You're lucky security sucks around here."

She cut their binds, starting with Mia. But despite their embrace, Carol wasn't smiling.

"Don't thank me yet. It's gotten worse out there."

And it had, but as they exited the box and Mia began to realize just how sore her arms and shoulders were from their binding. The scent of spent gunpowder was heavy, as were the sounds of brewing conflict. The pop of shots, the grunts and dirty sounds of human struggle, the somehow angry groan of giant engines. But the fighting hadn't yet decayed to chaos, and for that Mia was thankful. This was her second attempt at getting free, and she hoped to do it right this time.

Hollis looked at his watch. "Those cube things last sixty-six minutes, right? I'm guessin' we've got about ten left." He paused to inspect the conflict. "I don't think this fighting's gettin' worse, so that means ten minutes left to get out of town. I sure hope there's at least one good car with keys in it across the bridge."

"What about the car you drove here?"

"I must not have put enough into the meter, because ..." He pointed. There was a second skirmish happening near the Long Center, and a whole lot of fire, presumably swallowing his car in the blaze.

Mia grabbed Carol's sleeve then they slipped out, moving low and fast. For the most part, she kept her feet going because Hollis was right, their sixty-six minutes was almost up. But mostly she didn't want her brain to take too much time thinking. Despite Hollis's flip attitude, finding a car that hadn't been fried by the electromagnetic pulse, had gas in the tank, and keys or a fob inside an unlocked cab seemed unlikely. Add the criterion of being nearby and able to reach minimum safe distance in the remaining time, and their chances of surviving this fell nearer to zero.

The groups were violently clashing. The cube would blow.

But they had to try. There was a span of two seconds during which Mia considered trying once more to convince those in charge to *stop fighting* and keep the bomb from blowing, but even she wouldn't believe her right now. If Mia were in the governor's shoes, the *last* thing she'd do would be to lay down her defenses. That's how assholes got into power — when good people stopped fighting for what they felt was right.

So they ran. Away.

And smacked into a man with a soot-smeared face. Trim, military bearing, and the burnt remnants of a jumpsuit clinging to his body over plainclothes. Too late, she realized why he looked so familiar. The light was different than when she'd seen him last. Specifically, there was some.

Until right now, Carol had also failed to recognize Burning Man without his flamethrower.

But he saw them fine and raised his gun — a pistol, now, from a holster on his belt.

They hadn't even made the middle of the bridge.

"Turn around. Keep walking."

At first, Hollis didn't. He hadn't met Burning Man and didn't know how eager he was with his weapons.

"Outta our way. There's ten minutes left before this place becomes a crater. You really wanna spend it rasslin' three people that don't wanna be here? There's a war about to happen, and we're chickenshit civilians haulin' ass to safety."

Burning Man hit Hollis with the butt of his weapon. "Turn around, and keep walking."

He herded them back toward the Capitol.

"We been here already," Hollis said.

"Twice," Mia added — more to Hollis than to Burning Man.

"Shh. I know who you are." Then, talking to Mia, "He told me all about you. Nobody screws with the boss, lady. You get into the aliens' computers, that makes you a collaborator far as I'm concerned."

"We weren't *in their computers,*" Carol said.

"Quiet now." He poked Carol in the back with the pistol. "I don't wanna miss this."

The entire show had moved north like a hostile caravan. But there was still a forum of sorts ahead, and a place to grandstand even as cross-group violence bloomed in a semicircle around them.

Mia spied the governor, but there wasn't much to see. Yet. "You don't want to miss us getting covered in fallout? Or, in the best-case scenario, a mothership falling onto us?"

"'Are you stupid or something?" Burning Man asked. "Look where the ship is. You think you're gonna get crushed?"

Mia looked up. To her surprise, it wasn't directly overhead, though she was sure it had been.

"Governor talked a while back. Said he'd wait until it was at the end of its arc."

"What arc?" Hollis asked.

"It moves back and forth. Real slow. Sometimes it's over us, but other times it's actually over near Dripping Springs. It's just so big you don't always realize. And the winds. He says he's waiting for the winds."

Mia didn't feel line engaging in more conversation with the man who'd tried to kill her but thought she knew what he meant. Garrett must be waiting for the prevailing winds to shift, so they'd carry fallout away from town. Mia, with her limited knowledge of all things nuclear, found it unlikely that they'd be unaffected by a blast a few miles out of town regardless of where the wind was blowing.

They'd probably all grow extra limbs or genitals twenty years from now — but it's not like they'd live another twenty *minutes* at this rate. The nuke strike might not kill them, but the cube would.

Burning Man spoke as if reading her mind.

"The governor told Brendan what you said, about us laying down our guns and bending over for the aliens."

"That's not *exactly* what we said," Hollis told him.

"Seems to me, you're always on the aliens' side. You don't want us to fight back. Or stand our ground and hold onto what's ours. You're tryin' to convince the governor to let that actor run us over, so his people can have their way. But you tell me, lady. You tell me how doing *nothin'* is the way we beat these things."

"The theory is that—"

Torchy poked Hollis in the back, too. Harder than Carol. "Your theory is stupid. You don't know what these things want."

"Neither do you," Carol said.

"Guess I don't. Same for the governor. And Mr. Banks. But their way's better than picking daisies. Since we're all guessing, let me tell you *my* theory. *I* think that if they sometimes blow up and sometimes don't, that means they're being controlled by someone up in the mothership. We blow it up, then *I* think the cube won't do shit because the operator will be dead. *I* think blowing up the mothership's the only way to be sure."

"You can't be sure," Mia said.

"Neither can you!" Burning Man's body language changed, exuding something like pride. "Listen. I've been a grunt all my life, but I'm a *good* grunt. How much front-line battle have you seen? How much enemy tech? How much behavior have you studied, from the heart of a warzone?"

He looked up at the mothership. Took a second before he continued.

"I've been watchin' these things. When they've been shot at, they get hit. There's no force field or anything like that. They got vents in the sides, up high, and we can see how big they are. Mr. Banks has technology that can *easily* guide a warhead through one of 'em. Are you seriously tellin' me that if we shoot a *motherfucking nuclear weapon* right into that thing, we won't hurt it?"

He shook his head and laughed. "Is your argument that, knowing a weakness in their ships, we seriously shouldn't use it? That's what McCafferty's group thinks. But we'll show them, same as we'll show the aliens. First *them*. Then *them*."

Burning Man pointed up, then past the full-lawn scrum, presumably toward the human enemy.

There was activity at the grandstand, where Mia could see the governor orbiting. A young man rushed across the group and began chattering animatedly with him. The group pressed in — those from both camps in the same small space, hatred pungent in the air.

"Something's happening," Carol said. "Something's gone wrong."

Mia reached for Hollis's wrist. He seemed to think she was taking his hand, but really she meant to look at his mechanical watch.

Five minutes left.

If not less.

49

Hollis watched the scene, no longer sure what to think.

This had been the world's longest day, and it was only beginning. Last night was a million years ago.

At the time — and definitely while driving all night — he'd been convinced that Socrates was right. He'd arrived to find Mia sure, despite her lack of evidence, and that assured him even more.

But now, he wasn't so certain. The governor had been as level-headed as Socrates (more so, maybe), and claimed to have even more data. So who was to say what was right? Even the weirdo with the burned clothing and an apparent history with Mia and Carol made some excellent points. The vents were holes into the ship, so why *did* Hollis think a nuke shot into one wouldn't cause damage.

Too much Hollywood, painting aliens as invincible until the third act.

Maybe they were right, and the cubes *were* under manual control. Maybe someone, in the ship, was flipping a coin as to whether it went off or went away.

And if that was true, maybe shoving a nuke up their ass *was* the best option.

It didn't feel right. Hollis was still nervous, from the pit of his gut, when he saw humans fighting in clear view of that cube with the weird mechanical display forever shifting on its front.

But what did Hollis Palmer know ... *really?*

Nobody at the grandstand had a microphone or bullhorn — fried in the EMP, probably — but something about the acoustics amplified their argument just fine.

The crowd went silent, straining to listen. Whatever may have been going smoothly before had hit a glitch.

Hollis began to put it together.

The missiles were finally prepped and ready. They could be fired — then guided into the vents — at will.

But the mothership was swinging toward Austin.

And, worse, the prevailing winds had shifted. There was a burst coming from directly behind the mothership, directly toward downtown.

Brendan Banks had been on the sidelines but approached the governor when he started arguing with the runner.

The crowd began to shift. Hollis thought they might start fighting harder versus the simmer in the hour since his return. But instead they moved around, grumbling low, figuratively circling each other like gunslingers about to draw.

More arguing from the governor, from the runner, from Brendan.

We have to abort.
But then, the bomb might go off.
If we fire the rocket, people will die.
Brother, people are already dying!
The mothership will fall on people's homes.

But not on us.
Fallout will happen over the population.
But not here, right now, where we *are.*

And on and on. Hollis kept glancing at his watch, nowhere near sure about the time he was keeping. He assumed those who pretended to be in charge knew how much was left of the typical sixty-six minutes, but they weren't announcing shit.

There should be a display of some sort. A scoreboard, so the home audience could play along.

But if he had to guess ... four minutes remaining?

At most?

"Governor," came a voice.

Forest McCafferty was walking through the open space in the middle, same as before.

"Governor Garrett," McCafferty said, still projecting.

Garrett turned and faced him.

"You can't do this. You can't fire that weapon."

Brendan, beside and arguing with the governor, had lost all his decorum. "Fuck off!"

"We can all see the ship swinging back over downtown. You'll kill people if you fire."

"Necessary collateral damage," Brendan barked.

"Governor," McCafferty said. "Don't do this."

A man in the front row on the governor/Banks side of the conflict, looked at the person to his right, then to his left. With an air of *I-guess-I-have-to-do-it-if-nobody-else-will,* he racked his shotgun, took a single step, and aimed the barrel at McCafferty's chest.

Before centering on the man himself, his gaze ticked toward the cube, now a bit back from the shifted group's center. "Back off, McCafferty. You're gonna get us all killed."

McCafferty's hands went up. He spoke to the governor still, ignoring the shotgun. "There must be another way."

"I said *back off!*" the man shouted.

Now others were raising pistols, lowering shotguns from up-facing hold positions. On *both* sides.

"Let's everybody just breathe," McCafferty said.

"Piss off," said Banks. "We're doing this."

The governor, uncertain now, held a hand out toward Banks. Brendan was holding what looked like a massive remote control, with a massive silver antenna. The governor's fingers brushed the thing.

"Now, hang on just a second, Garrett. Let's at least think about this."

"Think? Shit." Brendan scoffed as if cogitation was for weaklings. "We got five minutes. Ignition and flight time probably take two by themselves. The time for thinking is over."

Five minutes? Bonus. That's more than I expected.

Brendan stepped back and turned away with the remote, moving like a squirrel protecting a nut. The governor followed, and the ensuing scuffle unsettled the crowd, set neighbors to bickering. Cracks were forming even within the two camps, the pressing decision forcing them into an impossible choice.

Garrett had one hand on the remote, but the man to his side — a bodyguard, perhaps — had two.

Banks lost his grip, reached again.

Now a new person — a woman, this time — stepped out of line. She'd been in the governor's camp, but now turned and pointed her weapon at Garrett himself.

"Sally?"

"Give him back the box."

But then someone hit Sally. She fell, and the whole group began to shift.

Hollis and the others were jostled back. He realized as he looked back, trying not to trip and fall, that they'd lost their escort. The burnt man who'd driven them into this huddle was gone ... only, no, Hollis could see him shoving through the crowd, moving toward the governor.

Hollis tried to shout — to whom, he had no idea because as people broke ranks, too much was happening too fast — but then a great number of minor fights erupted. Guns came out. There was shouting and shoving and, toward the edges, another few shots.

But it stopped in a second, and the entire lawn turned into a Mexican standoff.

Hollis's attention went to McCafferty, who had at least a dozen guns aimed his way. Then to the governor, who had a dozen more pointing in his direction. The scene had frozen like a diorama. The governor with the big sliver remote, Banks behind him looking murderous, a hundred weapons raised to kill.

McCafferty's eyes were darting in every direction, his smooth charm finally departed. He seemed afraid to flinch, as did Hollis, at whom no guns were pointed, for a change.

A battleground stopping to pose for a photo: *Nobody move, now. 1 ... 2 ... 3.*

Very carefully, very slowly, the governor consolidated his hold on the box.

He moved behind his guards, uneasy and daring the first person to shoot and throw a match into the tinder, but in the second it took for the governor to retreat, no one found the guts.

"Time's almost up," Brendan said, his movements and

voice careful. "Give it to me, Jefferson. Give it to me, so I can do what has to be done."

Nothing from the governor, who Hollis could no longer see.

"If you do nothing, we're dead."

"If I do *anything*," came the governor's voice, "we're dead."

Hollis watched Brendan stare at the unseen governor. Then his body language broke and he stalked away and out the back like a petulant child. A few of those closest to him stopped pointing their guns and went with him. The clock was nearing zero, and their decision, it seemed, would not be the one to win.

After that, the governor's head resurfaced. By no means should he feel safe with all the guns still aimed at his head, but Hollis had a strange thought. *If they haven't shot him yet, it's because they want to believe.*

The fact that both the governor and McCafferty were still alive meant that everyone in the circle had made their decision. There was no time left for *doing* to make a difference. The die had been cast.

The governor, slowly, found his feet.

"Let's just ... see where this goes," he said.

50

Everyone seemed to understand that an invisible threshold had been crossed. With the big remote in Governor Garrett's hands and out of Brendan's, no rockets would be fired. They *couldn't* be, Mia imagined.

With Banks out of the picture, there was no clear path to launch. It'd take time to arm the missiles. Or for them to fly, reach the ship, and steer through one of the tiny holes, somehow using the remote.

By then, the timer would run out.

Whether or not destroying the mothership (or trying to) would render the cube inert was no longer up for consideration. There was nothing anyone could do to stop it, and no time to run.

"How much time is left, until sixty-six minutes are up?" someone asked.

One of the governor's aides said, "Two minutes and ten seconds."

Beside Mia, Hollis showed his watch. Together, they could see the second hand sweeping the dial. Together, they could watch the final sands fall through the hourglass.

She caught movement out of the corner of her eye. Mia looked up to see Garrett doing a strange thing. He walked to the edge of his makeshift stage, extended a hand, and beckoned toward McCafferty.

The crows murmured. It almost felt like a trap.

"Come on, you dirty hipster, I think I can tolerate standing beside you." Garrett said it kindly, and incredibly, it even came across that way. Amid all the threats, adrenaline, and gun-waving, something had changed. Or broken.

It was as if they'd all reached their limits, ready to kill and die in unison. When that tense moment was over — coming and going without incident — they had nothing left inside.

Mia looked around. There were sides, of course. But in the end, they were people.

A few chuckled at Garrett's joke. McCafferty, who'd so recently been the target of dozens of weapons, actually smiled.

Burning Man said, "So ... what? Now we're just supposed to hold motherfuckin' hands?"

Garrett looked at his watch. "I'll make you a deal. If we're still here in ninety seconds, we can all go back to fighting."

Burning Man huffed. "This is bullshit. You're doing exactly what they want — *lying down*."

McCafferty said, "Maybe. But no matter how much you all suck, I can wait one more minute to knock you out."

There were a few laughs, but not as many. McCafferty's mention of "one more minute" returned the imminent threat, and everyone felt it. Only difference was that instead of the multi-pronged animosity, it was all now focused on the ship and its cube. For the next sixty seconds, the city had a single enemy.

"What happens when time runs out?" Burning Man asked, clearly itchy, and loving none of this.

"It goes off or it doesn't. We die or we don't."

"And *if* we die ... with a winning plan and a bunch of nuclear weapons sitting here, unused?"

McCafferty shrugged at the governor. "I can live with that."

It was so strange, seeing them sharing the stage. They'd been the bitterest of rivals, and surely would continue to be. But there they were, side by side, and the world hadn't ended.

Yet.

Mia felt the seconds tick by. Watched the hand on Hollis's watch.

Forty seconds.

Burning Man, all of a sudden, was *not happy*. He ripped the pistol from his belt and, from his position just in front of Hollis, aimed it at the governor. "Give me that control."

"You can't fire it."

"I can. Even if the missile doesn't hit in time, *it will hit.*"

"You'll just piss them off!" someone blurted from the crowd.

"Bad idea," McCafferty said.

"You shut up! I'm not talkin' to you!" Burning Man swung the gun toward McCafferty before centering again on the governor.

Garrett now had both hands on the control box, holding it tight. His gaze kept flicking down, probably to his watch, hoping he could filibuster for the final twenty-five seconds, until the time ran out and this all stopped mattering.

"Give it to me," said Burning Man, taking aim. "I won't ask again."

Three seconds. A beat of held breath.

Then Hollis picked up a discarded length of small-bore pipe that had been between his feet, and pressed it, like a gun's muzzle, against the back of Burning Man's head. He had a real gun, of course. But given where they all stood, real guns were against the rules.

"Lower your weapon, or you won't ask *anything* again."

Still the gun centered on the governor. "Give it to me."

Hollis pressed harder. The bluff wasn't working. Either he knew it wasn't a gun, or the man had stopped caring.

"No," Garrett said.

"Fifteen seconds," Mia whispered.

"If any of you want this," the governor said, looking at all of his recent allies and foes, but mostly holding Burning Man's eyes, "then *come and take it.*"

Hollis pushed once more against his head. Mia watched, knowing his bluff was called. He'd shoot. Out of spite — out of a simple human need to not contradict his former convictions — he almost *had* to pull the trigger.

But then the gun finally drooped in his hand. He took his fingers off the butt, letting it sag in the trigger guard until it fell to the concrete. Hollis picked it up and stowed it.

The clock hit zero.

There was a long, long wait.

Ten seconds passed.

Twenty.

And then, as suddenly as it had come, the cube disappeared.

Hollis must not have been able to help himself. Burning Man turned, and he pulled the man into a hug.

When the cube went, so did the animus. For a few minutes at least, factions ceased to exist.

Enemy smiled at enemy.

Cowboys, with their big mustaches and bigger hats, embraced Austinites with small hats and smaller 'staches.

Lines blurred. The open bubble between them lost its borders, then all definition. The sense of relief was a real thing, sudden like a sigh. For the few minutes it took for everyone downtown to appreciate the fact that they were still alive, nothing else mattered.

Hollis took Mia's wrist with one hand, Carol's with the other.

"Where are we going?" Carol asked.

"Away."

"But *where*?" Carol wanted to know.

"Anywhere."

"But—"

"Right now, everyone just got high on life. Think it'll last?" Hollis ticked his chin toward the mothership. "And what about them? Think they'll just go away?"

Mia was about to ask Hollis to elaborate, but he continued to drag them away.

She'd felt the euphoria, too. Only now was the ugly reality reasserting itself.

This wasn't even a battle won. But at least it was a battle survived.

"C'mon," Hollis said. "We got promises to keep, and miles to go before we sleep."

Mia stared at him.

"Yeah, that's right. Robert Fucking Frost. I know shit."

He dragged. Mia still didn't know where they were going, but Hollis was right.

He'd told her, while they'd been in the back of that tractor-trailer, about the other things Socrates said. Things Hollis needed Carol's thoughts on. Things, if he'd still had the attaché case, that should be stopped.

Mia looked up.

This wasn't over. Not by the longest of shots.

They crossed the bridge and found Hollis's car, right where he'd left it.

"I sorta figured, maybe we go back to that weirdo bar?" Hollis suggested. "At least for the night?"

Mia closed her eyes. Hollis and Carol could decide. She was too tired.

Promises to keep, she thought as her mind drifted. And miles to go before I sleep.

But Mia — who'd run from aliens and humans, who'd been tied up and tied down, who'd nearly died at least three times today — couldn't wait.

Sleep descended.

And until they arrived at their destination, she saw and heard no more.

51

Hollis figured he should look for a job, and that the need for a viable black market would only grow. He planned to be well-positioned. He had the temperament for dealing and knew all the players in town before the arrival, many resurfacing now. Maybe he could start as a runner, heading into occupied areas to steal supplies. In time, he could graduate to a boss. Benevolent, of course. And if he stayed out of Thomas Davies's circles, he'd do fine.

And Sonny Malone's, of course.

The cell network, like the Internet, was patchy. When it came back online, Hollis was deluged by messages meant for Ricky, whose phone he still hadn't — and wouldn't — return. Except for that one message meant for him, sent by Sonny. Seemed he'd found the paper inside the tennis ball and opened the case. The contents had self-destructed, and Sonny, judging by his words to Hollis, wasn't amused.

After the non-event downtown, Hollis made a run, then returned to find the Spider House Ballroom empty.

No creatures were stirring, not even Mia and Carol.

"Hey, you guys avoidin' me?" Hollis asked the empty building. "Does my breath stink?"

And that was funny for a second, until he realized it probably did.

"Mia? Carol?"

There'd been others, too, but Hollis still hadn't learned their names. They weren't a community — just a cluster of similarly-minded freeloaders. Ricky and Ember hadn't returned, for Ricky's phone or anything else. Maybe they were dead. Or maybe, as Mia liked to fantasize, they'd gone on to better places and circumstances.

They seemed like tent-in-the-woods people. The forest might be free of aliens, and they'd be there too, if not for his profession. And yet, for some reason, she'd still been unable to leave him behind.

Hollis crossed the quiet space, feeling a strange sense of dread.

They might just have run out.

Together? Without saying anything?

For what ... a walk?

But Hollis kept his calm, until he saw that someone had dragged a round table into the dead center of the ballroom space. A piece of jewelry lay on the table — a locket that Hollis had seen before.

Mia's.

And inside the open locket was a small piece of electronic equipment. Hollis picked it up and looked it over, but he knew it was a tracker already. An audio surveillance device. A Wi-Fi snooper, capable of pulling decoded wireless communications out of the air.

Deeper inside the locket, behind the spy device, was a Post-It Note folded very small.

BRING ME THE CASE OR THEY DIE

Mia. Carol. And the case that Sonny's opening attempt had destroyed.

... *OR THEY DIE.*

The joke was on Hollis.

Because the note said what the governor had so recently told the man with the pistol...

Come and take it.

THE STORY CONTINUES...

Save The Girl is the thrilling continuation of the Save The Humans series —with more action, more secrets, and more twists than ever.

GET SAVE THE GIRL NOW!

A QUICK FAVOR

If you enjoyed this book would you please consider writing a review of it on your favorite bookselling site so other readers can enjoy it too? Just a couple of sentences would be fantastic.
　Thanks!
　Johnny B. Truant

ABOUT THE AUTHORS

Avery Blake doesn't want you to know where she lives, or what she does. She travels the world, moving from place to place quickly to ensure she can't be tracked. It's safer that way.

When she's not looking over her shoulder, you can find her in the corner of a cafe, facing the exit, typing as fast as she can.

Johnny B. Truant is the bestselling author of *Fat Vampire*, adapted by SyFy as "Reginald the Vampire" starring Spider-Man's Jacob Batalon. His other books include *Pretty Killer, Pattern Black, Invasion, The Beam, Dead City,* and over 100 other titles across many genres.

Originally from Ohio, Johnny and his family now live in Austin, Texas, where he's finally surrounded by creative types as weird as he is. His website at JohnnyBTruant.com features his Creator Diary, additional works, fan extras, behind-the-scenes peeks, early access, and a whole lot more.

ALSO BY AVERY BLAKE

The Invasion Series

Longshot

Invasion

Contact

Colonization

Annihilation

Judgment

Extinction

Resurrection

Save The City Series

Save The City

Save The Girl

Save The World

Stonefall Series

Alienation

Stonefall

Snowfall

Downfall

The Taken Saga

The Taken

The Changed

The Hidden

The Saved

The Next Evolution

Transition

Convergence

Evolution

Stand-Alone Novels

Analog Heart

Family Royale

Ruthless Positivity

Vicarious Joe

ALSO BY JOHNNY B. TRUANT

The Dead World Series

Dead Zero

Dead City

Dead Nation

Dead Planet

Empty Nest

The Fat Vampire Series

Fat Vampire

Fat Vampire 2: Tastes Like Chicken

Fat Vampire 3: All You Can Eat

Fat Vampire 4: Harder, Better, Fatter, Stronger

Fat Vampire 5: Fatpocaplypse

Fat Vampire 6: Survival of the Fattest

The Fat Vampire Chronicles

The Vampire Maurice

Anarchy and Blood

Vampires in the White City

The Beam Series

The Beam Season One

The Beam Season Two

The Beam Season Three

Robot Proletariat Series

En3my

Robot Proletariat

The Infinite Loop

The Hard Reset

Cascade Failure

Reboot

The Invasion Series

Longshot

Invasion

Contact

Colonization

Annihilation

Judgment

Extinction

Resurrection

The Tomorrow Gene Series

Null Identity

The Tomorrow Gene

The Tomorrow Clone

The Eden Experiment

Stand Alone Novels

Pretty Killer

Pattern Black

Burnout

The Target

The Island

Devil May Care

www.ingramcontent.com/pod-product-compliance
Lightning Source LLC
LaVergne TN
LVHW031536060526
838200LV00056B/4522